Seventeenth Summer

— for Rosemary Courtney

— Maureen Daly

Seventeenth Summer

MAUREEN DALY

SCHOLASTIC INC.
New York Toronto London Auckland Sydney

To My Mother

Maurice Sanders, 17, a student at Sylmer (Calif.) High School, won an Honor Award for the cover photo in the 1967 Scholastic Photography Awards conducted by Scholastic Magazines and sponsored by Eastman Kodak Company.

ISBN 0-590-02554-6

31 30 29 28 27 26 25 24 23   6 7 8 9/8   0/9

Printed in the U.S.A.   01

CONTENTS.

JUNE

I DON'T KNOW JUST WHY I'm telling you all this. Maybe you'll think I'm being silly. But I'm not, really, because this is *important*. You see, it was different! It wasn't just because it was Jack and I either — it was something much more than that. It wasn't as it's written in magazine stories or as in morning radio serials where the boy's family always tease him about liking a girl and he gets embarrassed and stutters. And it wasn't silly, like sometimes, when girls sit in school and write a fellow's name all over the margin of their papers. I never even wrote Jack's name at all till I sent him a postcard that weekend I went up to Minaqua. And it wasn't puppy love or infatuation or love at first sight or anything that people always talk about and laugh. Maybe you don't know just what I mean. I can't really explain it — it's so hard to put in words but — well, it was just something I'd never felt before. Something I'd never even known. People can't tell you about things like that, you have to find them out for yourself. That's why it is so important. It was something I'll always remember because I just couldn't forget — it's a thing like that.

It happened this way. At the very beginning of

the summer I met Jack — right after graduation. He had gone to the public high school and I went to the Academy just outside of town which is for girls only. I had heard of him often because he played guard on the high school basketball team and he sometimes dated Jane Rady who sat next to me in history class. That night (the night when things first began) I drove down to the post office with my father to mail a letter and because it was rather late Dad pulled up in front of McKnight's drugstore and said, "I'll just stop here and keep the motor running while you run in and get a stamp." McKnight's is where all the fellows and girls in Fond du Lac get together and I really would rather not have gone in alone — especially on a Friday night when most girls have dates — but I didn't want to tell my father that.

I remember just how it was. I was standing by the drug counter waiting for the clerk. The sides of the booths in McKnight's are rather high and in one, near the back, I could just see the top of some-one's head with a short crew cut sticking up. He must have been having a Coke, for he tore the wrapping off the end of his straws and blew in them so that the paper covering shot over the side of the booth. Then he stood up to see where it had landed. It was Jack. He looked over at me, smiled, and then sat down again.

Of course I didn't know him yet, he just smiled to be friendly, but I waited for a few minutes look-ing at magazines in the rack near the front door, hoping he might stand up again or walk up to the soda fountain or something, but he didn't. So I just left. "You certainly took long enough," my father said gruffly, "I might have been arrested for parking double like this."

The next night my sister Lorraine came in from

8

Chicago on the 2:40 a.m. train. She has been going to college for two years and wears her hair long, almost to her shoulders, and puts her lipstick on with a brush. We drove to meet her, Dad and I. It was raining a little then and the lights from the station shone on the wet bricks. The two-wheeled baggage carts were standing in a line, their long handles tipped up into the air. We waited while the train came out of the darkness, feeling its way with the long, yellow headlight beam. When it stopped, a man jumped out and ran into the station with a package under his arm. A conductor swung onto the platform and stood waving a lantern while the train waited, the engine panting out steam from between its wheels. Dad and I walked along, peering up at the windows. A boy at one of them woke up and waved to me sleepily.

Then we saw Lorraine half stumble down the steps with two suitcases and a black wool ram under her arm. "I fell asleep and almost forgot to get off," she said. Her hair was mussed up and her cheek was all crisscrossed red where she had been leaning on the rough upholstery. "One of the girls had this goat in her room and didn't want to pack it so I brought it home for Kitty. (Kitty is my sister who is ten but still likes toys.) You've got to hold it up straight or the rubber horns fall out." Lorraine laughed. "I'm glad I'm home — this should be a good summer, don't you think, Angie?" Dad kissed her gingerly — because of so much lipstick — and I took one back to the car and he took the other and we went home.

That was Saturday. Monday was the day summer vacation really began.

It was just after nine o'clock and I was in the garden picking small round radishes and pulling

9

the new green onions for dinner at noon. I remember it was a warm day with a blue and white sky. The garden was still wet with last night's rain and the black earth was steaming in the sun, while between my toes the ground was soft and squishy — I had taken off my shoes and left them on the garden path so they wouldn't get caked with mud — and I remember thinking how much fun it would be to go barefoot all the time. The little tomato plants were laid flat against the ground from last night's downfall and there were puddles like blue glass in the hollows. A breeze, soft with a damp, fishy smell, blew in from Lake Winnebago about three blocks away. I was so busy thinking about the weather, the warm sun, and the sleek little onions that I didn't even hear Jack come up the back sidewalk.

"Any baked goods today?" he called.

"I don't know," I answered, turning. "You'd better ring the back doorbell and ask my mother." I sidled over a little and stood in the thick quack grass beside the garden path. I don't like to have people see me in my bare feet.

"Why don't you ask her for me?" he called. "You know her better than I do." I stood still for a moment hoping he wouldn't notice my feet. "Come on, hurry," he said. "I don't care if you haven't any shoes on."

Now, it wasn't that I was shy or anything, but it's awkward when a boy has on a clean shirt and his hair combed and your hands are all muddy and you're in your bare feet. I tried to wipe off the mud on the quack grass before I went down the garden path.

"What were you doing," he asked, "picking radishes?" (I still had the bunch of radishes in my hand.) "That's kind of silly, isn't it?" he added laughing. "It's just my salesman's personality coming out — anything to start a conversation. Twice already this morning I caught myself saying to customers, 'What's it going to do — rain?' I've got to be careful not to get into a rut." He laughed again and I laughed too. It was such a warm, bright morning.

We talked together for a while and I told him I didn't know he worked for a bakery, and he said he hadn't until school let out and that he was going to drive one of the trucks for his father during the summer, and when I remarked that I didn't even know his father owned a bakery, he said, "You don't know much about me at all, do you?"

"I know your name," I answered.

"What?" he asked.

"Jack Duluth. I remember reading it in the paper when you made that long shot from the center of the floor in the basketball game with Oshkosh this winter."

"Good for you — just another one of my fans." He laughed. "What's your name — as if I didn't find out after I saw you in McKnight's the other night. Angie Morrow, short for Angeline, isn't it?"

I was glad he had asked about me, but for some reason it was embarrassing and I tried to change the subject. "I remember when you used to go with Jane Rady," I ventured. "She used to sit next to me in history class. She talked about you a lot. She told me about the time you drove to the city dump — "

"Forget it," Jack said sharply. "Forget all about it, see. All that is down the drain by now." For a moment I thought he was angry. "Go ask your mother if she needs any bread or doughnuts or anything, will you?" He sat down on the cement doorstep and I opened the door to go inside. All of a

11

sudden he turned and said slowly, with a thought in his voice, "Say, Angie, you don't go steady or anything, do you?"

My heart jumped a little. "No, I don't," I answered and then added quickly, "My mother doesn't like me to go out much." It wouldn't do to say that I wasn't often asked, either. I waited a moment. "Do you, Jack?"

He laughed. "Of course not. None of the fellows I go around with do. Silly to tie yourself down to one girl. But, say, seeing you don't — how about going sailboating with me tonight? Me and Swede Vincent have got a little boat we bought last fall. Do you know Swede? He's a good guy. He'll come with us and sail it and you and I can just — ah — well, just sit. How about it?"

I didn't know, I told him. I would have to ask my mother first.

"Go ask her now," he urged, "when you ask her if she needs any bread. I'll wait."

"Oh, I can't do that!" I could hear my mother upstairs running the vacuum cleaner noisily over the rugs and I remembered I hadn't tidied up my bedroom yet. "Now's not such a good time to ask but I'll tell you by one o'clock," I promised, trying not to be too eager. "I'll try to fix it and if you'll call me then I can let you know."

"I'll call you at one then and let's skip the bakery goods for today. Please try to go," he added. "No girl has ever been out in our boat before so you'll be the first one. Something kind of special."

That was the first time I ever really talked to Jack. When I went back into the garden to get my shoes I noticed how the little tomato plants seemed to be straightening in the sun. And there were small paper-thin blossoms on the new pea plants.

My mother always lies down in the afternoon — at least, she has for the past three years, anyway. Right after lunch she went upstairs as always, turned down the chenille bedspread and drew the shades. Out on the side lawn in the shade of the house Kitty was sewing doll clothes and talking to herself in a quiet, little-girl singsong. From Callahan's, across the back garden, I could hear the drone of the baseball game on the radio. All the little children were in taking their naps and already our street had settled into the quiet of afternoon. I'd have to ask my mother soon for I knew that in a few moments she would be asleep.

Outside her bedroom door I paused. "Maybe I'd better count up to seventeen first," I thought. "Seventeen and then I'll ask her." So I counted slowly, deliberately, being careful not to skip. When I was younger I used to count up to fifteen while trying to decide things, then it was sixteen, and now it was seventeen — one count for each year. But when I got to seventeen I still hadn't figured out in my mind how I should say it. "Better count up to eighteen," I decided. "Eighteen because that's how old Jack is. After that I'll go in for sure."

My mother was almost asleep when I pushed open the door gently, lying on top of the blankets with my old blue flannel bathrobe thrown over her. Sunlight filtered through the drawn shades in a brownish-yellow glow and the crocheted circle used to pull them down twirled in the breeze. I swallowed hard and it made a noise in the quietness of the room.

"Mom," I ventured, "a boy asked me for a date tonight." She opened her eyes. "It will be all right and I'll be home early," I assured her hastily. "He'll come over first and you can meet him and make

13

sure it's all right. They're nice people — he plays basketball and his father owns the DeLuxe bakery." I rushed the words after each other without stopping, before she could say no.

Rolling over toward the wall and nuzzling her head into the pillow she asked sleepily, "What's his name? I don't think I ever heard you mention him, did I?"

"Jack Duluth," I answered and waited. The room was quiet except for the sound of the window shade flapping in the breeze.

"Duluth as in Minnesota?" Lorraine called out. She was in her own room down the hall taking the curlers out of her hair. She keeps them in all the time except when she's going out. Lorraine wears her hair very long with just a little fluffy curl on the end like they all do in college. But already my mother was breathing lightly as if she were asleep.

"Mom," I said quietly, trying to keep the impatience out of my voice — my mother doesn't like it if we tease, "can I go or can't I? It will be all right — really it will."

"See what your sister thinks," she answered. "I suppose it's all right if you're home early. And see if you can fix that window shade so it doesn't flap so — put a book on the cord or something."

It had been as easy as that and my heart was beating fast as I closed the door softly behind me while downstairs the telephone rang. It was Jack.

We walked out to the lake, he and I. It was about half-past seven in the evening and the summer sky was still brushed red with the sun. "Looks like ostrich feathers on fire," Jack had said. We had cut through our back garden and through two empty lots and then crossed the highway between our house and the lake. Jack had held the barbed wire

14

of the fence apart for me to crawl through and we went into the field behind the boathouses. "This is my own special short cut," I remember his saying. "I like it better this way than walking through the park."

Along the path by the fence was a row of wild plum trees with hard green knobs of fruit hidden in the leaves. Little sparrows twittered excitedly and fluttered among the branches as we passed. Not many people came by this way. Just past the last fence was a row of whispering willow trees lined along the ditch by the railroad track. Water from the spring rains still gurgled and ran in ribbons between the swamp grass. "You'll have to jump," said Jack. "It's marshy here. Step first on that flat stone and then over onto the sewer top." There was a round cement sewer with a heavy, knobbed iron lid padlocked shut and almost hidden in the weeds. "Let me go first," he said, "then I'll catch your hand and help you across." The ground was marshy beneath my feet and I almost lost my balance on the smooth stone. Jack caught me and I remember his hand was tight and warm.

We hit a flat grassy spot a little farther on — just on this side of the tracks. "This is Hobo's Hollow," Jack told me. "Lots of times I come through here and see the fellows who have jumped the trains lying here sleeping. Sometimes there are four or five of them and they make a fire and cook things. I saw a man dead drunk here one day lying right in the sun with flies on him and a bottle in his hand and the next day he was gone. They never talk to me when I go by at all. Just sit and look."

I shivered a little. It was weird there with the air half gray-green from the thick trees and lush weeds and the coming night. There were bits of charred wood and old rusted cans sticking up in the grass.

The wind sighed a little as it wove its way through the long line of willows. Jack pulled my hand suddenly and we scrambled up the cinder embankment of the railroad track. Directly beyond was a broad gravel drive and then the gray and white boathouses.

It was early in the season and many of the houses were still padlocked shut from the winter. Between them the little waves slop-slopped against the heavy wooden piles. "Swede said he'd have the boat out by the steps of the Big Hole," Jack told me. "He came out to clean her up a bit before you came. We had a sort of picnic in it last week and it's still all full of old sandwiches and stuff." The Big Hole was built by the city a few years ago to harbor small boats against the sudden vicious squalls that come up so quickly on Lake Winnebago. It's bordered on one side by the boathouses, on the other by a shrub-edged drive, and on a third by the Point with a tall, white lighthouse on the end. Over on the right the water sloshes into a mass of treacherous water reeds and thick seaweeds. Beyond this is bare red clay scattered with water pipes and heaps of black dirt — an uncompleted WPA project.

I saw Swede bending over in the boat arranging canvas. Jack whistled at him shrilly through his teeth and Swede straightened and waved. "You'll like Swede," Jack told me. "Some girls think he's kind of fast but I told him to be nice to you." Swede was rather fat with kinky blond hair and had on a very tight, very clean white sweat shirt.

"Hello," he called. And when we got up to the boat, "You're Angie Morrow, aren't you. I thought maybe at the last minute you wouldn't be able to come. Jack said he thought maybe your mother might not want you to go sailing," and he grinned at me.

16

"Everything's all right so long as we get home by eleven," Jack told him. "Anytime after that's no good. We won't go out far — just until we find the moon." He squeezed my hand. I couldn't help shivering a little — it was such a beautiful night.

In the Big Hole the wind barely wrinkled the water with waves. We moved slowly at first — Swede up in the bow and Jack and I sitting in the stern, until we had passed through the narrow space between the lighthouse and the breakwater. Already cars were parked along the Point with their headlight beams poking out into the thickening dusk. Almost everyone in Fond du Lac goes out for a drive in the evening and then stops for a while to look at the lake. Someone honked a horn and leaned out a car window to wave at us. "People do that just to be friendly," said Jack. "I don't know who it is."

"Are you comfortable?" he asked. "If you get chilly say so and you can put my sweater on." I just nodded. It was too lovely to talk. The boat rose and fell gently as it topped the waves. Swede was letting out the sail and the loose canvas flapped in the wind. Occasionally the greenish water slapped hard against the side of the boat and sent spray over the edge. "Here," said Jack. "We'll put this canvas over your legs — no sense in your getting wet. You're a good scout, do you know that? Lots of girls are scared to go out in boats."

"I love it," I told him. He was sitting almost on the point of the stern with his red and white basketball sweater tied around his neck by the sleeves and a light wind was ruffling his hair from behind.

I sighed and he said to me, "You're not cold, are you? Remember, just say the word and the sweater's yours. I really brought it along for you — I never get cold myself." Leaning over, he put it around my shoulders and I remember thinking

17

when he was so close how much he smelled like Ivory soap.

We were sailing in silence for a long time and way up in the sky, past the boathouses, was pasted a thin tissue-paper curve of moon. Swede had hung a lantern that swung in the darkness on his end of the boat and it licked red light over the tops of the waves. Just then he finished a cigarette and flipped it out over the water. We were far out by that time and the car lights were only star dots along the pier. It was very still. I looked back at Jack and he was sitting with his head thrown back, gazing at the sky. Far beyond him was only the darkness of the lake. The wind blew lightly, brushing through my hair. Jack moved forward suddenly and slipped up beside me on the narrow seat. "Angie Morrow," he said quietly. "You look nice with the wind in your hair."

And I remember just how he said it.

"That's one thing about the lake at night," he whispered. "No other place is so beautiful or so quiet. Sometimes Swede and I come out here and just drift for hours and don't talk at all. We just sit and watch the sky and think. You should see the water when the moon's out — I mean a big yellow summer moon. It looks just like it does in movies. Sometimes I almost cry. Swede mostly just thinks about girls when he's out here, but I like to think about clouds and God and things." He sat silent for a moment, watching the water. The sweater had slipped from my shoulders and he put his arm around me to hold it in place.

"I didn't know," I told him, "that boys thought much about *pretty* things. The fellows around Mc-Knight's never act like they think about anything much."

"Most of them don't, but some of them do. We talk together a lot about girls and life and things. It's funny what some of those fellows think. Some of them have got big plans for what they want to do and who they want to marry and some of them never think at all."

"I just want to read a lot and learn everything I can," I told him. And then thinking that sounded dull I added, "I'd like to know about everything beautiful."

Jack sat up suddenly and looked at me. "Do you?" he said. "Do you really think that, Angie? You know, all my life I've wanted to know about beautiful things — to be cultured. Maybe that sounds funny to you. I haven't any background or anything. My mother and dad are swell, but I could never talk about a family tree or my grandfather who had whole stables full of horses . . . see what I mean? I've got to find out about all that sort of thing — my father's father was a farmer and my mother's father had a meat market out in Rosendale. Do you know," he said, "that until a couple of months ago I didn't even know what side a salad plate goes on?"

I wanted to tell him then about the silver fish service my mother has with the mother-of-pearl handles and the big curved-blade serving knife to match that looks like a Turkish dagger. I thought he might like to know about it because it was different and beautiful, but I couldn't think how to tell it so it didn't sound like bragging so I just said, "Salad plates go on the left, Jack, with the forks."

"And another thing I want to do is go to an opera someday. I'd like to have a big black cape and a cane and a folding silk hat and I'd come in the door and slap those old white gloves in the hat and walk right down the aisle. I don't know much about music," he said. "I don't even like it a lot but I could learn."

I wanted to tell *him* something too. There were so many things I had always thought about to myself and never wanted to tell anyone before. I almost told him about how I used to lie in bed at night and imagine that I was married to Nelson Eddy just so I could pretend he took me places — night clubs and dances and things. "You know, Jack," I ventured, "once last winter when I went down to Chicago to see my sister Lorraine — the one that was sitting in the living room with curlers in her hair when you called for me — we went to see a play. It was called *Kiss the Boys Good-bye*. It wasn't a good play or anything. I mean, it wasn't like Shakespeare but it was a big hit and had a run on Broadway. A lot of it I didn't understand very well — I think it wasn't nice."

"We read *The Merchant of Venice* in English class," Jack answered. "Parts of that I didn't understand very well either — maybe that's because it's too nice." He laughed a little. His arm was on my shoulder and I relaxed and leaned back. He leaned over closer saying, "That's right. Just sit comfortable. Lean way back if you want." We were drifting then and Swede was sitting with his head resting on the side of the boat, half asleep. It was darker by that time and the moon was half hidden, cushioned in cloud. The boat rose and fell gently with the waves. "All I know is that I just want to be happy and turn out good, that's all," Jack mused, half to himself. Somehow it made me shiver a little.

For a long time no one spoke, I remember. Once Swede raised himself on his elbow and looked toward shore and then put his head down again. We were far out, drifting slowly, and the silence over the water seemed soft and thick. It was then I got that queer feeling. Maybe you won't understand what I mean. You see, I was just sitting there thinking of nothing in particular when suddenly I felt a warm tingling and then an almost guilty feeling — almost as if I were doing something I shouldn't. And I remember the wind blowing very cool on my cheeks. No one had even moved or said a word. I could see the glow of Swede's cigarette in the stern of the boat. It was then I felt that strange urge to turn my head and look at Jack to see what he was thinking, and an odd fear that if I did he might be looking at me. I could feel my thoughts loud in my brain as if they were hoarse whispers. A panicky, excited pulsing started in my throat. My cheeks were hot. I knew Jack was looking at me and I turned my head just a little so I could see his face. His arm tightened suddenly around my shoulders and a warm, contented feeling went through me like when you drink hot milk.

Jack straightened just then and said quietly, "I think I'll light my pipe," and reached into his back pocket. I was strangely hurt that he should want to move just at that moment, so I pulled the sweater tighter round my shoulders and sat up very straight, away from him. Jack filled his pipe, cupped in the hollow of his hand, pressing down the tobacco with his thumb, and then hunched over to light it. The first match guttered out. The wind snuffed out the second before he even got it near his pipe. He turned in the seat, pulled up his knees, and bent almost double with his shoulders pulled up to shelter it from the wind. The third match went out. "I'll tell you what, Angie," he said. "Give me that piece of canvas from round your legs. You hold it over my head and keep the wind out and I'll light my pipe." I unfolded the canvas and he

21

ducked under. A moment later he pulled his head out explaining, "That doesn't seem to work either. I can't hold the canvas off my face and keep the match lit at the same time. I'll tell you what. You put your head under, too, and strike the match and I'll light my pipe and keep the canvas up. Two heads ought to be able to hold it."

So we put the canvas over our heads and it seemed suddenly quiet and hushed, in out of the wind. The first match I struck broke and its head flipped off onto the bottom of the boat. "Try again," Jack said. He shifted toward me. It was very dark under the canvas. The second match flared.

My hand shook a little and Jack held it to steady it as he brought it over the pipe, drawing in deeply till the tobacco glowed, then puffing out the smoke. He took the pipe from his mouth, blew out the match, and dropped the burnt end to the bottom of the boat. I could see the glowing bowl of the pipe in his hand. Neither of us moved. And I remember wondering why it was so silent, so very silent, and why I didn't seem to be even breathing. I knew then that we were both thinking the same thing. I sensed the very warmth of his nearness.

It was only a moment, a long, tense silent moment, and then suddenly I pulled the canvas off my head and it brushed my hair forward over my face. I pushed it back and against my cheek the night air was damp and cool.

Swede was sitting up straight. "Hey, you," he said to Jack, "what were you doing with your heads under the canvas?"

"Lighting my pipe," Jack answered.

Swede smiled and winked. "Yeh?" he said, knowingly. "That's a new name for it."

I tucked the canvas tightly in around my legs, looking out over the lake, and said nothing. Jack

22

was leaning back, slowly puffing at his pipe, watching me and not saying anything. After a long while he leaned over and knocked the ashes from his pipe into the water. Then, looking at me, he said quietly, "We might as well have, you know."

About half-past nine it began to get rough. The wind changed and the lake grew dark and choppy. "We'd better turn her around," Jack called. The wind whipped the words out of his mouth and he waved his arms and pointed toward shore. Swede nodded and pulled at the ropes. The sail billowed out and swooped down toward the waves as the boat swung around to face the lighthouse. Little waves lipped over the sides and sloshed under the crossboards on the bottom. "Don't get scared," Jack said, "it's a little rough but Swede can hold it." I pulled the canvas tighter around my legs and the wind blew my hair around my face. Off in the north thunder rumbled and sharp lightning slit the sky. It took us almost an hour to reach shore in the shifting wind and there were only a few cars parked along the drive when we swung into the Big Hole.

"If you kids want to start home before the rain it's all right with me," yelled Swede against the wind. "I'll put the boat up and see that everything's covered. It looks like we're going to have a real rain, but you two have just about time to make it home."

"Thanks," said Jack. "I'll stop round to see you on the route tomorrow. Put my sweater on again, Angie. It's still chilly," and he pulled it down over my head. "Come on, we'll take the park road home."

"Good night, Swede," I called back. "Thank you, and I'm very glad I met you. I hope I see you again sometime." Swede was running down the sail and it was flapping wetly in the wind. The

23

waves were dashing against the boat and he didn't hear me.

"Don't worry, Angie," Jack said. "You'll see him again."

My dog Kinkee ran out to meet us as we came up the walk, giving her tail a brief wag for me and then nosing around Jack's trouser cuff with a low growl. Kinkee is a chow and doesn't like strangers. "Go 'way," I told her. "It's all right. Maybe, Jack, she thinks you're a strange man who followed me home." It wasn't really funny but we both laughed.

"You know," said Jack, "when I was younger I used to think that if a chow licked you that black stuff on their tongues would come off." We were by the front steps now. My mother had heard the thunder and set the two potted ferns from the living room out on the steps to catch the rain. There was one lamp lit on the corner table in the living room and the light shone out onto the walk. The trees on the lawn were bending in the wind and the air was full of the damp, fishy smell of water that always blows in from Lake Winnebago just before a storm.

"Here's your sweater, Jack," I said and pulled it off over my head. His hand touched mine as he took it and I kept my fingers there for a moment, thrilled by my own daring.

"I'm afraid I have to go too now," he said but I waited. He had flung his sweater around his shoulders and tied the sleeves in a knot and then we both just stood without saying anything. You can't ask a boy, "When will I see you again?" or "Will I *ever* see you again?" I had meant to find out from my sisters what fellows usually say when they leave. I thought maybe I should tell him I had

24

liked the boat or that it had been a pleasant sail or something, but all those words seemed silly. Already the first drops of rain were spotting the cement sidewalk dark.

"It's raining," Jack said and held out his hand to see if he could feel the drops. "That will be good for the gardens."

You can't say to a boy "Have I been fun tonight?" or "Don't you like me more than other girls — wouldn't you like to go out with me again?" A girl just can't say that sort of thing to a boy — especially when he's talking about gardens. So I just stood there and all of a sudden the rain started coming down hard and the wind tossed the trees with quick gusts and blew my skirt around my legs.

"Good night, Angie," he said. "You'd better get in the house quick. I've got to run for it. Get in quick so you don't get wet." He turned and cut across the front lawn with his sweater over his head.

And he hadn't even said. I didn't even know if he would call me again.

Softly I tiptoed upstairs. Far out over the lake, thunder rumbled like a slow freight. As I passed by my older sisters' bedroom lightning lit the sky and in the yellow flash I could see the two of them sleeping quietly, their hair in metal curlers and cold cream shining on their faces.

And that was the first night.

I woke early the next morning — so early that the first flaming slashes of dawn were just beginning to be reflected pinkly on my bedroom wall. For a long time I lay in a warm, sleepy haze, looking at the alarm clock and knowing it was too early to get up and yet not wanting to go back to sleep again. It was so pleasant lying thinking comfortable, blurred thoughts about summer and about the night before.

My sister Kitty lay beside me sleeping soundly with her arms flung up over her head. She wears her hair in long pigtails and it was all fuzzy from tossing on the pillow. Once she turned over wearily, muttering something to herself, and then smiled contentedly in her sleep. Outside the window there were birds twittering excitedly about new plans for the day and inside I lay looking at the ceiling and thinking.

In the brightness of the morning last night didn't seen quite real — as if it had been a movie which I had sat and watched but of which I had not really been a part. It could hardly have been me who felt almost beautiful just because wind was fingering through my hair and the moon was thin like a piece of sheer yellow silk. I knew in a little while I would be getting up and putting on blue denim slacks and eating cereal at the table beside the kitchen window and dusting window sills and talking to my mother about garden flowers and what to have for dinner just as I had for so many summers. There would be no more of the exquisite uncertainty of last night, no queer, tingling awe at the newness of the feeling, and no strange, filling satisfaction out of just being alive. All that was last night because it *was* night and because it was the first boy I had really been out with. Not because it was a special boy — a boy different from other boys — but just because it was the first one. After a while, maybe after years when I had had so many dates that most of them were hazy, I would think of last night and remember it and that breathless loveliness, the same way and with the same amused pleasure that I think now about how I used to wait for the first look at the tree on Christmas morning or about the sweet pink froth of cotton candy at carnivals. Maybe, I thought to myself, if I were to see Jack this morning in the bright sunlight his eyebrows might be scraggly or his face might be pale and silly.

What if he tells every girl she looks pretty with her hair blowing around her face. And what if I didn't look pretty at all and it was just because there was no one else around and nothing else to say. What if Swede had sat in the bow of the boat laughing to himself because Jack was being smooth and I was being silly by listening. There is a crack over in one corner of the ceiling of my bedroom and I found myself unconsciously lining my thoughts up on either side — the good and the bad. The nice things to remember and the things that maybe in the sunlight wouldn't be the same at all.

It might be that he would never call me again and I would spend the rest of the summer evenings going for rides with my mother and father and lying in bed trying to repiece that night in the boat and wondering where I could have failed. Maybe when I went away to college in the fall I would have to write all my themes for English class about water spraying over the side of boats and wet sails flapping in the wind and thin moons that were hardly there, because that would be all I could remember, all I could think of. Maybe all my life my heart would jump a little when I saw a short crew cut or a boy with a basketball sweater knotted around his neck. Maybe every time I heard the name "Jack" I would hold my breath and be afraid to turn around to see who was there in case it might be he.

The sunrise flush was fading on the wall and I shut my eyes, trying to sleep again. But the darkness was like the soft, hushed darkness had been with the canvas over my head in the boat and the wind outside ruffling the water. I caught my breath a little, knowing I was being silly and not being able to help it every time I thought of his hand and mine holding the match. . . . Maybe if I got up quickly everything would be all right and I would forget. It could be, I thought, that I am still sleeping a little and holding a nice dream by the tail so it won't get away. But I could hear Kitty breathing quietly beside me and I could see the long crack zigzagged on the ceiling and the early sun shining in the window and I knew that I was wide awake. And I knew that even getting up quickly wouldn't help, that it was something that had nothing to do with waking or sleeping. Something that would be there all the time. And if I looked at myself in the mirror that morning I would see something different. My face would be the same but yet something had changed, and I would try not to look straight at my family all day in case they might see it too, and smile at each other and say, "Angie's growing up." And somehow I was afraid to have anyone know because I wasn't sure myself. I couldn't be sure at all until I saw Jack again.

About seven o'clock I heard my mother's bed creak across the hall and I heard her open my door softly and look in. Quickly I shut my eyes and sighed as if I were asleep. I didn't want to get up just yet. I wanted just a few minutes more to lie there and think. Just a few minutes more. She went into the bathroom then to get washed, and soon the morning noises began. There was the water running in the kitchen sink and the sound of five plates, four coffee cups, and one glass of milk being set on the table. The smell of freshly made coffee drifted upstairs and made me start thinking wide-awake, daytime thoughts. I could see in my mind just how it would be. My sister Lorraine would be sitting at one side of the table and my sister Margaret on the other. Lorraine would be rushing to get to work and Margaret would be in her house coat, all ready except to put her make-up on. My mother would pour the coffee and say, perhaps, that it was strong or weak or should have percolated longer or something. Then one of them would remember last night and say, "Oh, Angie. Did you have fun?" or maybe, "Do you think he'll ask you out again?"

And I would put cream in my coffee and tell them all about the boat and how good Swede was at sailing it and how it had started to rain just when we got home. And they would ask a few more questions while I said yes or no or whatever the answer should be, but I would never mention the moon or the cool clean smell of the wind or that I had worn Jack's sweater all evening or all the other small, warm thoughts that kept nudging at my memory even as I lay awake watching the sun grow brighter on the ceiling. I would eat my breakfast like any other morning, clear the table like any other morning, and do the housework like any other morning; but somehow inside myself I would be waiting for the phone to ring or listening for a bakery truck to pull up at the curb in front of the house.

I got out of bed then without waking Kitty, dressed, and went downstairs. Just before I went into the kitchen I stopped and pinched my cheeks to make the muscles relax. Somehow my face felt stiff and unnatural. I had a queer feeling that when I sat down at the breakfast table I might not be able to eat at all. I might just look at everyone

29

drinking their morning coffee and then suddenly blurt out foolishly, "I like a boy. And I never knew it would be like this!"

But that wasn't quite what happened. Lorraine was standing by the kitchen stove in her house coat, curling her hair with the curling iron — she had just washed it the night before.

My mother was sitting now in a clean blue print dress at the table next to the window drinking her coffee, and her hair, where it is turning white on the sides, was brushed back high off her face. She used to get very bad headaches and would have to lie in a darkened bedroom with cool cloths soaked in vinegar on her forehead. The vinegar had bleached her hair snow-white at the temples. My mother is the only person I know who looks completely wide-awake and fresh when she wakes up in the morning.

"Your tomato juice is in the icebox," she said to me. "I didn't think you'd be down for a while."

Outside, the garden earth was dark from last night's rain and cobwebs, dew-sparkled, were stretched on the grass. Everything had a fresh, clean smell. "I think it's almost cool enough to wear a sweater and skirt," Lorraine said. "You know, after being used to collegiate clothes I just hate wearing summer dresses that wrinkle so easily."

She had a job for the summer at the Elite Canvas Company, just sitting all day folding and addressing circulars which were sent all over the country to advertise awnings, golf bags, and canvas laundry bags. Every summer the Elite took on about twenty extra girls. My father is a good friend of one of the men in the office — they had played some early golf together the weekend before and he had arranged it.

30

At first no one mentioned the night before. "We'll put the winter things in the attic this morning," I remember my mother saying to me. "Just let Kitty sleep and you get the stepladder from the garage and I'll hand the things up to you." Ours is the old-fashioned kind of attic that you get into through a trap door in a bedroom ceiling. "We can get all Lorraine's school clothes put away so the closets won't be crowded all summer," she added.

My sister Margaret came down just then, all ready for work. You would like my sister. She is tall, thin, moves very quickly, and is engaged to a boy from Milwaukee who looks and acts just like a giant baby panda. Leaning over she kissed Mom, or rather brushed her with her cheek so she wouldn't rub off her lipstick. "No tomato juice this morning," she said and drank her coffee standing up by the stove — Margaret is always in a rush.

There was the usual breakfast talk: "Did you hear the rain last night?" "What would you children like me to get for supper?" (Mom always calls us children), and "We should have a big day at the store today." Little everyday things that could be said on any morning and I waited, just drinking my coffee and eating my toast, knowing that at any moment someone would remember. I could almost feel the words just hanging in midair. My mother reached over to snap off a loose thread hanging from the hem of Margaret's dress. I remember that so well because that was just before Margaret turned to me, remembering, "— Oh, Angie, how was last night?"

"Fun," I answered. Then I told them about the rain and how good Swede was at sailing and that Jack used to date Jane Rady and how I remember her talking about him when she used to sit next to

31

me in history class and about how many people had been out riding because it was such a nice night and all the cars with bright headlights that had been lined up along Lighthouse Point. Maybe, I thought, I'm talking too much; maybe I'm talking too fast. My voice seemed not to be coming from me at all, and I was surprised to hear it so calm and casual when inside my head the thoughts were all warm and shaky.

"I used to know Jack's cousin," Lorraine said. Her hair was curled in rows of shiny sausage-curls, and she was holding the curling iron as far away from her head as possible so she wouldn't burn her cheek, talking with a funny grimace as if any movement might bring the iron too close. "He was a drip though. He used to wear real baggy pants and always got to school late and had to be sent to the office for tardy slips."

I tried to think of something to counteract that slur. It wouldn't do to have the family think that Jack had dull connections before they even knew him — it's important that the family like a boy — but nothing came to my mind quickly enough.

In the green clumps of marguerite daisies along the garden path, round knobby heads stuck up with the green sheaths half open, showing the white silk petals underneath. Mom pushed back the kitchen curtains to look at them, commenting absently that next spring we would plant only a few rows of vegetables and have the rest of the garden all in flowers. Lorraine looked at Margaret and she looked at me and we all smiled, because every summer, for as long as we could remember, my mother had said that.

Then Margaret glanced at her wrist watch and gave a little gasp, though she had known all the time that it was late, gulped down the rest of her

32

coffee, and rushed out, leaving the front door half open, calling back, "Be sure to have something good for supper because I'm going to be real hungry!" Lorraine went upstairs to get dressed and Mom finished her coffee and a last piece of toast before clearing the breakfast things away.

Though I don't know just what I expected, I was vaguely disappointed that this was just like any other morning. The sun was bright on the kitchen floor, the coffee was steaming as always, and my mother looked just as calm and shiny clean as she always did. Maybe, I thought, I was wrong about last night and maybe everything is just the same. Maybe it wasn't — well, what I thought it was.

But all morning, puttering with the housework, I was really waiting for Jack to stop round on his bakery route, and my mind was far from finger marks on the white woodwork and dustcloths that smelled of oily furniture polish. But by eleven o'clock he had not come. And by eleven o'clock, with the beds all made and the housework done, I knew this was not an ordinary day; I knew definitely that everything was not the same.

We had had scrambled eggs and toast and tea for lunch, just the three of us, my mother and little sister and I, sitting at the end of the kitchen table. "Just a pick-up snack," Mom had said. "Whatever you can find in the icebox." At twelve o'clock I began to get a queer restless feeling, as if I wanted to sit drumming my fingers on the table top, and I could hear the big clock in the dining room very plainly as it ticked.

Perhaps, I kept thinking, Jack will call me now, while he is home for lunch; but by one o'clock I had decided that probably he didn't like to call when his mother and father were around — some

33

boys are like that — and maybe he would stop off at McKnight's on his way back to the bakery and call me from there. Or perhaps he would even come over for a few minutes — my mind made up a series of pleasant little excuses for him as the time went by.

But by the time two o'clock came and I had put away the lunch dishes, the house had grown quiet and the trees were beginning to turn their shadows eastward on the lawn; that excited feeling of waiting seemed to turn hard and make an aching throb in my throat. I had been so sure he would come.

Kitty was in the garage making bright, tinkering noises, trying to straighten out a dent in her bicycle fender with a claw hammer, and she said, "Sure, I'd like to walk to the lake with you," when I asked her. "Wasn't doing much anyhow."

There were men working on the road that goes along the wide breakwater with the lighthouse on the end. One of them was leaning his chest on a pneumatic drill, pressing it hard into the gravel road and it made a loud rut-ta-tutting that echoed in the stillness of the afternoon, spitting up dirt and sprays of gravel as it dug. We stood to watch for a while. The rest of the men were working slowly, swinging their pickaxes in wide, lazy arcs, or just leaning on the yellow, wooden trestles with the red danger flags fluttering, put there to turn the slow afternoon traffic away from the shallow gap in the road. Beyond them the lake was very blue. You could just barely see the strip of green and the thin fingers of smoke that was Oshkosh on the opposite shore.

Just behind me, inside the breakwater, was the Big Hole where the smaller sailing boats were tied. I knew if I looked I could see it. But I didn't want to — not yet. There is that funny fascinating suspense in waiting, like wiggling a very loose tooth with your tongue. And besides it wouldn't do to have Kitty know what I really came out for. She is a good scout but — well, I just didn't want her to know, that's all.

So we went over to watch the children swimming and splashing first, and then I pushed Kitty in a swing until she said she was beginning to feel dizzy, and we walked all the way to the refreshment stand at the other end of the park for an ice-cream cone and a bag of popcorn. By the time we had walked back she had chocolate ice cream dribbled down the front of her shirt and her chin was shiny from the butter off my popcorn and both of us were ready to go home.

Just as I had planned we took the long way, back through the park, and we had to pass the Big Hole on our way.

The afternoon sun was sparkling and glinting on the tip of each small, quick wave so that the whole stretch of water in the harbor seemed to be giggling in the sunlight. There was a long row of small green and white sailboats tied to the shore, nodding up and down as the water licked the anchoring piles. They all had single, slim masts jabbing upward and gray canvas stretched neatly over their cockpits and, to me, they all looked exactly the same! I couldn't even tell which one was Jack's! I felt suddenly so relieved that I could have laughed out loud just standing there, looking at the boats dancing at the ends of their short ropes and the blue water shining in the sun. I don't know just what I *had* expected to see — one boat standing off by itself, looking different from the rest or a sign on one of them saying, "This is the boat that Angie Morrow fell in love in!" or something equally as silly. But whatever it was, it wasn't there at all!

Just then a horn honked close behind us and Kitty and I both jumped in fright and turned to look. There was Swede. He pulled up alongside us and leaning out the car window, said, "Hi-yah, Angie. Want a ride home?"

It was annoying that he should come along just then. In the first place I hadn't wanted him to see me standing staring at the boat, and besides I could just hear him saying later, "Hey, Jack, that Angie don't look so good in the daytime! I saw her this afternoon out looking at the boat and she didn't look so good as at night."

I had on old slacks and I knew my nose was shiny, but Swede was smiling at me with his funny warm grin so there was nothing to do but say, "Hello, there. You scared me, honking that way. This is my sister Kitty, Swede." They nodded to each other and she bent down in an embarrassed little-girl sort of way, pretending to take a stone out of her shoe and softly whistling a breathy tune with no particular melody.

"Been looking at the boat?" Swede asked. I nodded. "Nice little job, isn't she? Did you have fun last night, Angie?"

Now is my chance to find out, I thought. Swede is sure to know if anyone does! "Oh, I had a wonderful time," I told him, and then added casually, very offhand, "Did Jack have fun?"

"Yeh, I guess he did."

"Don't you *know?*"

"No, he didn't say nothing."

"Did you see him today?"

"Sure."

"Well, what did he say?"

"Nothing much. At least nothing — about you."

36

So he hadn't said anything! After last night and the way he'd looked and my wearing his sweater, and after what had happened while trying to light his pipe and everything — and he hadn't said anything. I couldn't believe it! Swede was sitting running his finger up and down, playing with the grooves in the steering wheel. I looked at him and I could feel a question forming on my lips, "But didn't he even —" and I checked myself just in time, saying instead, "Thanks anyway for the ride, Swede, but I guess Kitty and I will walk home. It isn't very far. Thanks anyway."

"Okay," he said. "Glad I met you, Kitty. See you later, Angie," and the car pulled away.

The sun didn't seem quite so bright on the water now. We passed two little boys coming home from swimming with their hair sleeked back and damp canvas knickers pulled on over their still-wet swimming suits. They had stopped at the public drinking fountain where the water comes out so cold that it hurts your teeth, and were squirting mouthfuls of water at each other, their cheeks puffed out like chipmunks'. One yelled hello to Kitty, sending the water out of his mouth in a spout. He was in her room at school, she explained with injured dignity.

Mom was sitting in a canvas lawn chair in the shade at the side of the house when we got home, reading the evening paper. It is an unwritten rule in our house never to ask for a piece of the paper until my mother has finished with it, so Kitty and I both sat down to wait. The short-clipped grass was cool and fresh and full of little clover, the kind whose heads flip off like small pink and white balls before the lawn mower.

"I see where Grace Mary Wuerst is going to be married," my mother said. I raised an eyebrow in acknowledgement and Kitty just sat chewing a clover stem. She turned a page and after a moment or two — "Remind me to tell Dad that there is a new hospital going up in Sheboygan. They are open for bids next Monday." I raised the other eyebrow. My mother leafed through the last few pages quickly and then, without saying a word, pulled out an inside sheet and handed it to me and gave Kitty the page with the comic strips. We sat reading together and before long it began to get cooler and the shade from the house stretched out over the side lawn on which we were sitting, over the neighbors' driveway and printed the crooked shadow of a chimney halfway up the side of the neighbors' house. "You two had better go in and set the table for supper," my mother said. "Margaret and Lorraine will be here soon and perhaps we might all like to walk up and see a movie tonight."

I thought it over as I spread the cloth on the dining-room table. Of course, I couldn't say I didn't *want* to go, but if he should call when we were at the movie I'd never know! It might be that he hadn't said anything to Swede because, like me, he wasn't sure. And maybe Swede was just teasing me. Probably he and Jack had talked it all over and he just didn't want to tell me, that was all. Outside, long shadows lay on the grass and I could hear robins in the trees on the front lawn singing that lilting question they always ask from tree to tree as the sun is going down.

In the kitchen Kitty had been opening two cans of pork and beans and she popped something quickly in her mouth and was wiping her fingers on her slacks with a guilty look when I came in for the silverware. I still couldn't believe that he hadn't even *mentioned* last night, hadn't said anything at all.

No matter what you tell her, Kitty always eats

the little piece of fat pork off the top of a can of pork and beans like that.

Even when you say prayers for it, a thing almost never happens the way this did. In five minutes more we would have been halfway down the block and I'd never have heard the phone ring at all. It was just as if it had been planned. Kitty and my other two sisters were already on the front steps with their hair all brushed and ready to go to the movie, and I had just run back upstairs for a clean handkerchief for my mother when the phone rang. It was Jack calling.

He knew it was late, he said, and he would have called earlier, but his father hadn't decided to let him use the car until a few minutes ago and would I like to go out for a while? Probably drive to Pete's or something. . . .

"Of course *not*," my mother said firmly. "Tell him that you were just going to the movies with us. The idea of thinking that you can go out any night in the week! Does he think you have nothing else to do?"

"Oh, let her go, Mom. With school just out it's good to fool around."

"Sure. It's a wonderful night to go out and Pete's is on the lake — let her go, Mom. The show isn't very good anyway."

"It won't hurt, Mom. Let her go."

My sisters were talking. I said nothing.

She mused a moment. "Well, all right. You may go this time but don't let this boy —" she *knew* his name was Jack — "think that you can be running around all the time. You have better things to do. I thought this was the summer you were going to get so much reading done. But you may go this time."

39

Halfway down the front sidewalk she turned and called, "Angie, you'd better put on your blue linen. You don't look very dressed up for an evening."

And I hurried upstairs to get ready, trying to calm the crowded, fluttery thoughts in my head. "I'll see you in ten minutes then," Jack had said.

You would like Pete's, I know. There is no other place quite like it. When we were little we used to go for drives on warm summer evenings with my mother and father and stop there for ice-cream cones. Everyone did. And now that the children were grown up they still stopped — to dance now and have Cokes or beer instead of ice-cream cones. Mr. Mingle (everyone calls him Pete) is past eighty and can just barely shuffle around, but he remembers everyone and can call each by his own name. The building, old and square, is built right on the lake shore about three miles out of town and the inside hasn't been painted for years. Outside, the lawns and flower beds have all run into one and stretch to the water's edge in a tangle of weeds. On one side is a gravel parking lot, for Pete's is always jammed at night with the crowd from high school.

We went in the side door, Jack and I, and sat in one of the booths which are set back in latticework arches with little black painted tables, the tops rough with carved initials. The edges of the carving are worn smooth by hundreds of Coke bottles and glasses of beer and by hands that have held each other tight across those tables. Off in one corner is Pete's old and irritable parrot perched on a wicker stand, scrawking at anyone who comes too near, continually rolling its yellow eyes in anger, and perching at the pumpkin seeds in its food dish with an ugly beak that is chipped in layers like an old fingernail.

I felt a little scared. It was almost like making my debut or something. I had never been out to Pete's on a date before, and in our town that is the crucial test. Everyone is there and everyone sees you. I knew of a girl once who went out to Pete's with her cousin and no one else asked her to dance or paid any attention to her, and so she went away to college in the fall and never had dates at home for any of the dances at Christmas or Easter. If you don't make the grade at Pete's, you just don't make it.

"What will you have, Angie?" Jack asked. He hadn't said much to me on the way out — not much *about* me, I mean. Halfway to Pete's he had asked if I heard anything funny in the motor of the car — like a faint knocking or something, so we drove almost two miles in silence, he with his head cocked to one side and a scowl on his face and I sitting very still trying to look as if I were listening hard. In the end, just as we got to Pete's, he decided it had been his imagination after all. So you see, when he said, "What will you have, Angie?" that's when my evening, the evening of my "coming out," really began.

At Pete's you choose from only four things — beer, root beer, Coke, and peanuts salted in the shell. No one ever wants anything else. I wanted a Coke and he wanted a glass of beer and we both wanted peanuts, so Jack went up to the bar to get them to save old Pete the trouble. The bar is in a smaller room in the front and the juke-box is there, too, and that's where all the boys who haven't dates sit and play cards and watch the other fellows and girls as they come in.

While he was gone I traced through the maze of initials on the table top, trying to make out someone's I knew. Maybe, I thought, his is here some-

41

where. There was a heart with a J and another letter in it, but the second initial had been carved over so I couldn't make it out. I thought of scratching my own A.M. in a small, smooth space — just so it would look as if I had been there before, as if someone had wanted to carve my initials like they did other girls' — but I couldn't find anything to do it with. If I took a hairpin out of my hair the curl on top would fall down and I would have to fix it all over again.

I took the little mirror out of my purse to look at myself — I didn't often wear my hair with that big curl on top, and because they had all gone to the movies there was no one at home to consult before I left. It looked all right to me, but then Pete's is so hazy-dark that everything looks different anyway.

Swede walked in from the bar just then with a glass of beer in his hand and slid into the booth across from me. "Hi-yah, Angie," he said. "Jack will be back in a minute. He's talking to some of the fellows." He paused to take a sip of his beer. "Well, what's the good word?"

I didn't know just what he meant by that so I smiled, telling him I hadn't known he was going to be out here, and we began to talk about little things — did I drink beer, and whether or not the kids would like Pete's as well if it was all fixed up, and how come a good girl like me had wasted my talents by not going up to high school? I liked Swede. His hair was blond and kinky and he looked so well-fed and healthy that it seemed as if his chest would burst right through his sweater. Besides, he made me feel like a pretty girl, talking as he did — "A good girl like me wasting my talents by not going up to high school." Maybe it wouldn't be so hard to talk to the other fellows after all.

When Jack came back with my Coke and peanuts

he brought two of his friends, boys who had played basketball with him, and in the beginning I felt quite at ease with them. After the introductions they didn't pay much attention to me, but just talked about school, and that they had heard "Old Baldy" wasn't going to be teaching math next year after the way he had thrown that book at Chuck Wilkins that day, and who was the new girl from Ninth Street that Dick Fox had had out for the past three nights? I just listened and laughed and drank my Coke and didn't seem to be out of place in the least. I'm sure none of them thought that this was my first night out at Pete's on a date and that I'd never sat in a booth with four boys at once before. I tried to act very natural and casual and didn't say much.

I didn't know Jane Rady was there that night at all until she came over from one of the darker booths near the back to talk with us, saying, "Well, Angie Morrow, I didn't know *you* were here!" in a funny surprised sort of voice that really sounded as if she were saying, "Well, Angie Morrow, I really never thought I'd see you out on a date!"

Jane is much shorter than I am with fluffy blond hair that she lets hang loose with no hairpins or bow or anything. And for some reason when you look at Jane you always see her mouth before you see the rest of her face.

All four of the boys said, "Hi, there, Janie!" and one stood up to give her his place but she said, "Oh, don't bother, I'll just squeeze in." It was so crowded that Jack had to put his arm around the back of the booth to make room and she looked at him with a little smile and purred under her breath, "Uum, nice!" and everyone laughed and said, "What a girl, Janie!" and I laughed, too, but my face felt stiff and the laugh came out funny though I don't think anyone noticed it for they were all listening to her.

I sat and listened too. It wasn't because I hadn't gone up to high school then; Jane hadn't gone up there either but she knew the things to say. She knew what they were talking about when they said, "Remember the night after the Sheboygan game when there were seven of us coming home in the back seat?" and "Did you hear what happened to Bartie when he broke the drum at the graduation dance last week?" Jane did remember and she had heard and she added a few more things that made the boys laugh and look at each other and then back at her. And of course I laughed too but I felt very uncomfortable and conspicuous; and though I drank my Coke in little sips it did not last long enough, and I had to sit sliding ice round and round in the empty glass and rack my brains for something to say, something that would make them remember that I was there or make them at least think that I thought what they were talking about was interesting too.

I thought of saying brightly, as if the thought had just come to me, "Did Jack and Swede and I ever have fun sailboating last night!" But they might all turn and look at me, saying with a questioning inflection, "Yeah?" and I wouldn't know how to go on from there. Maybe Jack wouldn't want them to know we had been sailboating — after all he hadn't mentioned it himself, had he? He was lighting a cigarette for Jane just then and she blew the smoke in his face in a playful puff as she said, "Thanks," and smiled a little half-smile with the side of her mouth that didn't have the cigarette in it.

Through my mind mulled all the things she used to tell me about Jack when she sat next to me in

44

history class. The evening dragged on and on. The Coke had left a sweetish, sickening taste in my mouth and my whole body ached with wretchedness.

Swede's beer glass was empty and he stood up saying, "Can I get anything for anybody?" and balancing the empty glasses in a pyramid, he went out to the bar. In the other room someone had put a nickle in the jukebox and music began to come through the round amplifier all hung with crepe paper above the door. Jane gave a little gasp and made her eyes and mouth very round. "Oh, that song — I love it! Jack, dance with me!" She stood up, holding out her hand.

Jack looked at me and said, " 'Scuse me, will you?" I didn't blame him. Anyone with a date as dull as I was would naturally want to dance with someone else. Out of the corner of my eye I watched him. I didn't care, I said to myself. I was all wrong about last night anyway. It didn't make any difference — he was just like any other boy, any boy at all. I was all wrong.

The music seemed to fill the whole room at Pete's with its poignant tilt, and the little liquid waves of music seemed to curl in and out the latticework that arched the booths. I sat staring at the table and slid my Coke glass so that it covered the carved heart with the initial J in it. Of course I was all wrong about last night.

There were other people dancing now but it didn't seem to matter; Jack and Jane weren't looking at anyone. She was much shorter than he and danced with her arm crooked around his neck and her head back so that her fluffy hair hung halfway down her back. Neither of them seemed to be saying anything, just dancing and letting the music float round them. I tried to keep from watching them too hard. One of the fellows in our booth became restless and muttering, " 'Scuse me," went out to the bar. "I don't care," I thought. "Let him go. I know I'm dull. I don't care if he wants to go — everyone can't be like Jane Rady." It seemed as if my whole face was stiff with scowling and my eyebrows must be growing straight across my nose, dark and heavy.

The full disappointment of the evening struck me all in a lump. It was the rollicking sadness of the music that made my heart feel sore. It was that and the thought of last night and all the silly, wonderful things I had been feeling all day and the way my heart had jumped when the phone rang and it was Jack. And it was because he was there now dancing with Jane Rady when he hadn't even danced with me once and I was his date. And the other fellows didn't like me either and I was awkward and didn't know anything to talk about. It was all that and the sudden, sickening realization that I couldn't fool myself. I did care! It wasn't because it was the first boy I had ever really been out with — this was something different. I had never felt this way before — and he didn't even care! Someone had put another nickel in the music box and they kept on dancing.

So I just waited, toying with my empty glass, and the corners of my mouth seemed suddenly tired and a peculiar lonesome ache went through me right down into my hands. I just sat, not thinking of anything in particular, feeling as useless, as emptied, and as hollowed as a sucked orange.

Lying in bed that night thinking it over, slowly and clearly, I decided it was *me* that was all wrong. Other girls knew what to do. Other girls could talk with fellows and laugh with them and say funny things. Jane Rady could do it. Jane knew how to dance with her head back so her hair fell long and smooth as silk thread. Mine was curly all over and no matter how much I brushed it there were always little wispy curls around my face, as if I had just come out of a steamy shower. I wasn't the kind of a girl who could ever go into Mc-Knight's drugstore and have a crowd of boys come over to sit with me, wanting to buy me a Coke. And I know I'd look silly if I shook my finger as if I were trucking and clicked time with my tongue, swaying from side to side the way some girls can do, when good dance music came on the radio. None of the fellows at Pete's had even offered me a cigarette because they could tell just by looking at me that I was the kind of girl who wouldn't know how to smoke!

And of course I had acted all wrong too. It made me squirm inside to think of it. When Jack and Jane had finished dancing I should have smiled as if I hadn't cared at all and said something smart like "smooth stuff there," or "just like Veloz and Yolanda," as any other girl would have done. But I didn't. My face had been stiff with misery, and seeing everyone else laughing and having so much fun I couldn't help thinking how much better it would have been if I had just gone to the movies with my mother and sisters. You know, if you don't see all the fellows and girls out on dates you don't think about it and then you don't feel so unhappy. If I hadn't gone out to Pete's at all things could have gone on as they had before — "Angie Morrow doesn't go out on dates because her mother doesn't let her" — and no one would have known I was such a drip. But now even Jack knew.

Only once during the whole evening had there been a trace of that strange, warm feeling of last night when, just before we went home, we had gone outside and down to the water's edge behind Pete's. The lake was rough and the waves tossed up, white with spray, sucking at the shore, and the wind went soughing through the line of old willows, swaying them with a sonorous, restless rhythm. We stood quiet, listening to the night sounds and watching the pale moon, half hidden by the gray cotton cloud stretched across it. Inside, Pete's had been so full of music and laughing, but out here the whole stretch of dark water and the thick weeds and the swaying trees on the shore seemed tormented by a strange, aching lonesomeness, and the wind blew in cool and damp from the lake with the familiar, moist smell of fish. Out here something in me relaxed; all the awkward restraint that had haunted me through the evening was lifted and I felt like taking off my shoes and dancing in the grass.

As we were going back to our car I noticed all the silent, dark cars parked around the gravel lot and remarked to Jack, "There don't seem to be nearly as many people inside as there are cars parked out here."

He looked at me a moment, as if he thought I was joking, and then said with an odd laugh and an inflection which I didn't quite understand, "You're a good kid, Angie." That's all he said and it may have been just my imagination mingled with the mysterious spell of the lake but for a moment, for the only time during the whole evening, I thought he looked at me as he had last night.

But the feeling couldn't last when, during that short ride back to town, I realized again with doubled humiliation what a terrible date I'd been. Jack didn't look at me once all the way home, or try to talk and as soon as we got in front of my house he jumped out of the car and came round to open my door. It seemed so funny, walking up the sidewalk, that just this time the night before I had been doing the same thing and wondering if he would call me again; and now he *had* called and I *had* gone out with him and here I was, still wondering if there would be another time. But tonight it was tinged with a little hopelessness. After the way I had acted what would any boy do?

Standing on the front steps, I had an uncomfortable feeling that there was something I should say; yet a girl just can't blurt out an apology for not being like other girls! I could almost feel the right words on my tongue, but when I opened my mouth to speak there was nothing there at all. I broke off a bit of the tall spruce that grows beside our steps and smelled the pungent piny odor rising in the air. Jack was standing running his finger round and round one of the scrolls in our wrought-iron stair railing. "Angie," he said slowly, "Angie, I'm going to be out of town for a couple of days." My heart slipped down a little. This was his way of saying that he wouldn't see me for a couple of days — a couple of days that would probably merge into a week and then turn out to be the rest of the summer. "Going up to Green Bay," he explained, "to see a cousin of mine and I won't be back till Friday afternoon some time." That's all right, my mind said hurriedly. That's all right, Jack. You don't have to tell me anything. I know how I've acted tonight. "I wondered," he went on, "if you'd like to go to the dance at the Country Club with me on Friday night. It's the first one of the summer and I thought maybe you'd like to go!"

Lying in bed that night I thought it over. I had wanted an invitation to that dance more than anything else in the world, but now that I had been asked I hardly wanted to go because I could tell beforehand just what it would be like. My mother, who is always good about things like that, would buy me a new summer evening dress to wear; and my two older sisters, who would probably be going too, would arrange my hair and lend me perfume to dab behind my ears and on the hem of my dress so I would swish up a glamorous smell when I walked; and there would be Kitty, sitting on the edge of her bed in her pajamas, watching each step and saying over and over, "Oh, how nice you look!" When we were all dressed my mother would stand back to look at us with her eyes shining, thinking, probably, how short a time ago it seemed since we were just little girls. Of course, I would smile and pretend to be excited and so glad to be going, but all the time, inside, I'd keep remembering how it had been at Pete's when I hadn't been able to talk to the fellows at all and I would keep thinking how I had watched the cross parrot, pretending to be very interested in his chipped beak and yellow eyes just because no one bothered to talk to me.

I had never been to a dance at the Country Club before but my sisters had told me about them. Almost anyone could go. The people divide into crowds and cliques when they get there, the older ones, when they're not dancing, sitting at the bar, and the younger crowd at little tables drinking Cokes or walking around outside on the flagstone terrace. It was easy to imagine the girls like Jane Rady out there with their soft formals fluttering in the night breezes, laughing up at fellows in white coats whose cigarettes made bright holes in the darkness. And it was easy to imagine me too, not ever saying anything smooth, not knowing what to do with my hands, and laughing too often in a stiff, self-conscious way, just because I wouldn't be able to think of the right things to say. Even with a new formal and perfume on my hair I wouldn't be any different. If I hadn't been able to do it at Pete's I wouldn't be able to do it at the dance. I knew it. Other girls could have fun and get along with boys but I wasn't *like* other girls.

I turned over, shutting my eyes, trying to sleep, and on my fingers I could still smell the pungent spice of the spruce tree.

It was odd to remember that just this time last night the thoughts in my head had been as pleasant and sweet as warm, thick honey.

Doing the supper dishes next evening, Lorraine and I discussed what kind of a formal I should get, though we knew very well that in the end it would be my mother who would decide. All of us had agreed at supper time that it should be "something young and not too sophisticated." Margaret had suggested a blue and white sprigged dimity — very quaint and little-girlish, which had just come in at the store — but Lorraine thought something "less ordinary" would be better.

"You know," Lorraine said to me later, "a girl should always choose something different so she stands out on the dance floor. If you really wanted to do something unusual you should take a very, very long piece of ribbon and tie it in a small bow on the top of your head and let the streamers hang right down to the hem of your skirt. One of the girls at school did that at our spring dance this year. And another had a black net formal so she got some black veiling and wore it on her head with a red rose like a Spanish mantilla — but that would be a little exotic for Fond du Lac." My sister always

51

knows a lot of original, clever ideas about clothes and even if she wasn't going to the dance herself she didn't mind talking about it.

No one had mentioned it out loud, of course, but we had all been hoping someone would ask her. When the older and younger go it's hard for the middle one to stay home. Lorraine never dates much in Fond du Lac. When she was at college in Chicago she used to go out a lot — at least as much as the other girls. There wasn't a chance for meeting many boys when you went to a girls' college with no college for boys nearby. She used to write home about the smooth blind dates she had for school dances and they almost always asked her out again afterward. Somehow the boys around our town didn't seem to appreciate her — there weren't many fellows who knew about books and English literature and the things that Lorraine learned in college. Of course, she never said anything about it but in the summertime it is handy to have a boy.

Kitty was outside playing "One, Two, Three, O'Leary" on the driveway and the ball made a pleasant, rhythmic bounce-bounce on the pavement. The man next door was cutting his lawn and between the noise of the lawn mower we could hear Margaret and my mother talking in the back garden. "You know," my mother was saying, "if you're sure it isn't too old looking, I think that blue sprigged should be nice for Angie."

"You'll like it!" Margaret assured her. "You and Angie come down to the store tomorrow and she can try it on. It's the prettiest one we have in right now and we certainly don't want her in one of those aqua or rose taffeta things." And then the lawn mower drowned them out again.

A few moments later Lorraine was just shaking some soap chips into the dishpan for me when we caught the tail end of a sentence from the back lawn — "well, it's a little late but Art can probably get hold of *someone* who will go, though, you know, Mom, most fellows wouldn't want to drive all the way up from Milwaukee just on the chance of a blind date!"

My mother's voice was very maternal and concerned. "I know. It wouldn't be so bad if Angie weren't going, too, but — " and then came the whirring sound of the lawn mower.

This was something we hadn't been meant to hear and I hoped perhaps Lorraine hadn't, so I made a clatter with the dishes and tried to pretend nothing had happened. But suddenly she turned to me and said in a tight voice, "Why if that isn't absolutely silly, Angie. Honestly! If I really *wanted* to go I could always ask one of the fellows up from Chicago, couldn't I?"

I checked myself just in time with the logical question on my lips — "Why don't you, Lorraine?"

A moment later she threw her dish towel over the back of a chair and without looking at me said quickly, "Got to go upstairs a minute. Be right back to finish." I dried the rest of the dishes, swept the kitchen floor, and hung the dish towel on the rack to dry. The bounce-bounce of Kitty's ball on the driveway was beginning to get monotonous so I turned on the living-room radio to drown out the sound. The breeze coming in the window was fresh and clean with the smell of newly cut grass.

When Lorraine finally came down I pretended to be very busy with the evening paper and she leafed through an old magazine, neither of us saying anything. Her cheeks were very white with powder but around her eyes was still red. It was funny that I had never realized before that Lorraine *minded* not dating.

On Friday night before the dance I stood in the garden, wondering what it was all about. Just a short time ago Jack called to say he would pick me up at a quarter-past nine. I was all ready except to slip my evening dress on over my head. In the end we had decided on the sprigged dimity and my mother had pressed it so the full skirt hung in soft, billowy folds and the small sleeves stuck up stiff and puffed as it was spread out on my bed. I had come out to the garden to pick bachelor's buttons for my hair in my long white slip, holding it high to keep the hem above the cool dew on the grass. And as I stood in the garden with the soft air against my cheek and a night breeze fingering through my hair, I couldn't help wondering a little.

From the house came familiar sounds — the radio in the living room purring out soft dance music, the noise of Lorraine clicking down the stairs as the telephone rang, and Kitty in her own bedroom talking to someone excitedly in a high, small voice. When Jack had called I had thought it would make me excited, after not having heard him for three days, but it didn't. It was just a boy's voice. Just a low, friendly boy's voice that might have belonged to anyone. I hadn't felt any particular thrill at all — at least I believed I hadn't; but now out in the garden with the night air so still and soft, the thought of him came back to me and played through my mind till my lips felt warm and my heart beat fast with the wonder of it.

In the past few days something had changed. I had never felt things inside of me before and now I wasn't even sure if I really felt warm and eager because it was my first Country Club dance and my dress was new, or if it was really because in such a short time, such a very short time, Jack would be there — or was it only that the night was so beautiful that I just wanted to feel something? That evening at Pete's had left me with a cautious soreness, half in my mind and half in my heart. And yet, out in the garden, I realized that some of the strange feeling of the first night still lingered. But I couldn't tell, really — it was all still so puzzling and so new. And the night breeze blew till the thin silk of my slip licked against my legs, cool and clean.

Beside the garden path was a rose vine clinging to a rough lattice support, the tender trailers tied with bits of string. The heavy-headed red roses looked black in the darkness, their perfume floating upward, bewitching the air. Over the whole garden the crickets sang with a steady, rhythmical cheeping, keeping time to the music of the night. The air was soft and warm with the smell of damp earth and the lush darkness of summer. Somewhere, off where lights were bright and the night was moving, I heard a car's brakes screak. The echo waited a moment and then all was still. One thought in my mind sang a beating refrain with the crickets — "in just a few minutes Jack will be here." Far up in the darkness was a thin yellow arc of moon, turned over on its back, and the night sky was faintly stardusted. Something deep within me stirred and a throbbing warmth surged through my whole body until the very tips of my fingers tingled. The whole night was drawn out like soft, silver music. Dew from the plant was cool and clean on my wrist, and as I stooped to pick the little flower heads in the darkness a small night moth with white tissue-paper wings fluttered upward from the leaves. I remember suddenly my lips felt soft, as if I had just smiled, and with a hushed feeling of breathless awe I heard myself whisper a single-word prayer, "God!"

I know you will think it's terrible, after I had

only been out with him three times but in a way I couldn't help it — even if I did know from the very beginning of the evening, or at least from the first dance, that it would happen. If I had heard of any other girl's doing it I would probably think the same thing you will think but, well, I did it — and I wish I could make you understand.

I can't explain much about it — the dance itself, I mean. So much happened that I don't remember any of it very distinctly; but it doesn't matter much, because it wasn't the dance, it was the evening as a whole that was so important. I do remember seeing Lorraine dance by several times with the pale, blind date who had come up from Milwaukee with Art. He looked a little odd to me, gaunt and dry — like something you should soak overnight before using, but Lorraine didn't seem to mind. Having been to college, she knows how to act at dances. She had on purplish lipstick and was dancing with her head back, laughing very hard and having a very gay time, but he was looking at her in a surprised sort of way, holding his head back at a funny angle as if his neck were stiff.

At times I could hardly believe I was actually with Jack. When he was talking to someone else and I was watching him he seemed so tan and clean, so familiar and yet so far away; he was so much fun and everyone liked him so well that it didn't seem as if he could possibly be my date at all. It didn't seem that a boy so nice could really be with me. Several times I felt quite sure that when the music began again he would be off dancing with someone else. Once when he introduced me to a friend of his, Dick Fox, who said, "So this is the Angie we've been hearing so much about," I looked at Jack quickly but he was looking at Dick just as if he hadn't even heard him at all.

One dance I had with Tony Becker, a boy from Oshkosh, whom Jack didn't seem to like very well. They had played basketball together on opposing teams during the winter and that night Tony didn't have a date — he was just out with the fellows, he told me. I liked Tony. I liked the way he held me when we danced and I liked him for telling me he thought my formal was pretty and for commenting on the flowers in my hair. Of course I knew it wasn't all true but it was fun talking to him — and he said he hoped he would see me again sometime.

But what I really wanted to tell you about is this. After that dance with Tony, I had all the rest with Jack. At first I tried to dance like Jane Rady with my head back so I could look up at him, but that way I had to look right into his eyes and it gave me such a funny, panicky feeling that I would forget what I was saying and get mixed up in my dancing. Once Swede came up, tapping Jack on the shoulder, asking to cut in, but he told him to come back later and Swede just shrugged and went away smiling knowingly, as if he had a secret on his mind.

I don't know just the minute it began to happen but soon, after each dance, when the music had stopped, I would feel less and less like taking my arm away from Jack's shoulder and he kept holding my hand as if the music were still playing. And yet he would never look at me and as I watched his face it was perfectly still, as if nothing were happening, while all the time his hand was in mine sending warm shivers all up my arm. Once Swede danced past and said under his breath, "Break it up, break it up!" and Jack grinned suddenly and I couldn't help laughing.

The band was playing something slow and hushed — I don't remember what it was — but it filled the room from the floor to the ceiling. No one seemed to be actually dancing but the crowd moved with a slow, rhythmic swaying and Jack and I seemed to be part of the whole gentle movement. I shut my eyes and the sound of the other dancers, the full, sweet swelling of the saxophone, and the thin magic of the clarinet floated above us in a haunted cloud while we danced in a breathless stillness beneath. I knew then I couldn't go on feeling this way — I knew something had to happen.

The rest of the evening passed quickly, like a movie film being run off in a rapid blur, rushing to the climax. When the dance was almost over we went out on the terrace, Jack and I. I think there were several other people out there, I'm not sure, though I vaguely remember the scattered glow of cigarettes burning in the half darkness and the warm sound of people laughing. It seemed to me then that I had two hearts, one where it should be and the other pulsing rapidly in the soft hollow at the base of my throat. Leaning against the clubhouse wall I could feel the roughness of the stone and the coolness of the Virginia creeper leaves on my shoulders. Even out here the air throbbed with music. It was better to say something casual than just to wait in that breathless silence saying nothing at all. "Did you have a good time in Green Bay, Jack?" I asked.

"I did, Angie. I really had fun," he answered. "I meant to send you a postcard but, well, I just didn't get around to it." He paused. Now it was his turn to be without words. "Did you do anything special while I was away? Anything interesting?" It was silly to be standing there with my hands closed tight behind my back telling him about the new book I had read and that Kitty had started to take swimming lessons at the lake to try to earn a Junior

Lifesaver's badge and other unimportant things, when we both knew we were just trying to make conversation, just marking time; and the words lumped in my throat, not even wanting to be said. It was silly just standing there. Both of us knew.

"I used to caddy on this course," he told me suddenly as if the thought were an inspiration. "It's a beautiful course. Beautiful, Angie. One of the best in the state. I practically know it by heart. There's a little elevation over by the second hole, you can't see it from here, but standing on it you can look out over the whole course. At night it's wonderful. There's just enough moon — would you like to look at it with me?" I nodded and he took my hand to guide me over the grass. "Hold your skirt up," he said softly. "There is dew on everything."

Standing on that elevation, the whole course seemed to be rolled out broad before us in the moonlight, smoothness and shadow. From this distance a sand trap looked like a big open scar on the smooth face of the green and the moon gave a weird yellow half-light that made the whole night a two-tone picture of highlights and hollows. Behind us tall old elm trees on the edge of the course stretched their black leaf-lace high against the sky. Jack took a handkerchief out of his coat and the dubonnet dress handkerchief from his breast pocket, spreading them together on the grass for me to sit on. I have never known anything so lovely as that night.

At first neither of us spoke but sat feeling the softness of the breeze and watching the fireflies winking in the grass, while from the clubhouse music floated out to us, muted by the almost tangible stillness of the night. Jack lit a cigarette and in the match glow I saw his face, so young and clean, and the sheer joy of just being with him made me shiver a little. He smoked in silence for a time and then, turning to me, said unexpectedly, almost as if he relished the words, "Everyone I introduced you to tonight liked you, Angie. A couple of the fellows are mad that they didn't find you first." I didn't say anything but sat looking at the moon — by squinting my eyes I could make it shoot out into long yellow jags of light.

"Swede told me he saw you out looking at the boat the other day," he went on. I still made no comment. He was puffing out the smoke from his cigarette thoughtfully, watching it in the air as it floated into nothingness. All around us the crickets were keeping up a steady cheep-cheep, so constant that after a while it was no sound at all, just a rhythm keeping time to the faster beating of my heart. Then without looking at me, without turning his head, Jack asked, "Why, Angie?" The night was so quiet that the words seemed to stand still in mid-air, echoing over and over softly till at last they faded away. Why? I could hear my thoughts brushing past each other in my head, none of them coherent enough to be spoken. There were no words for an answer. I felt Jack's hand on mine as it lay on the grass, his fingers warm and hesitant. He flipped his cigarette away and together we watched the stub glowing until it burned itself out in the grass.

Really I don't know how it happened. If I could tell you I would. Maybe I shouldn't even mention it, seeing it was only the third time I had been out with him. But I knew it was going to happen, and I wanted it to.

It was wonderfully strange knowing even before he moved, even before he put his arm around me, that he would. It gave me a new sense of power to think that from the very beginning of the evening — at least, from the first dance — I knew this would happen.

Then suddenly, and yet it wasn't sudden at all, I remember myself with both hands pressed against the gabardine of his coat so hard that I could feel the roughness of the cloth. My head seemed to be throbbing wildly and still I was thinking very clearly and precisely. Behind him I could see the high stars and the golf course stretched out silver-green in the moonlight and the fireflies flickering in the grass like bits of neon lighting. I felt a new, breathless caution as if I were sitting in a bubble. And then, I, Angie Morrow, who had never done anything like this before, who until last Monday night had never even had a real date, could feel his cheek on mine, as warm and soft as peach fuzz. And I knew if I moved my face just a little, just a very little . . .

In the movies they always shut their eyes but I didn't. I didn't think of anything like that, though I do remember a quick thought passing through my mind again about how much he smelled like Ivory soap when his face was so close to mine. In the loveliness of the next moment I think I grew up. I remember that behind him was the thin, yellow arc of moon, turned over on its back, and I remember feeling my hands slowly relax on the rough lapels of his coat. Sitting on the cool grass in my new sprigged dimity with the little blue and white bachelor's buttons pinned in my hair, Jack kissed me and his lips were as smooth and baby-soft as a new raspberry.

The night was so still I hardly noticed the small breeze that brushed past us, as soft and silent as a pussy willow.

That's the funny thing about Fond du Lac. It isn't such a small town — we have at least eight churches, three theatres, and a YMCA — but everyone seems to know everything about everyone else. Early Saturday morning Mrs. Callahan called over from her back garden to my mother who was cutting flowers, "Did Angie have a nice time at the dance last night?" and then I saw her walking up her garden path and my mother walking down ours to talk it over.

At noon I heard Margaret on the phone saying, "Why, yes. She had very much fun. He's rather young but nice, I think. She's been out with him a couple of times before." Everyone seemed to know.

Probably if I'd walked into McKnight's that afternoon girls I had never even met would look up and say to each other, "That's the girl Jack Duluth has been taking out!" It's funny what a boy can do. One day you're nobody and the next day you're the girl that some fellow goes with and the other fellows look at you harder and wonder what you've got and wish that they'd been the one to take you out first. And the girls say hello and want you to walk down to the drugstore to have Cokes with them because the boy who likes you might come along and he might have other boys with him. Going with a boy gives you a new identity — especially going with a fellow like Jack Duluth.

Lorraine and I were talking about it the night after the dance. Jack works late Saturday nights so I hadn't even hoped to see him. Kitty goes to bed by seven-thirty and Lorraine and I were alone. "It's different when you go away to school," she had said to me. "You seem to have a broader outlook. Most of the girls in town here have nothing to think about but fellows — they just get out of high school, work in the dime store or something for a year or two, and then get married. They don't have anything else to think about!"

She was sitting in her flowered seersucker house coat with her hair twisted in curlers. It was only half dark outside and we were in the living room with the lights off, listening to the radio and enjoying the stillness of the house. I wasn't really listening to her — warm, slow thoughts of last night kept brushing through my mind and sending tingles up my spine. "You know," Lorraine went on, "there are girls who graduated with me from high school who have babies two or three years old already and I'm not even through college!" I didn't quite get the connection but didn't want to say so. By not listening hard I thought maybe I had missed the first part. "Like my date last night," she continued.

"What about him?" I asked.

"Well, lots of girls in this town would be crazy to go out with him." I looked at her to see if she was really serious — Lorraine doesn't usually talk that way. "But," she went on, "I don't even care if I see him again or not. He's a good dancer and everything but I've just got other things to do. Of course," she added with condescension, "it was nice of Art to bring him up, but it wasn't as if I *had* to have a date — it's such a short time since I was in Chicago and I know boys down there. . . ."

We sat saying nothing for a while, me thinking about Jack and she thinking about I don't know what. Occasionally a car went down the street past the house, its headlights making a sweep of light before it. The dog, Kinkee, came into the living room and stretched out on the rug, settling her nose on her paws with a contented sigh. Lorraine reached over and twisted the radio dial to dance music.

"You know," she said suddenly with unexpected emphasis, "there is nothing I dislike so much as girls who are boy crazy!"

A little later the telephone rang and she answered. At first I couldn't tell what she was talking about, catching only snatches of the conversation: "How tall did you say?" "Where will we go?" and "Who else will be along?" and then she came back into the living room very excited and already twisting the curlers out of her hair. It was a blind date, she told me, and her words were jumbled with excitement — a friend of a friend of one of the girls she knew. He was a little older; he graduated from the university about six years ago; he was a fraternity man but she couldn't remember which one; he was now in town working with an insurance company and he wasn't too tall but tall enough!

"He wouldn't have been looking for a date this late on a Saturday night but he's new in town and doesn't know many girls yet," she explained carefully. "We're not going anywhere special — just dance somewhere or something." She snapped off the radio and said, "Come on upstairs with me, Angie, and help me decide what to wear — I want to look nice."

I sat on the edge of the bed, watching her. After she powdered her face she stood in front of the mirror with her eyes opened very wide as if she was amazed at something and put Vaseline on her eyelashes. Her lipstick she put on with a brush — a small, pointed one like the kind that came in the tin boxes of paints we used in grade school. She talked to me with hairpins in her mouth as she fixed her hair. It had been dampened when she put the curlers in and now the curls weren't quite dry so she combed them out into a fluff, curled it all around her finger, and then combed it out into a fluff again.

"You know," she said through hairpins, "if he went to the university he is probably a smooth boy — probably drinks Scotch and things. I wish I knew what kind of girls he likes. I don't know if I should pretend I'm the real intelligent type or pretend I'm sophisticated and have been around. It's different," she added, "with a town boy who knows all about you. Like with you and Jack — he knows that you've never gone with another fellow anyway."

I'd never thought of "pretending" with a boy. I'd thought either you had been around or you hadn't, either you were the intelligent type or you weren't. Lorraine talked as if she were dressing up a paper doll.

I had meant to tell her about Jack right away. When something as important as that happens to a girl she ought to tell someone. But the words were hard to pick. Every statement I figured out seemed to require a "so what?" answer. What if I did like Jack, she might say. What did I expect to do — dislike him?

The date came before she was ready so I opened the front door for him and asked him to come in and sit down. He wasn't very tall and when he smiled only his lips moved, as if his eyes were thinking of something else. He introduced himself very politely, saying he was Martin Keefe and how was I tonight. He said it nicely enough, but the way he looked at me made me feel like one of those pale, eyelashless girls used in magazine advertisements to sell mascara. Lorraine didn't come downstairs at once.

He took out a cigarette and tapped it on the back of his hand, lit it, and then sat there holding the burnt match end. We have no ash trays in our living room. None of us girls is supposed to smoke and my father gave it up years ago. I went into the kitchen and brought him a little crystal sauce-dish to use. "Thanks," he said in a half-angry tone and then added abruptly, "What grade you in in school?" I explained that I had just graduated last week and he nodded in an approving sort of way without even listening and said, "Well. Do you like school?" I assured him I did though I had found senior chemistry a little hard and he answered vaguely, "Good. Everybody should like school. Is that a picture of your sister on the piano?"

It was Margaret's picture he was talking about, taken one day when she was nineteen and someone had just told her that she looked like Merle Oberon. She had posed with her eyebrows arched and her lips pursed a little, with a very ethereal, faraway look on her face. Martin looked at it a moment and then walked around the room, stopping to examine the things on the knickknack shelf. He picked up a carved wooden Indian head with a worn, brown face.

"Real Indian stuff?" he asked. "Ever been way up North? Can pick this stuff up for nothing. Round the reservations it practically grows on trees. It's nice to have around though if it's a novelty to you."

It was disconcerting to have him pacing up and down as if I weren't even there, so just to make conversation I said, "Do you like living in Fond du Lac? It's a nice town when you get to know the people."

"I don't live here, you know," he told me with

unnecessary emphasis. "And I don't know anybody except a few fellows I've met around and that girl your sister knows. Maybe I'll like it here and maybe I won't. You can never tell if a town's any good until you've been out in it on a Saturday night." He sat down on the edge of the davenport, pulling his trousers up carefully at the knee before he crossed his legs. As if it were a sudden thought he took a fresh cigarette and then, changing his mind, pushed it back into the package. He kept looking at his hand, flexing the knuckles, turning them over and over, finally laying them palms up on his knees. His fingers were short and fat as a girl's.

Just then Lorraine came down, stopping a moment at the foot of the stairs with one foot a little ahead of the other the way models do. She had combed her hair high up on the sides, pinned in two sweeping rolls on top. I looked at Martin to see if he noticed how nice she looked, but he had just about the same expression on his face as when he was looking at the Indian carving. Lorraine put out her hand saying, "And you must be Martin Keefe. I'm so glad to know you."

When they left she turned back and called to me in the same careful, bright voice, "Good night, Angeline."

I could tell by the way she said it that Lorraine had decided to be the sophisticated type.

The next morning was Sunday and Sunday is always almost the same at our house. After church in the morning we had a very late and very large bacon-and-egg breakfast and waited for Art, the boy Margaret is going to marry, to drive up from Milwaukee. He came just after breakfast, shaking hands with my father and kissing us all on the cheeks as he always does. He is a big, soft-voiced boy and his kiss always reminds me of a large, wet marshmallow. Margaret patted him happily on both cheeks saying, "Hello there, Arthur, you fat-faced one. You haven't written to me since Thursday!"

Kitty spent most of the morning on the living-room rug with the funny papers, while my father cleared all the sales circulars out from the back seat of his car onto the front lawn, swept the floor and the seat with a whisk broom, shined the windshield and polished the headlights, and then put all the circulars back in neat piles. My father is a traveling salesman and his car is as important as his house to him. Every Sunday after church he takes off his coat and tie and goes out to straighten it. It is all part of the contented, weekend ritual, and he puffed and blew as he worked, bustling with importance while he polished the windshield till his neck was red with exertion. Then he stood back with the chamois cloth in his hand to admire it. My mother sat by the living-room window watching and we all laughed to ourselves, for we knew that by next weekend the car would be as dusty and untidy as ever.

Lorraine and I made the beds together, and the house smelled of roast and cauliflower from the kitchen, and everything was so pleasant and Sundayish that I forgot to ask what she had done last night and whether or not she had had fun with Martin Keefe.

Margaret and Art had gone for a ride and didn't get back until just before dinner was served. Art went out to the kitchen with his hands behind his back, walking in his funny way like a Teddy bear. In one hand he had a jar of green olives and a can of black olives in the other. Each Sunday he stops at some grocery store that is open late and brings home a contribution.

My mother was just lifting the roast out with two forks, dripping with sputtering hot fat, and Art set the olives down on the table to hold the meat platter for her. She saw them and looked at him with a softness in her eyes. "What's that for — a bribe?" she laughed, and patted his cheek.

Until she met Art, Margaret had always gone with a different kind of boy — tall fellows who moved fast and laughed deep down in their throats and showed square white teeth when they talked. But after she met Art she never went out with another boy. He was just a little taller than she with thick, dark hair and warm brown eyes that were as soft and mellow as his voice. We got used to his queer humor and odd gentleness till we liked him so well that to say "Margaret and Art" was as easy and natural as "bread and butter" or "dark and handsome."

Later, when dinner was over and we were sitting around the table in a contented, Sunday-afternoon apathy, Kitty pushed back her chair, excused herself, and went out to play on the front lawn. She walked about listlessly, flipping off clover heads with a short stick, humming to herself in dejection. Every now and then she stopped to stare down the street.

My mother looked out at her and shook her head. "Really, we're going to have to do something about that child," she said. "When you three girls were younger you had each other — but there is no one on this street for her to play with. Angie, you don't seem to have any more interest in her than the man in the moon. If she wants to play dolls, you're dusting; if she wants to go swimming, you're just washing your hair. It will be a good many years before she can go dancing!"

It's funny how, having nice thoughts in your head, it is so pleasant to pull them all out and think them all over again. And I wanted to think about Jack just then, so I said, "Mom, if you'll excuse me, I'll take Kitty for a walk in the field. We can pick violets or something . . ." and my conscience didn't even prick at the deception.

Our house is the second from the last on our street from the edge of town. Beyond the end house runs a gravel road and then a broad stretch of undeveloped real estate, run wild with weeds and low, scraggly bushes. We have always called it the Field.

That afternoon Kitty and I just wandered aimlessly through the long grass that was still lush and fresh with the last rains of spring, not going anywhere. It was early summer and the water was still puddled in the ditches along the grassy road and underfoot the ground had a soft, spongy feeling. The sky was dotted with cotton cloud-puffs and Kitty walked along, zigzagging with her head back and watching it till she was tired, and then plumped down to rest. I sat beside her. The breeze was like a gentle breathing and the sun hot on our faces till both of us were mellowed with contentment, basking in the almost liquid warmth of the sunshine.

Kitty rolled over on her back. "Angie," she said, her voice slow with thought, "did you ever wonder where the butterflies go when it rains?" I had to admit that until that moment I hadn't even thought of it.

"Well, I was thinking about it the other day, Angie," she told me, "and I figured that seeing they don't have holes or nests or anything, they must hide under leaves. That's the only place they *could*

70

be. Probably under big leaves like on the rhubarb plants. Next time it rains remind me, and I'll go to poke the leaves with a stick. I won't hurt anything. I just want to see if the butterflies come out. . ." and she lay mulling the thought over carefully.

After a while we got up from the soft grass and walked out farther across the Field until we came to the creek. It is a muddy, fast-moving tributary of Lake Winnebago and at this time of the year it is swollen with the early summer rains. We leaned over the wood bridge to watch it, Kitty and I, and it rushed past beneath, eddying around the cement piles of the bridge and stirring up the red-brown clay. There was a small dead tree fallen part way across the stream, and the water churned around the trunk and ribboned its way through the bare branches. She picked some flat leaves from the roadside and dropped them over the rail, watching them float a moment and then rush on down the stream. Later in the summer the water would be green and sluggish and there would be fat bullfrogs squatting in the mud along the bank, loudly clearing their throats as they sat hidden among the river rushes.

Tired of just standing, we edged our way cautiously down the bank, feet heavy with damp clay, and stood on the cement ledge under the bridge near the water's edge. The stream is only a few feet deep here but it was whirling along in such full, angry haste that it gave me a queer fear at its strength, and I took Kitty's arm with one hand, gripping the rough cement wall with the other. A car came along the gravel road and thundered over the bridge above our head, sending a few bits of gravel hurtling over the side into the water.

Besides enjoying the loveliness of the afternoon

I was stalling for time and I knew it. The minute I got home I would be hoping and waiting for Jack to call, but here, not knowing if he had called or if he would call, even the suspense was pleasant.

We walked away from the creek slowly, pushing aside the grass with our feet as we went, looking for the meadowlarks' nests hidden in the grass. Often in the summertime we had run across four of the small eggs with the red-brown speckles, secure in a nest, while the mother bird would fly above us in wide swoops to distract our attention, singing desperately, her high breast feathers throbbing with song.

When we got home my bare legs were nipped with small grass cuts and from even that short time in the sun Kitty had new freckles on her nose. The family were sitting in the shade of the side lawn and Lorraine was lounging on a canvas lawn chair, putting polish on her nails right down to the tips and holding her hands straight out in front of her till it dried. She is always very careful to wear her nail polish and lipstick to match.

"Angie, that boy called," my mother said as I came up the walk.

"What boy?" I asked, careful to make my voice sound surprised. I felt an instinctive need for caution. Individually my mother likes them well enough, but as dates she regards all boys with a vague, general disapproval — just in case.

"That boy, Jack," she answered, never looking up from her knitting. "Margaret spoke with him."

"He said he would call later, Angie," Margaret explained. "That he thought maybe you would like to go to some party at somebody's cottage tonight with him and some other fellows and girls. I told him you probably could and he said he would call back sometime before supper. You can wear my yellow sweater if you want, Ang — but be careful of it. I'd like to see him when he comes to pick you up — he sounded cute over the phone. He talks as if he has brown eyes — has he?"

There was a hot tingling round my face and I waited to be sure my voice wouldn't sound too eager, for my mother was knitting with fast, jerky movements as if she were annoyed and her needles clicked. "Do you mind if I go, Mom?"

"I don't know," she shrugged. "Ask your father."

I turned to him. "May I, Dad?"

"Whatever your mother says," he answered lightly, dismissing all responsibility. If he takes time to reprimand us, my father is always very stern but otherwise he doesn't bother at all. He was sitting then in a loose golf shirt that he always wears on weekends, and his neck showed soft and white at the throat where it is usually covered with his weekday shirt and tie. I stood waiting as he leafed through the paper.

My mother cleared her throat crossly. "I would certainly like to know with *whom* you are going, *where* you are going, and at what *time* you will be home. I don't like the idea of you girls just going out any time with anybody!"

It isn't that my mother doesn't like boys, as I explained, but because we are girls and because we are the kind of family who always use top sheets on the beds and always eat our supper in the dining room and things like that — well, she just didn't want us to go out with *anybody*.

"That will be the third time this week that you've seen that boy!"

This was just what I had been shying away from. For all the warm glow in my thoughts, thinking about Friday night, I didn't want anyone else to know or to ask questions.

"But, Mom, I'll find out about it first," I assured her hastily. "When he calls I'll ask where the party is and everything and I promise we'll be home early. It will be all right."

Later that evening when I was sitting in my bedroom waiting for Jack to come, I heard the phone ring downstairs and went down to answer. But Margaret had got there before me and she was standing holding it, with her hand over the mouthpiece, saying, "Honestly, Lorraine, if he wants a date and you go I'll just be furious at you — anyone calling for a date at this time of night!"

Lorraine was absently shining her fingernails on the sleeve of her blouse. "I don't know," she said slowly, not looking up, "I can't quite see why I *shouldn't* go, after all. I'm the only girl Martin really knows in town — maybe he's been busy all afternoon and didn't have time to call before." She looked over at Art but he just shrugged his shoulders.

"If he thinks he can get a date with you any time he calls! Last night may have been all right at the last minute because you haven't been home from school so long yourself; but two nights in a row . . ." Margaret stood jiggling the phone impatiently. Even when she was only in high school she didn't have to worry about not having boys like her.

"Hurry up," she urged Lorraine, "and decide what you're going to say to him. But I certainly know what I'd tell him!"

"Just say that you're busy and then you and your mother and father can go to a late show so you won't just have to be sitting here," Art suggested in his quiet voice. "From what you told me about last night, he sounds like one of those 'big men on campus' who never quite got over going to college.

74

Do what you like, Lorraine, but I know what I'd think if I could get a girl at the last minute."

Margaret held out the phone. "Here," she said, "tell him you're busy."

It was just beginning to get dark outside and the room was thickening with dusk. We could hear the drone of my mother's and father's voices as they sat on the side lawn, but the rest of the house was quiet.

"If you want to go out so badly," Margaret added, "you can come along with Art and me."

"I know. I know that," Lorraine said slowly. "But, Margaret, I can go out with you and Art *any* Sunday night — I want to go out with *him!*"

Just as Jack and I pulled out of our driveway, Martin Keefe swung up to the curb in a low green coupe, screeching the tires against the curbstone, and as we turned the corner I looked back to see him crossing the lawn with his long, insolent stride to shake hands with my father.

Another couple drove out with us, friends of Jack's from high school, a girl named Margie and a tall, thin boy called Fitz. He had a very bad complexion and a shiftiness about him, as if by not looking directly at me he could avoid my looking at him and seeing his ugly skin. Margie was a tall, slim girl with quick, bright eyes and she talked continually, laughing between the words. Her hair hung long in the back but was swooped up into curls on the sides and crisscrossed with hairpins. Nervously, she kept adjusting the pins as she talked to me.

Leaning over the front seat she commented affably, "You're the girl who knows Jane Rady, aren't you? Us girls have a bridge club that meets every couple of weeks and she happened to mention you.

Jane said she might stop out tonight with that new boy from Oshkosh she has a date with."

"Say, this is going to be some party," Fitz said with significant enthusiasm. "Is Tony Becker going to be out?"

"Don't know," Jack answered, keeping his eyes on the road. "I was talking to him at Pete's this afternoon and he said he'd be over if he could get the car." He looked back at Fitz. "But if he gets the car I don't think he'll waste his time at the party — huh, Fitz?"

"No, sir, that boy don't waste no time," Fitz agreed and whistled shrilly through his teeth. Margie laughed and there was some giggled whispering in the back seat, but I couldn't understand what they were talking about.

The cottage was only a few miles out of town along the lake shore, set far in off the highway. I had a feeling of apprehension as Jack swung into the rutted mud road. The car lurched sideways and Margie squealed with delight in the back seat. There were three other cars pulled up in the cottage drive and inside someone was playing Viennese waltzes on an old victrola. Already an early moon was showing through the lace of the trees.

It was a shabby cottage. Jack explained to me later that it belonged to Fitz's family but they used it only during the last month of summer, and the rest of the year it lay vacant except when some of the bunch came out to go swimming or to have a party. The front of the house was flush with the lake so we went in the back way into a kitchen smelling damp and musty, like old wood, with layers of yellowed newspaper on the shelves and a big wooden table.

No one had lived in the cottage since the summer before and the front room had the same damp, close smell as the kitchen. One of the girls took me off into a side room to powder my nose. There was a mirror on the wall and a bare bulb hanging from the ceiling. She seemed younger than the rest and more talkative, and as she edged around her mouth carefully with bright lipstick she remarked with emphasis, "Honestly, I'm so glad we're not having anything but beer, 'cause after *last night* I couldn't stand to look another mixed drink in the face." Her name was Dollie, and Jack told me later that she was only fifteen and had been dating the fellows in his crowd for only about three weeks. She was what the boys called "a find."

Until she had mentioned beer I had never thought just what people did do at parties like this — we couldn't just sit around and listen to Viennese waltzes all night. I hadn't really gone to parties since the days when we were small enough to care about ice cream and cake with pink frosting, and play drop-the-clothespins-in-the-bottle or Going to Jerusalem. Some of the other girls had come in and I thought of saying very casually, "What are we going to do — just sit around and talk?" but I didn't want them to know that I'd never been at a party like this before. It was important to act as if you had been around. Maybe they would whisper to their dates later in the evening, "You know that girl that Jack Duluth is with? She doesn't even know the score. She asked me before what we were going to do. I'll bet she's never even been at a party before!"

One of the girls said to me casually, "How long have you been going with Jack, Angeline?" I explained that I hadn't known him quite a week and that I'd just been out with him a few times. "That's what I thought," she went on, "because last thing *we* knew he was dating a couple of girls from high school and then Jane Rady off and on and then all of a sudden he turned up with you at the dance. . . . We kind of wondered," she added slowly. She was sitting on the arm of an old stuffed chair smoking a cigarette with deep puffs and holding the smoke in her mouth for a long time before blowing it out. I could tell by the way she spoke that she was a friend of Jane Rady's.

When we went back to the living room two of the boy were rolling back the old grass rug — "just in case someone might want to dance," and Dollie and the other girls got down on their knees to help roll, laughing and talking loudly. I tried to help too, but gave up because I felt awkward and in the way. Dollie sat down backwards suddenly with her legs sprawled in front of her and cried with a petulantly accusing voice, "Johnnie, you pushed me on purpose!" and everyone laughed.

I went out to the kitchen then where the others were crowded around Swede who had just come in. He was trying to screw a spigot into a barrel of beer. We never had beer at our house and I had always felt that there was something disgraceful about it. For a moment I wished I hadn't come. Jack was holding the barrel for Swede and when the first beer dribbled out onto the floor he yelled, "There she goes! Wash out some glasses, somebody!"

I was glad to have something to do rather than just stand watching, so I opened the cupboard and took out some glasses to wash and the other girls came to help. There were half a dozen pink glass tumblers and three tall, heavy glasses with thick edges that looked as if they must have once been peanut butter jars. The faucet made a choking sound far down in the pipes as I turned it on and then water spouted out very brown and muddy, for it had been standing in the pipes unused for so long. We waited till it ran clear and then rinsed the glasses, setting them upside down on the newspapered table top to drip dry.

Everyone crowded round the barrel holding out his glass to be filled. Jack came over with one for me and when I shook my head he said suddenly, "That's right! I forgot you didn't drink beer! We should have stopped and picked up some root beer for you but I never even thought of it. I can't give you a glass of water either because the water out here isn't very good for drinking, and besides these glasses look too dirty to drink out of unless there is beer in them."

It was all right, I told him. Really it was all right. I didn't mind the least bit and I wasn't thirsty anyway. I hoped he wouldn't say anything to anyone else, for the other girls were all drinking it and having fun. For a minute I was tempted to take a glass myself. But then I thought of having to walk up the stairs when I got home and perhaps my mother would call from her room, "Angeline, come in a minute and tell me if you had a nice time," and I would weave my way over to her dressing table, fumble for the lamp, knocking over the perfume bottles in a glassy-eyed stupor — I had seen people in the movies who had had too much to drink.

Later they moved the beer keg into the living room and we all sat around on the chairs and on the floor, laughing and singing. I couldn't make myself sing with the rest, for my voice sounded queer, but no one seemed to notice. Swede was next to me and Jack sat on the arm of the davenport, singing and winking at me at the same time. A lamp with a parchment shade was lit on a corner table and the room was in a half-glow as if by firelight. Large night moths fluttered low around the shade and made vague shadows on the circle of light on the ceiling. There were musty brown-and-cream print drapes on the windows, full and shadowy, and I noticed that high on one of them was pinned a large yellow butterfly of waxed crepe paper with bent wire feelers and wings edged with a dust of gilt paint — the kind unemployed women used to make to sell from door to door during the depression. The floor and chairs were scattered with cushions stiff with painted roses and bright sunsets, or made of soft leather with doeskin fringes printed with pictures of tall pines and low yellow moons — souvenirs of the north country and the Indian reservations.

The whole room was filled with the damp smell of the lake and it was even a little chilly — the sort of chill that makes you feel more comfortable because you can snuggle against cushions and be grateful for their warmth and comfort. Those sitting on the floor joined hands and sang low songs as they swayed from side to side, and Jack slid off the wicker arm of the davenport and sat beside me. I was so contented and happy I felt as if I would like to sit right there without moving until I fell asleep. It was odd to think that just last week I hadn't known anything about this — about Jack, about girls who really went out and drank beer, about parties like this — the sort of things I used to hear Jane Rady talk about and never thought I would be a part of. Tonight had been easy. Everyone else had been laughing and talking so much they didn't seem to notice or mind that I just watched and enjoyed the whole thing without saying anything. The first misgivings I had felt when I saw them fitting the spigot into the beer barrel were gone, for after all they were just sitting in a circle singing now and there was nothing wrong about that! But back in my mind I had a vague guilty feeling that I probably wouldn't mention to my mother that there had been no older person there and that they had had beer — even if I hadn't drunk any myself.

Suddenly Dollie jumped up and said in her round, baby voice, "Come on, fill my glass and let's play 'chug-a-lug!'" Everyone passed around his glass to be filled and then, holding them high, began to sing a loud song with words which I couldn't catch for everyone was laughing so hard as they sang. Someone called out, "Dollie!" and they all went on laughing and singing like deep-throated bullfrogs — "chug-a-lug, chug-a-lug, chug-a-lug" — while she stood up, tilted her glass of beer and drank to the bottom without stopping. Then the song was started again and someone else's name was called and he drained his glass while the others kept up the rhythmic chant. They kept it up till they had gone the round of the circle and everyone was laughing so hard they could hardly catch their breath and I found myself laughing, too, with my mouth open.

Finally they laughed themselves quiet and Dollie gathered some of the painted cushions into a heap and leaned against the victrola, sleepy-eyed and contented. Someone shuffled through the pile of old records again and put on an old scratchy recording of a dramatic baritone singing "In The Valley of Sunshine and Roses." Fitz looked over at Margie and they both got up, rinsed their glasses at the kitchen sink, and went out to sit on the front porch. Soon we heard the creak-creak of the glider. Fitz and Margie were "going steady," Jack told me later.

Swede gathered up some cushions and made himself comfortable beside Dollie, and some of the others got car robes from their cars and went out to sit on the front lawn. I didn't quite understand how, as if at a given signal, the whole party broke up into couples and drifted off by themselves. Jack and I still sat where we were, not saying anything, mostly because I didn't quite know what to say or what I was supposed to do now. Dollie, snuggled against the cushions, was rubbing over Swede's short curly hair with the back of her hand, saying over to herself softly, "Just like a kitten. Swede feels just like a kitty."

One of the boys came over to us saying, "Mind if we sit on the davenport — if you kids aren't going to use it?"

"Sure, sure," Jack said. "Go ahead. We can sit on the porch. Do you want to sit on the porch, Angie?" I nodded.

The front porch was built across the full length of the cottage and was screened in with long, black screens that ran from the floor to the ceiling. Out there, the darkness was warm and thick, for the broad front lawn stretching down to the lake was covered with trees and their branches, heavy with the full, lush foilage of early summer almost hid the moon. On one side was the glider and on the other a lumpy couch covered with the same musty brown-and-cream chintz as the drapes inside. Jack and I sat there. Out on the lawn near the lake's edge someone was building a bonfire and we watched it grow, flickering at first till the fire dried out the damp wood and then suddenly bright and leaping against the darkness of the water. It was very quiet with just the steady lap-lap of the water, the hush of the wind through the trees, and the occasional creak of the glider on the other side of the porch. Attracted by the light of the dim lamp inside, heavy-bodied June bugs bumped clumsily against the screens and night moths kept up a dainty flutter. Out on the lawn there was a wink of light like a firefly as someone lit a cigarette.

"Angie," Jack said, "let's get a robe from the car and sit out on the grass. It smells so damp and musty here that I'll bet if we turned this couch over centipedes would crawl out from under it like from under a rock." He spread out the robe on the lawn and lay flat with his chin in his hands, smoking his pipe, and I sat beside him with a funny, choked feeling in my throat because I suddenly felt self-conscious being alone with him. I was running the fringe on the edge of the robe through my fingers, wondering whether or not it would seem funny if I suggested that maybe Swede and Dollie would like to come out to sit with us, when Jack turned to me and said in a puzzled voice, "Angie, you didn't have fun tonight, did you?"

"But I did. I did," I told him. "I liked it very much. The girls were all nice and the boys were funny and I really liked it — what made you think I didn't?" I watched him puff-puffing at his pipe, making the tobacco glow as he drew in.

"You didn't talk much," he explained, "and I thought maybe you were mad because of the beer or because we made too much noise or something. You seemed different Friday night. I don't know. Just thought maybe you were mad," and he reached over and I felt his fingers on mine. "If you ever don't like anything, Angie, just say so."

For the first time in my life I felt that warm, possessive power that comes from knowing that you are able to worry a boy. It wasn't fair I know, but I left my hand flat on the robe, pretending that I didn't even know he was looking at me, pretending that I didn't even know his hand was on mine.

"Is it about Friday night then?" he urged in the

same worried tone. "Tell me what's the matter." After a moment's hesitation he added slowly, "Are you sorry, Angie?"

"Friday night?" My voice sounded high and incredulous as if I had never even heard of such a thing as a Friday night before.

"I don't know," he said. "I just thought you might be mad about it later on. I was almost afraid to call you this afternoon."

"Why? I certainly don't see why you should be," I heard myself saying in the same high, surprised voice, while my thoughts went slowly, carefully through my head as if they were on a tightrope. I had never thought of being angry about Friday night, but it just made me feel shy to think of it now that I was with him again. I had kissed him once, but what are girls supposed to say the next time they go out with a boy after a thing like that; what are they supposed to do?

"It's just that you're different from other girls I've known," he went on. "Most of them wouldn't give it a second thought but I didn't know what you would think about it the next day." His pipe had burned out and he sat tapping the bowl on the palm of his hand. The thick leaves were whispering above, and behind us the wind made a thin whistle in the screens of the porch. "It wasn't *wrong*, Angie!"

How queer all this is, I thought. Here am I sitting in the dark with a boy I didn't even know a week ago and he's worrying about what is in my head and I'm so mixed up I can't even tell him. He's worried about whether I'm angry at him because I haven't been talking all evening, and I haven't talked because all the other girls were so much prettier than I was that I couldn't think of anything to say.

84

It made me feel older than he to have him talk to me that way. "Of course it isn't wrong," I told him. "Things like stealing or telling lies are wrong but kissing someone you . . . well, it isn't . . . you know what I mean, Jack." I couldn't quite see his face in the darkness but I could feel his hand on mine, so I added softly, "Kissing someone you *like* isn't wrong!" and the words felt warm on my lips.

And all within a week I, Angie Morrow, was sitting there saying things I'd never dreamed of saying, things that belonged in a movie.

We mused over the thought for a while and soon the quiet stretched into long minutes till our thoughts cleared and both of us were conscious of the silence with nothing but the hushed night noises going on in it.

A car pulled in to the gravel drive, the door slammed, and someone called out, "Hey, anybody home here?" and Fitz and Margie left the front porch to go inside and we heard Swede talking. "That's Tony Becker who just came," Jack said. "I can tell by his voice. He always gets places late because he finds so much to do on the way. I wonder who he's got for a date tonight?"

I suggested that we go in to find out and say hello to Tony, but Jack held my hand. "Let's not go in quite yet, Angie — unless you really want to see Tony. . . ." His voice turned the end of the sentence up into a question. "He told me that you and he got along pretty well at the dance."

"What's the matter, don't you like him?" I asked.

"Sure, I *like* him," he hastened to explain, "but Tony's just one of those guys. . . ."

He sat with his hands locked around his knees and said, "Let's just sit here a little while longer and then we'll go in and round up Fitz and Margie — it's getting late and I'll have to be getting you home soon. I'd like to talk to you a little more and if we go in we'll have to talk to Tony and everyone and I won't have a chance."

Inside someone was winding up the victrola again and overhead the moon inched its way from behind a cloud and showed in glimpses as the wind swayed the thick trees. It seemed so natural for me to be lying there listening to the waves and it wasn't surprising at all to feel Jack's hand in mine. I wondered contentedly if my mother was still sitting knitting the yellow sweater she was making me for college, and I wondered with a troubled feeling if Lorraine and Martin were having a good time. My thoughts bobbed in my head as if they were floating, as if they were airy, impersonal ideas resting lightly above my more solid and serious thoughts beneath.

I wonder, I thought, what I am really thinking. Last week I would have known definitely but now everything seems vague and evasive. Every time I tried to think clearly about Jack and especially about Friday night there was a warm feeling in my heart and a very pleasant confused jumble in my head. Lying there on the car robe, I tried to imagine what I would have thought last week if someone had told me about a girl who had kissed a boy the third night she had been out with him. I tried to turn my thoughts so they looked inward; so I could really find out what was going on inside my head. Lying very still, my forehead wrinkled with concentration, I wondered.

"What," I said to myself, "will I do if he should want to kiss me good night?"

Just then Jack leaned over and said with a laugh in his voice, "Angie, Angie, what are you doing? You look so funny that at first I thought you were looking cross-eyed!"

The door of the screened porch slammed and two

people stepped out onto the lawn. Jack sat up and listened in the darkness. Their voices came toward us and then a low, deep laugh, and Jack turned to me, his words twisted with annoyance. "Well, we might as well go in the house now, Angie, here comes Becker. I don't know who the girl is with him but I'd rather be where the bright lights are when that boy's around."

The next week passed quickly. Each morning I woke with an eager, expectant feeling as if I had just had a good dream. The days were filled with the mellow warmth of sunshine and the air was fresh with the smell of green leaves and damp earth that comes with early summer. Jack called every noon at a little after twelve and his calls punctuated the day like periods. It surprised me that my mother never seemed to mind that I talked with him so often, though we might just be sitting down to lunch when the phone rang. Once after he called I happened to look at myself in the mirror and was surprised at the bright, wide-awake look in my eyes.

Even my thoughts seemed changed. When I woke in the morning and looked in the bathroom mirror as I was washing my face the thought might strike me, "What would Jack think if he could see me now with lathery soap all over my face?" or when I was puttering in the garden I might wonder, "Does Jack ever notice the queer, cool smell that comes from nasturtium leaves?" When I did leisurely things like ironing or peeling potatoes for dinner I found my mind making up little stories about Jack and me, pretending that he had walked into Mc-Knight's while Jane Rady was there and that he looked at her and then came over to sit with me, or pretending that he had come to visit me for a dance at college and all the other freshmen were so nice to me after that, thinking that I must have been a popular girl in my home town to have such a nice looking boy come all the way down to see me.

One morning Kitty was out playing on the front sidewalk. She had taken her old box of half-used crayons left from school, laying them in a row in the sun until they melted to a pliable consistency, and then bending them into bright-colored rings or melting the ends with a match, sticking several together to make a bracelet. "Costume jewelry," she called it. Every few minutes she came running into the house with excited plans of how she could make a fortune with just a few boxes of crayons by getting one of the local department stores to sell the crayon jewelry. Each summer Kitty is full of schemes to make money in a hurry. Once she had a lemonade stand that served soda crackers with each drink, and another time she had a route mapped out for the children in the neighborhood to sell the vegetables from our garden, door to door. None of the projects lasted more than two days.

Jack drove up in the bakery truck and was standing listening to her chatter that morning when I glanced out the window and saw him. I hurried up to my room and carefully edged on lipstick with the tip of my finger before I went out to talk with him. That evening the two of us went out with his cousin from Oklahoma who was about twenty years old and drank more beer than any boy I have ever seen. He and Jack talked mostly about what they had done together before Jack had moved North — he and his family had lived in Oklahoma until five years ago and his cousin said something about the girl that lived in the white house with the pines in front whom Jack used to like. So Jack must have been going with girls, at least *liking* them, since he was thirteen! The cousin talked to me too, and said that any time I happened to pass through his state to be sure to look him up. I told him that since Wisconsin was almost walking distance from Oklahoma I would probably see him often and they both laughed and I felt almost pleased with myself.

Lorraine went out with Martin three nights in a row that week. I never knew when they made their plans for dates for he never called the house. She explained that she "ran into him" almost every day after work. He was rooming at a house not far from the Elite Canvas Company, and if she didn't bump into him in front of his house she usually saw him having a Coke at the drugstore on the next block. Lorraine always said there was nothing she liked so much as a Coke after a day's work and always stopped at the drugstore on her way home.

When I asked what they did when they went out, she explained that they didn't go to any of the places that the younger crowd went like Pete's and McKnight's, but that Martin knew some nice places a little farther out of town — the kind of place he had been used to going to when he had been at the university. Each night she got in very late and I always woke with a start as the car pulled silently up to the curb with headlights switched off, so as not to rouse anyone. My room is at the front of the house and I would lie awake till I heard the car door close and Lorraine tiptoe upstairs and undress silently for bed. She always smelled of her own perfume and the heavy man-smell of cigarette smoke and went through the rituals of getting ready for bed in the dark, being careful not to waken my mother. That third night she sat in bed for a very long time with her hands around her knees, thinking. I said nothing, pretending I was asleep, and much later she got up again and I could hear the water trickling as she washed her face in the bathroom. The sky was already beginning to get light before she fell asleep that night.

Jack told me that Martin came into the bakery every morning at about seven-thirty for fresh rolls for his breakfast. He made morning coffee in his room at the rooming house but ate the other two meals out. "He gives you the impression that he's a city fellow," Jack had said. "He walks like he's got on silk underwear or has a ten-dollar bill in his pocket or something."

That week and the next were filled with such a new happiness that my whole mind sang with the sheer joy of it. One afternoon Kitty and I took our bicycles and rode out through the Field until we reached the creek bank, and then along the water's edge to the bridge on the gravel road, and I caught my breath at the loveliness of it. On the other bank a twisted cottonwood tree was shedding its white wool that caught in bushes as it fell, drifted with the creek or fluffed along the road, pushed by the breeze. Blue-bodied dragonflies hovered low over the stream, their gauze wings shimmering in the sun, and river plants laid their broad leaves flat on the surface of the water. Kitty leaned over the iron railing of the bridge trying to rouse frogs by dropping stones straight down into the water with the same full, plopping sound they made as they dive in. I leaned over the railing too, thinking of Jack with the warm, hushed feeling that came into my mind whenever I thought of him too hard. I felt the breeze brush my cheek like a soft hand and below me, under the water, I watched the seaweed ripple with the current like long, green hair.

We rode farther along the gravel road till we came to the stretch that is lined with slim, whispering willows. This is the place I had often heard girls talk about with giggles at school. Fellows like Swede or boys like Fitz who had steady girls always stopped at night to park on Willow Road. I felt almost sacrilegious riding along it on my bicycle in broad daylight. There were deep tire marks in the soft earth where cars had pulled in at the side of the road, and I had heard about how the police car used to ride up and down every hour at night with a powerful spotlight, scaring the parkers away. It gave me a queer feeling, as if we shouldn't talk too loudly even if there was no one there.

"Look," Kitty cried. "Look. There's a shoe in the ditch!" There was a high-heeled black pump half-stuck in the mud, the leather cracked and graying from the weather. What an odd place for a shoe, I thought, and all the way back I had a vague, guilty feeling, as if I should have known better than to go to a place like that — and as if I had let Kitty see something she shouldn't.

It was almost suppertime when we turned for home. The sky was still blue and the sun bright but the birds had already begun the usual contented rites of evening, flying from hummock to hummock and then circling high into the air with bursts of song. A low breeze hushed through the long grass, and along the roadside wild dill raised its dull yellow flower clusters high on thick stems and weeds, showed the silver-gray underside of their leaves, brushed forward by the summer wind. As we turned in our own sidewalk, we caught the smell of pork chops frying and strong, fresh coffee. My mother had already begun to make the supper.

Margie called a little later that evening and asked me to walk to McKnight's with her for a Coke — Fitz and Jack were going out with the fellows so she knew I wouldn't be busy, she said. We had got along well at the cottage party and driving back to town she had remarked coyly, "Angie, let's you and me get together some night when the fellows are taking out their *other* girls!"

Fitz made a muffled protest in the back seat, something that began, "Aw, Margie, you know that you're the only — " and I didn't hear the rest.

My mother doesn't usually approve of my sisters and me going downtown alone at night. "There's something so cheap about seeing girls just walking up and down as if they were looking for something," she always said, but in our town all the girls do it. They get as dressed up as if they were going on a date and walk slowly up on one side Main Street looking in the shop windows, picking out what they would like to buy if they had the money, and then down the other side, and everyone ends up at McKnight's to have a Coke about nine o'clock.

I had never liked to do it because I didn't know any of the fellows and I could sit in McKnight's for an hour if I wanted and no one would come over to have a Coke with me. But it would be different being with Margie — she had dated so many of the fellows and everyone knew she was Fitz's girl now.

There was the usual crowd standing in front of the drugstore when we went in. The younger fellows in our town have a system. To an adult or to someone from out of town it would mean nothing to see a group of young boys standing in front of McKnight's or on the nearest street corner. But I knew what they were there for — Jane Rady had told me before I had even known Jack — and all the other girls knew too. These are the "checkers." They are the more popular crowd at high school and every evening about half-past seven they gather to stand talking together with elaborate unconcern, while in actuality they are sharply watching the cars

going by to see what fellows and girls are out together; they watch to see who is having a Coke with
whom and to report any violations on the part of
the girls who are supposed to be going steady.

It is almost like a secret police system — no one
escapes being checked on. At least no one who
counts. The checkers also keep their eyes open for
new prospects among the young sophomore girls
who are growing up and show signs of datable
promise. They only watch out for the very pretty or
very popular girls, so it is the most serious catas-
trophe of all not even to be noticed by the checkers.
They were the ones who had spotted Dollie -- they
can start or stop any of the younger girls in town
just by passing the word around. Most of them
didn't even know my name until I began to date
Jack.

When Margie and I passed them that night she
smiled very wide and said brightly, "Hi, there, fellows," and they all smiled back with approval but
none of them seemed to notice me at all.

"Of course they know you," Margie exclaimed,
when I mentioned it to her later. "Any girl that
goes with Jack Duluth is checkers material from
then on. Just wait. First thing in the morning one
of the boys will stop in the bakery and let Jack know
that they happened to see you having a Coke with
me last night."

Margie was using a very instructive motherly tone
of voice, as if she were teaching me my catechism.
"I always tell Fitz exactly what I'm planning to do
when I'm not with him," she went on. "He so hates
to have the boys tell him what I've been doing before he knows it himself. You see," she added comfortably, "Fitz and I are very much in love."

We both sipped our Cokes slowly for a while,
watching others who came and went. Margie knew

almost everyone and said, "Hi, there!" to each in the same bright voice. Once two girls came in with a slow, hesitant air. They were palish girls, about my age, with their hair very carefully set in neat waves and very little lipstick. One of them had on flat black oxfords — and everyone knows that no high school girl should wear anything but saddle shoes or collegiate moccasins! All the booths were filled but they walked down the aisle between them, peering over the high sides, looking for a place to sit down. No one said hello or offered to move over to make room so the girls turned, talking to themselves very busily and giggling a little, and walked out. But their faces had a stiff, hurt look. I knew just how they felt for until I had met Jack it was the same way with me — except that I wouldn't be stupid enough to wear flat black oxfords. Any girl who does that almost deserves not to have fellows look at her.

Margie lit a cigarette and between short puffs said, "You know, Angie, I can't figure you out. Going with Jack Duluth is really something — because of his being such a good basketball player and being so cute and everything, but it doesn't seem to make any difference to you at all."

"Of course it does," I hastened to assure her. I knew anything I said would be relayed from Margie to Fitz and from Fitz on to Jack. "But what am I supposed to do, Margie? I am certainly nice enough to him and I'm glad to hear him every time he calls — "

"You're nice enough to him," she explained, "but you don't seem to *worry* about him at all. All the girls worry about their fellows." She said it in the same matter-of-fact tone that she might have said "girls brush their teeth every day." "When I first started dating Fitz," she went on, "I used to come here every day after school to find out what the girls knew. You know, the boys they were dating would tell them what Fitz thought of me and whether he liked me or not and then they would tell me. Of course, now that we're in love it's different."

While we were talking Martin Keefe came in and asked for a package of cigarettes. He stood up at the soda fountain near the front of the store and didn't see me. He looked at his wrist watch irritably and was holding it up to his ear when a little blond girl from the perfume counter at one of the department stores came in, said something to him, and they left together, laughing. I remembered Lorraine at supper saying that she had a date with him that evening and wondered.

Later when I got home she was sitting in the bedroom brushing her hair and I asked her about it. "Yes," she explained carefully, "I was supposed to go out with him but just after you left he called and said that he had a collection to make in Waupun and wouldn't be able to keep the date tonight. Of course," she said pointedly, "I could have driven over *with* him if I had wanted to.

"He has a very good job, you know, Angie. In college he majored in business law and this is just a filler-in until he gets into something bigger. This pays very well though — I can tell by his big car and the smooth clothes he wears."

I undressed for bed, opened both windows, and turned back the spread. As I reached to put out the light Lorraine added — just as if there had been no lapse in the conversation at all — "But I'll probably see him tomorrow night instead."

It was then that I decided I wouldn't say a word about having seen him and the other girl.

The next day passed like a bubble. In the afternoon there was a quick summer shower, the kind that blows up from nowhere in a blue sky and spatters the sidewalks with big drops and then spends itself in a brief torrent. My mother had just got up from her afternoon nap and I had put the water on for tea and was standing at the kitchen window watching the rain flatten the corn leaves to the ground. The last of the June roses on the bush drooped their heads and the rain pelted their petals to the wet ground.

Almost as soon as it started the storm stopped and there was a rift in the dark clouds, the blue sky showing through. My mother laid two clean napkins on the kitchen table and drew it close to the window so we could smell the damp, clean smell of the wet earth. The sun came out, glistening on the leaves and making the whole garden look brighter, like a sudden smile after a hard cry.

Along the block, children came out into the street, chattering like little birds after the rain and we watched them paddling about on the wet grass in their bare feet, pulling small sailboats along the water in the gutter. Why is it, I thought, that rain has never seemed so wonderful to me before? Each day since the beginning of summer something had seemed new and surprising, things I had never noticed before.

That was the first day I had ever seen Jack in the afternoon and I was surprised at how natural even that seemed. He knocked at the front door and explained that he had finished his route early and just thought he would stop in.

"We're glad to have you," my mother said. (I always liked the way she talked to boys.) "Won't you have a cup of tea with Angie and me?" I sliced lemon out in the kitchen and put the sugar and cream on the table, while Jack went out to the bakery truck and came in, all smiling, with six sugared doughnuts on a paper pie plate and a small chocolate cake with chocolate frosting, sprinkled with very dubious chopped nuts.

This was the first time too, I had ever eaten with Jack and every mouthful I took seemed too big and the tea made a noise in my throat as I swallowed it. Jack seemed perfectly at ease, holding his doughnut carefully with two fingers and not getting sugar on his sweater while he ate, and he and my mother talked about bakers and pies and whether or not many people make their own bread anymore.

I passed him the lemon and he dropped a slice in his cup and then unconsciously poured cream in after it, stirring the two together. I looked at my mother and she looked at me, raising her eyebrows in a signal not to laugh, and went on talking.

As I sat there I found myself being grateful for so many little things around the kitchen that I had hardly valued before. I liked the little red-and-white-checked hand towels hanging on the rail, and the way the afternoon sun glinted on the faucets and the clean, well-swept look of the linoleum. I was glad my mother's hair was in a neat bun instead of a fuzzy permanent, and that her eyes looked as blue as her dress, and that the dog Kinkee sat in the corner very politely, not drooling as some dogs do when they see people eating. I was glad that Jack could know what a nice kitchen we had and that we used quaint flowered napkins instead of oil cloth on the kitchen table.

When he left I walked out to the truck at the curb with him. He looked so strong and brown with his football sweater on and a white shirt open at the throat that I could hardly keep from touching him. When he looked at me I had a queer feeling that maybe I had chocolate frosting on my face or that maybe the freckles on my nose showed too much in the sunlight. A small wind shook raindrops from the trees onto the sidewalk, and on the lawn young robins with soft, speckled breasts hopped about, scolding for worms.

My whole head was singing with such a warm happiness that when the truck pulled away I felt that if the grass had not still been wet there was nothing in the world I would rather have done than lie flat on my back with my hands behind my head, watching the sky, clear and bright-blue in the sunshine, and just think.

It wasn't until that next Sunday that I noticed anything strange about Lorraine. The day went much the same as always. After the dinner dishes had been done my father got his brief case out of the car and spread his papers all over the kitchen table, working away at his prospects and order blanks for the rest of the afternoon. Kitty and Art played catch with a baseball out in the empty lot next to our house, while my mother sat in a garden chair knitting a pair of yellow wool ankle socks to match the sweater she had finished earlier in the week.

Upstairs, Lorraine had been listlessly sorting out the things in her dresser drawers, arranging neat piles of hankies, cosmetics, and odd jewelry on the bed, and then putting them back in as great a disorder as before. She looked very pale because she had put no lipstick on and nothing I tried to talk about seemed to interest her. I knew she hadn't even heard from Martin since he broke the date with her, and each night when she got home from work she would say brightly, "Anyone call?"

About five o'clock I happened to be alone in the

living room, leafing through the morning funnies, when she came downstairs and said, "Angie, I've just *got* to call Martin and see if he has my gold compact. I've hunted *everywhere* and the last place I remember having it was in his car. Honestly, I'd just *hate* to lose that." As she looked through the phone book she added, "He should be home about now. I really can't think how I didn't miss it sooner."

Carefully I folded the funny papers and put them in a neat pile on the davenport. That gold compact was in her purse. I had seen her use it when we went to church in the morning. But there was nothing I could say. She must have wanted to call him very much, for I knew the compact was there and I knew she knew.

"Hello?" Her voice was casually eager. "I'd like to speak to Martin Keefe — if he isn't busy." There was a short pause while someone on the other end of the line was talking. "Oh, I see," she said. "And when do you expect him in?" Her voice was high, cheerful. "Oh, I see. I see." The receiver clicked down and in a minute she came into the living room humming softly under her breath.

"When do they expect him in?" I asked, making my voice as casual, as noncommittal as hers. There are unspoken ethics between sisters.

She was standing by the table at the foot of the stairs, absentmindedly plucking the dead blossoms from the bowl of irises. With the same careful unconcern she answered, "They don't expect him. He's out for the evening." She looked up at me and then turned quickly to go upstairs. "Angie," she called back. "Angie, don't tell Margaret and Art I called him. They don't — they don't quite see it the way I do!" and then I heard her go into her room, shutting the door after her.

How sad, I thought. How sad to have to cry about a boy on such a beautiful Sunday afternoon.

You know how it is sometimes when things go along so smoothly that you feel certain something unforeseen must happen. To me it happened that Sunday at suppertime.

With no preamble, with no warning at all, my father said suddenly, his lips set in determination, "Angeline, I don't know as I like your going out so much!"

We were sitting at the dining-room table eating cold pork sandwiches made from the noon roast and fresh sliced tomatoes. I hadn't talked about Jack all day so I was puzzled to know what had made my father think of him. We had planned to walk to a movie that evening and except for feeling sorry for Lorraine, my mind had been humming to itself all day with a contented, muted sort of happiness. And now to have my father say that! It was like a blow at the back of the knees. Always he had been occasionally strict with us but his approvals and disapprovals usually came through my mother. And because he was only home on weekends he wasn't really cross very often.

"In the first place, you are too young to be seeing so much of one boy, and besides it seems to me," he went on severely as he stirred his coffee, "that your sister and you have enough to keep you busy helping your mother and getting some worthwhile reading done for college without all this running about." My mother didn't say a word and I could tell by her silence that he had discussed this with her before.

Then he cleared his throat and I could almost tell what was coming next, he had said it so often before, "You'll have plenty of time for dating later

100

on, Angeline. Your schooling is what is important now. Remember that. Education is one thing no one can ever take away from you!"

Lorraine went into the kitchen for hot coffee just then and the others ate in silence, not looking up or trying to put in a good word for me. Kitty was carefully taking her sandwich apart, cutting the white fat from the pork with frowning concentration and carefully putting the whole thing back together again.

Then that night seemed to me the most important night of the whole year. Here was I with a date with a boy that dozens of girls would like to go out with and I would have to call him up and say in a simpery voice, "I can't go out because my father doesn't want me to!" You wouldn't have to say a thing like that to a boy like Jack twice! Next time he wanted a date he'd know where to call. He'd get some girl like Jane Rady whose mother and father *understood* about her going out. I had such a lump in my throat that I couldn't swallow and had to keep staring at my plate so they wouldn't see the tears nipping at my eyes.

And Lorraine was eating quietly, talking to one or the other from time to time, not letting anyone know how *she* felt.

Later, when the dishes were done, the milk bottles set out on the back doorstep, and the floor carefully swept, I ventured into the living room. My father was reading an old paper and Kitty was lying on the rug with her feet in the air doing bicycling exercises. I stood for a moment trying not to look too eager, trying to work up the courage to ask.

"Dad," my voice didn't sound like my own. "Dad, may I go?"

"Eh?" he said, looking up from the paper, his eyebrows quizzical. "Go where? With that boy?"

My mind almost smiled inside of me. The mood had completely gone over. He had been having one of his temporary, fatherly spells and now he had forgotten all about it.

"You can go this time," he said, but added sternly, "I don't want you running about too often though, understand. Your mother has been speaking to me about it. It isn't good for a girl your age to go out with one boy so much," and he turned back to his paper.

The lump in my throat seemed to melt away as he spoke. "You'd better comb your hair, Angie. It's almost a quarter after seven!" Kitty piped up from the floor.

It was the sort of night near the end of June when everything is warm and hushed, steeped in summer. Jack and I walked along the side streets on our way to the movie and at each corner the air was filled with an indistinct murmur from the haze of insects circling round the bright street lights. We passed a garden hedged in with flowered shrubs and the fragrance from the white night blossoms hung heavy on the breeze. People were sitting on their front porches enjoying the cool of the evening and we could hear the creak of rocking chairs and the pleasant hum-hum of voices as we passed. It was then that I realized how much older I felt when I was away from my family. It wasn't that I felt taller or fatter but just more important. At home they cared about what I thought, of course, but in a different way. They cared whether I would rather have pork chops or steak for dinner or whether I would rather have a white collar on my dress or no collar at all, but they didn't seem to think much or care what was actually in my head.

When I was away from them it was different. In McKnight's, Margie had been interested in what I thought of Fitz; Jack had been interested to know if I liked Tony Becker — at home you are just part of a family, but away from them you really are somebody!

Before us the poles of the street lights laid thick shadows across the sidewalk and above us, above the houses and the trees, a high, lonesome moon was tilted against the sky like a half-slice of lemon. My mind was puttering with small thoughts as we walked, thoughts about the people rocking on the porches and the funny way the wind in the trees made restless shifting shadows on the road, when Jack said, "Angie, we don't have to meet Fitz and Margie at the movie till a quarter-past eight, and if we walk just a little faster we'll be in time to stop in at church for Benediction on the way." The first chapel bells for Sunday service had rung just as we left home about fifteen minutes ago and I remembered brushing the sound from my mind. It made me ashamed now that I hadn't had the courage to suggest going myself.

But there is something so final, something so husband- and wifelike about going to church with a boy. Religion is too personal a thing to share promiscuously and the thought of being there with Jack filled me with a kind of awe; made me feel as though I should tiptoe up the aisle and genuflect in careful silence.

The very air of a church inspires reverence, and that night the lower stained-glass windows were tilted half open and the breeze stirred the warm air that was thick with the scent of flowers, incense, and the damp smell of leather from the prayer books and kneeling-benches. Kneeling beside him I

103

felt so self-conscious and ill at ease I almost giggled, but Jack just knelt with his hands folded properly and his eyes ahead.

On the altar the tapers raised their flames in bright tiers and the squat candles of the votive lights filled the red glass holders with a warm glow like cups of wine. The ceiling of the church was vaulted into high shadowed arches and the organ music rolled out in full, rich swells above us; while the candleglow, the music, and the fragrance of the altar flowers filled the church with a heady, moving perfection. Jack knelt twisting his class ring round and round on his finger in unconscious thought. It was the first night I had seen him wear it and I remember noticing then the quick, clean look of his hands.

A series of pictures flipped through my mind — the way the wind had ruffled his hair that night in the boat, Jane Rady dancing with him, her hair falling like silk that night at Pete's, out on the golf course at the dance when the moon was pale and high above the trees . . . The candleglow on the altar and the thoughts in my head blurred together into memories so pleasant I could almost taste them. With a jolt I realized Jack was staring at me. I had been smiling in church! He passed me a little black prayer book he pulled from his back pocket and I turned my face toward the altar with the same small, humiliated feeling as if I had been caught chewing gum in school.

I will show him, I thought, and knelt very straight, my hands folded with my eyes raised the way figures do in the stained-glass windows. I made my lips just barely move in dainty, inaudible prayers, feeling very good and maidenly, but he never moved. With my eyes straight ahead I could still tell that he never turned to look at me. . . . And I never knew before that ordinary boys prayed.

Later, as we went down the broad stone steps of the church, Jack took my arm with a squeeze and said happily, "Come on, Angie. We'll have to step it up so we don't keep Fitz and Margie waiting."

I realized then with a half-proud, half-ashamed feeling, that Jack was a better boy than I was a girl.

Tony Becker called me the next morning just after I had cleared away the breakfast dishes. "Hi, there," he said over the phone. "Guess who's talking." I knew it wasn't Jack's voice and I didn't think Martin Keefe would call in the morning even if he did call at all. It might have been Swede but he was too good a friend of Jack's to call me.

"I just drove over from Oshkosh to deliver some stuff for my dad," he went on. "This is Tony talking." Even though he had liked me a little I hadn't expected him to call. It seemed too much luck to have two boys wanting to date me when just a few weeks ago there hadn't been any. He asked me if I would like to do something with him on Wednesday night and I told him I certainly would. When he hung up I went out into the garden and could hardly keep the elation out of my voice as I said to my mother, "Tony Becker just called me."

Later in the morning I phoned Margie and we talked about little things till I ventured casually, "Oh, by the way, Tony Becker asked for a date Wednesday night." I thought she sounded queer when she asked me if I were going, but attributed it to jealousy — even if a girl is going steady I guess she doesn't like other girls to be *too* popular.

At noon I made sandwiches and tea and we had lunch on the back lawn, my mother, Kitty, and I.

The sky was dazzling blue, and white cabbage butterflies flitted here and there over the garden in an
endless dance. We sipped our tea slowly, enjoying
the brightness of the day, while Kitty plucked hand-
fuls of the short grass and showered them down on
Kinkee who was sleeping beside her. The grass
tickled the dog's black nose till she sneezed and
then walked away in abused dejection. I kept waiting for the phone to ring till the one o'clock whistle
blew at the factories on the edge of town. That was
the first day in over two weeks that Jack hadn't
called at noon.

That evening Margaret and I put on slacks and
played baseball in the side lot with Kitty till the sun
went down, and after that we went inside and
played three-handed bridge with Lorraine while my
mother sat with her reading glasses on, letting down
the hem of one of Kitty's last summer's dresses.

Later, when I opened my window before going to
bed, last night's moon was out again, just showing
through the trees on our lawn. I tried to go to sleep
very quickly. It seemed better not to think about
Jack that night.

Lorraine told us when she came home from work
the next day that she had a date with Martin that
night. She met him having a Coke in the drugstore,
she explained all smiling. He was just as nice as
anything, asked how she'd been, and then suggested
that they do something that night. "Honestly," she
said to Margaret with enthusiasm, "you should
have Art find out subtly where he gets his things
. . . Martin has the most superb taste in clothes!"

She went upstairs and put her hair in curlers
and came to the supper table with apologies and a
film of cold cream on her face. No one mentioned
Jack's not having called. My mother had had a

letter from my father who was working on a prospect down in southern Illinois and he had hopes of closing a big deal in the morning. Kitty had spent the afternoon catching bumblebees in a canning jar and was rushing through her supper so she could let them loose again before they suffocated. All day long one half of my mind had been thinking about Tony Becker and tomorrow evening, and the other half was cautiously waiting for Jack to call. He might be in Green Bay visiting his cousin again, of course. Either I would get a postcard tomorrow or he would be certain to call.

That night I tried to stay awake until Lorraine came home to ask if she had had a good time. It struck me that I had been so busy thinking about Jack for the past few weeks that I hadn't taken the time to be nice to Lorraine or to talk with her the way we used to. I lay for a long time remembering how it used to be when we were all little girls and there was nothing to do on Saturday night but take baths and play pillow games in bed. I wondered if Lorraine thought about things like that anymore.

The old clock on the courthouse tower in the center of town rings out every hour, and late at night, when the town is still, the chimes echo out even to the edge of town. Lying in bed, I heard the clock strike midnight and then one o'clock. Outside the night was quiet and only an occasional car went down the street. Even the wind in the trees was hushed. Before long I lost hold of my thoughts and they slipped into dreams. I didn't hear Lorraine come in after all. I don't even think I heard two o'clock ring.

We drove back to Oshkosh on Wednesday evening. It is a twenty-mile drive from Fond du

Lac on a wide curve of highway that runs along the lake, almost touching the shore. My mother hadn't liked Tony very well — I could tell that. He had been polite and friendly but there was something in the way he had talked to her — as if he had known her a long time, instead of being a little shy the way boys are supposed to be. It was almost seven-thirty when we left and the sun was going down, with stretches of cloud like graying cotton against the faint rose of the sky. A cool, moist wind blew in from the lake. Farther on, the highway goes through a stretch of sodden marshland, thick with slim, green rushes and stagnant with green-scummed pools. Here and there were the dark mounds of beaver hills, half hidden in the tall grass.

From the very beginning I liked Tony. There was something different about him. He drove faster and didn't look straight ahead with his eyes on the road the way Jack did, but kept turning to look at me. In fact, he looked at me so much that I began to feel that I must be very nice to look at. He asked me what I'd been doing with my summer and what college I was going to in the fall and the sort of things that make easy conversation. One stretch of highway run directly along the lake shore and the water there was restless and choppy. There is a small island a short distance out with two heavy-headed trees on it. "Sometimes in stormy weather," said Tony, pointing it out, "the waves wash right over that island so that the trees look as if they are growing out of the water. I tried to land on it from a motorboat one afternoon but you can't do it. It's too rocky and the island's nothing but a piece of high marshland anyway."

He smoked one cigarette after another and I had to open my window to clear out the smoke, and the night air was cool and smelled of rain. We passed a long straight row of ash trees, bending gently with the wind and restless as before a storm. There is something fascinatingly secure about riding in a car at that time of evening. Along the road the barns and silos were changing into dark silhouettes against the sky, and fields were losing their fences in the dusk. The road to Oshkosh is dotted with taverns that thrust their bright neon beer signs out into the night. In a yard before one of them, an old white farmhouse converted into a roadhouse, early customers had already parked their cars, like a row of dark beetles. We passed an old billboard that sagged drunkenly on tired legs, its supports sunk into the marshy ground. The whole countryside seemed caught in the silence that comes over everything just as the sun goes down. First lights were just beginning to wink on in the farmhouses and trees stirred uneasily, apprehensive of the coming night. The wind had twisted the dark clouds into weird shapes and in the whole gray-green pall of half-darkness I felt as if I would like to sit closer to Tony, safe inside the car with the bright headlights before us, pushing aside the dusk.

Just on the outskirts of Oshkosh was a line of new white frame houses with warm lights in their shiny windows, the young evergreens beside the doors still squat and green and the lawn still grassless and fresh with red clay. Tony slowed up as we went by and said, "Look at that, Angie. Look at that, will you? All those people sitting reading the evening paper in their nice, clean white boxes. Looks nice, doesn't it? Just like playing house."

It was good to hear a boy talk that way and
Tony had talked like that all the way from Fond
du Lac.

He *liked* things. It was he who had pointed out
to me that the corn in the fields was higher than
usual for this time of year; he had showed me a
tavern where he usually stopped on Friday night
for crisp, hot little fish fried in deep fat; and he
had told me with pleasure to listen how clear the
music came through on the car radio since he had
had the aerial adjusted. He seemed to be *glad*
about everything. Each cigarette he smoked seemed
to taste good and he watched the smoke, blue in
the air. There was something about his mouth that
seemed different from other boys. When I looked
at him I felt so conscious of it. His lips were full
and red and when he talked the words sounded
slow and warm, as if he enjoyed saying them. I
had noticed too, that when he came up our front
sidewalk, though he came fast enough, he seemed
to be doing it slowly, to the fullest, and when he
looked at me I felt that my face must be warm
and smooth. I didn't get the same breathless feeling
of expectation I felt when I was with Jack but
rather a lazy, luxurious consciousness of being alive.

We stopped at a place called Chet's just on the
edge of town. Instead of going around to the other
side of the car to open my door, Tony just leaned
across from the driver's seat and turned the handle.
It struck me then what a big boy he was. Inside,
Chet's is divided into two parts, just like Pete's
— one half for the bar and the other half for the
orthophonic, the dance floor, and a circle of little
black-topped tables and chromium-and-leather
chairs. As we walked in several people turned to
say hello to Tony and the bartender hailed him

from the other room. This wasn't a tavern or a roadhouse or anything like that — in fact, it was the sort of place that every town has for the younger people to go — but I couldn't quite reconcile myself yet to being with people who drank beer and to going to "bar places."

The whole evening went quickly. Tony was fun, though he was the first boy I had ever been with who drank whisky and soda and I kept unconsciously watching him, expecting him to act as men in the movies do when they drink too much. We sat at a table by ourselves but several of his friends came over. The fellows seemed older and looked at me as if they were surprised about something, and the girls Tony talked to were the kind with very dark lipstick, short skirts, and low voices.

We danced together, Tony and I, and the music was slow and easy, and there was something in the way Tony moved that reminded me of how he had looked walking up our front sidewalk. I can't explain to you the feeling it gave me. There was something slow and conscious about the way he moved his legs — as if he were thinking about them.

Of course I was wondering about Jack. Little thoughts nudged at my brain all evening but I tried to fluff them away. It was just the music from the jukebox and the familiar things like cigarette smoke and Cokes that made me remember him. After all, three days without a phone call is nothing, and I busied myself talking with Tony to keep other thoughts out of my mind.

He kept watching me so intently that I found myself laughing in the wrong places and making small, uneasy remarks that didn't mean anything. There was something about him that I didn't

111

understand. He kept looking at me with such a slow, lazy look in his eyes that even with the table between us it seemed as if there were no table at all. And you can't talk to a boy when he's not really listening.

It began to rain just as we left for home, sending little drops spitting against the car windows while ahead of us the highway stretched lonely and dark. We drove with the car radio turned low and Tony reached over and took my hand in his. We went on in silence, he holding my hand lightly and me not knowing just what to do and feeling pretty silly, till he said in his same warm voice, "Are you cold, Angie?"

I was surprised. It wasn't a cold night. "Why, no. No, thank you, Tony. I'm quite comfortable — and besides I've got my sweater right in the back seat." He looked at me and then laughed hard, slapping his hand on my knee. He laughed so hard that I laughed too, and settled back on the car cushions, reassured. The music from the radio was soft and sweet and the windshield wipers were trucking merrily in the rain.

When we got home the storm had let up a little and Tony came right up to the door, standing on the top step with me.

"Would you like to do something Saturday night?" he asked.

My mind worked fast, feeling for the right, polite words. "I'd like to . . . I'd like to very much but — I'm busy this Saturday. . . ."

He didn't mind at all but just said, "All right, Angie. And thanks a lot for tonight. I liked being with you a lot. You know," he laughed, "you're a kind of *restful* girl to go out with."

After he left I set the potted plants from the

living room out on the front steps so they could catch the summer rain, while I turned over the odd thoughts in my mind to find out what Tony had meant. But I didn't understand. Outside, the rain fell again in a quiet, steady patter and the air was fresh with the smell of damp earth and wet cement.

Of course I wasn't really busy on Saturday night but I thought *surely* Jack would call by then.

Somehow when the telephone doesn't ring it seems even more noisily present than if it is constantly jingling. As each day went by it became more evident that he didn't mean to call. Every time I went into the dining room I could feel the phone on the corner table behind my back, almost as if it were someone staring at me. If it rang while I was upstairs I waited, breathless, to hear the mumbled conversation, praying that footsteps would come to the stair bannister to call up, "For you, Angie!" When I was washing my face in the bathroom I left the door open just a little so I could hear its ring over the noise of the water from the faucet, and when I was weeding in the garden between the vegetable rows my ears were strained with conscious alertness to catch any noise from the house. And as the end of the week drew near, each ring made that lump in my throat harder and heavier.

The days were filled with monotonous sameness. The mornings started out with bright, clean sunshine on the bedroom wall, the smell of fresh coffee, and my sister Lorraine at the breakfast table looking sleepy with curlers still in her hair. At first I tried to make myself feel glad that I was awake and that the morning was beautiful,

113

and to keep the toast from sticking dry in my throat, and I tried to make myself care when my mother would say cheerily, "Well, Angie, today we'll clean out the big spare closet," or "Angeline, today would be a nice day to wash the front windows, don't you think?"

Each morning was full of the pleasant drone of the serial stories on the radio and the usual little everyday tasks that dragged across my nerves in their routine dullness. When I dusted the living room there were furry night moths dead on the rug around the base of the floor lamp and the outside window screens began to be spotted with long-feelered Green Bay flies, those large, mosquitolike insects that sweep down like a plague for a few weeks of every summer. My mother enameled a kitchen chair white and set it on the back lawn to dry, and by night the paint was all stuck with their silly bodies.

The little boys next door found three dry peach stones one day and set them in a pan of water in the sun, waiting patiently to see them open, thinking they were clams. Kitty came in to tell me about it in her breathless, chattery way, but when I tried to talk to her the corners of my mouth felt heavy, and just moving my lips seemed too much trouble. I began to notice little things about her that I never noticed before — how her eyebrows turned up on the corners and the funny way she lisped when she got excited. I thought too how very nice it was to be young and not know about boys and things and still be happy about ice-cream cones and cutting paper dolls out of the Sears, Roebuck catalogues.

The days were beginning to get hot and the garden had that lush midsummer look when it seems that you can almost watch the plants grow. Early in the morning there were black and yellow spiders sunning themselves in strong webs stretched between the tomato plants, and the tomatoes were hard, green balls with the small twist of dried yellow blossom still stuck to the smooth skin. Little bright-green grasshoppers skipped on the grass of the back lawn, and along the cracks in the cement sidewalk the ants were busy mounding up their black mudgrain houses.

One afternoon we walked to the movie and in the soft, cool darkness I sat trying to keep my mind on the screen and hearing Kitty beside me making noise with a bag of peanuts, while all the time my heart was beating with an aching throb and I kept remembering that the last time I had been here was the Sunday night with Jack. I could re-act in my memory the contented feeling of being so near to him and the warm, clean pressure of his fingers on mine.

And as each day changed into evening and Margaret came home from work full of talk about Art and the store, and the setting sun slid long shadows onto the lawn, a queer, tired feeling crept over me and through me until even my hands went limp. I didn't even feel like a girl any more. And all my thoughts turned into little prayers which I meant so much that it made me ache all over. "Just once," I kept saying. "Let him call just once."

Lorraine asked me to go for a walk with her one evening. Martin hadn't called for several days and she had been sitting by the front window reading, leafing restlessly through the pages of a magazine and glancing up quickly every time a car went past.

I knew why she wanted to go for a walk and I didn't blame her. For the past few days I had wanted to do it myself. We closed the front door softly behind us and then walked down our street quiet and thick with summer shadows, till we came to Park Avenue. The night was different here. Any small town is the same on a summer evening and slow cars went by one after another with their windows open, sending out quick snatches of music from the radio and twice we passed fellows and girls walking hand in hand, going toward the park.

"Let's hurry," said Lorraine.

There is something almost disgraceful about two girls, especially sisters, even going out for a walk alone when other girls have dates, so we turned off the avenue as soon as we could onto a side street, a street with heavy trees and lampposts only twice in the block.

I wish now I could have said something to Lorraine. Something quick and bright with happiness in it. If I could have said the right things that night, her whole summer, her whole life might have been different. But there was a certain wordless pride that kept us both from talking. I couldn't admit, even though I knew it was true, that Martin had only been taking her out because he was new in town and didn't know any other girls. I had to pretend that I didn't know that every day after work she walked to the drugstore looking for him and that once I had heard her call his boarding-house and then hang up gently when a strange voice answered. I had to pretend that I thought she wasn't going out with him just because she didn't care to and that it was *she* who was turning *him* down. I had to pretend all that, and go along

116

in silence as if we were just out for an ordinary walk because we were sisters and because when we were younger we played tag together and never argued over paper dolls or tattletaled about each other and it was the same now.

She didn't mention where we were going but I knew where Martin roomed. Most of the houses on his street were already sound asleep but some still had low floor lamps shining through their eyes. "Let's cross over to the other side, Angie," she said quietly. "I wouldn't want him to see me if he should happen to be outside."

We walked softly on padded feet with the street lamps making heavy summer shadows from the old trees on the sidewalk. A quick cat jumped silently from the bushes and then, as suddenly, was nothing in the darkness. We went on until we were directly across the street from where Martin lived but the boardinghouse was quiet, its window shades pulled down like eyelids, and there was no green coupe pulled up at the curb. Lorraine said nothing at all but we both knew he wasn't at home.

The night was thick about us and the tree leaves whispered and small gnats made a moving fuzz around the streetlights. At the next corner we turned back automatically toward the avenue and out of the quietness of our thoughts, my sister said suddenly, "Angie, tell me — do you and Jack ever *neck*?"

She startled me and I could feel my face flush warm in the darkness. Necking was one of those words that everyone knew about but never said. I was embarrassed into confusion — Lorraine and I never talked about things like that.

"Do you mean have I — have I ever *kissed*

117

him?" I asked and the words felt slow and awkward on my lips. And the night silence was pregnant with thoughts.

"No, no," she answered, her voice impatient. I couldn't see her face in the darkness. "I mean — you know what I mean. Do you ever *neck?*"

I didn't really know, I told her, stumbling over the words. I wasn't sure just what she meant . . . and something inside of me, panicky, kept hoping frantically she wouldn't say the word again.

"Well, Angie, I've talked with girls at school, smooth girls, and they all . . . well, if you go out with a fellow a few times . . . it isn't as if you have to. . . . You know how it is, Angie!"

There was something in her voice that was asking me to answer but I didn't know what it was that she wanted me to say. There was something in her voice that was saying so much more than the words themselves, an odd pleading that didn't fit with the words at all.

"Things are different now from the way they used to be," she went on urgently. "People don't think anything of it anymore . . . I mean, if it's only one boy you're going with and that sort of thing. It isn't like it used to be when you had to be almost engaged . . . now *everybody* does it and nobody thinks . . . you know what I mean. . . ."

Her voice trailed off and she was looking at me hard in the darkness, waiting and I had to say something. I had to say something to get that worried, twisted sound out of her voice. I knew how she felt. She was thinking just as I was. There were little warm thoughts in her mind like soft fur, just as in mine; there were thoughts that made her lips tremble and set a quiet, steady beating in her throat when the gentleness of the summer night touched her cheek and the air was fragrant with the smell of flowers hidden in the darkness. I knew how she felt.

And suddenly I remembered how it was when we were still little girls and I wanted to reach out to touch her hand as we walked. "It's all right," I told her gently. "It's all right, Lorraine. If you really like a boy — it's all right to kiss him."

She went along in silence for a few moments, brushing close against the bushes, letting the cool, dark leaves touch her arm. "Angie, you don't understand," she said, wearily. "You don't understand at all." And there was no reproach in her voice. "You don't even know what I mean!"

* * *

I raked over that last evening with him carefully, looking for a sentence or even a word that could have made him angry, quickly skipping over the parts that were so lovely that it hurt to remember. And it wasn't because I had gone out with Tony. That was silly too. After all we weren't going steady. Just because you've kissed a boy doesn't mean you're going steady. That's silly, I told myself, but a little doubt dragged behind and stayed heavy in my mind.

The night after I had been out with Lorraine, Kitty and I took the dog for a walk. It was late and Kitty came pattering downstairs in her nightgown when she heard me open the front door; and though I would rather have been alone, I let her come with me. The dog walked on silent paws, disappearing in the shadow of bushes and coming out again in the patches where the moonlight lay light on the ground; while Kitty walked beside me, her bare feet making a padding noise on the cement sidewalk.

The night seemed to be deliberately hurting me with its lush loveliness. There was no need for the air to be soft and fragrant just then nor for the crickets to keep up their steady chant that blended with my thoughts till it was no sound at all. Why, I thought, do night moths rise up like small white ghosts from the grass and why are the trees so full of whispers? Why do I keep remembering the smell of pipe smoke that you can't even see, pungent in the night air, and that small, warm silence when someone is near you? Am I supposed to stand this? Am I supposed to go in the house and put the dog in the basement for the night and go into the living room and talk to my mother as if everything was the same as always? Am I supposed to keep my lips moving with small weekday words when my throat aches with longing and my mind keeps remembering that the night is breathless and the moon is looking through the trees, making silent shadows on the grass? It wasn't fair that everything was so full of loveliness and remembering, so full of everything I wanted. I wasn't old enough to have to stand all this.

A slow thought eased itself into my mind and grew and grew until I knew it was the truth. I knew it as certainly as if I had read it printed in the paper. Just thinking made my heart hurt with a throbbing ache till I felt that it would ease it if I could just hold it for a moment, with its pulsing ache, in the warmth of my hands. I knew. and the palms of my hands tingled with desire just to touch him, and thinking of it made my breath feel dry in my throat. I knew then there was no use pretending or trying to cajole my mind into silence or clouding my memory with forced, fluffy thoughts. Sometime, sometime I had to see Jack again and I knew it.

"We'd better go in," Kitty whispered in a small voice as if she, too, had caught the strange spell of the night, and she took my hand. Yes, I thought, we had better go in, and as I opened the front door a night moth flew in, drawn by the light, and fluttered against the lamp shade.

Later, lying in bed, I thought and thought so long that every thought in my head turned into a prayer, and the longing seemed to suck all other ideas from my head until the whole bed, the whole darkness of the room was keeping time to the words that beat and beat in my head. Through the window the night breezes came soft with the smell and warmth of summer and my prayers went on and on, ends linked to beginnings in an endless chain, till my thoughts were a steady chant of "Let him call, let him call!" and outside the moon, almost full, hung heavy and gold just above the trees.

And I kept seeing it, so round and close, even after I shut my eyes.

And the next morning I found out. My mother and Kitty drove to Sheboygan with my father — it was unusual for him to be home in the middle of the week and it made the day a sort of holiday. I waited till I heard the car back out of the driveway and the sound of it fade away down the street. Even though I knew I was alone I made myself walk down the stairs casually, slowly, as if it didn't matter at all. I stopped in the living room to dial the radio to a music program and took a last, cautiously casual look in the kitchen to make sure everyone was really gone before I picked up the phone. I even looked in the icebox and made myself pretend I was concerned over what I would

121

make for lunch. The dog Kinkee raised her nose from her paws as she lay under the kitchen table and it gave me a guilty feeling even to have *her* hear, but, after all, there was nothing wrong with calling!

Margie's voice on the other end of the wire was high and a little surprised. I could imagine her thin, red lips as she talked. "Well, gee, Angie, it certainly is a long time since I heard from you!"

"Why, yes. It is," I said, my mind feeling for the easy, noncommittal words.

"What you been doing?" she went on, and I told her nothing, nothing at all except the usual lazy things one does in summer and what had she been doing?

"Oh — Fitz and I have been going out to Pete's like always and then a bunch of us had a weiner roast the other night. . . ." Her voice trailed off a little.

Go on. Go on. Did you see him? Was Jack there? Tell me. Tell me. Don't make me ask. Don't make me ask, my mind said, but the words from my mouth came with slow unconcern, "That must have been fun, Margie. That must have been loads of fun with the weather so nice and everything."

The next words I seemed to see rather than hear, as if they came out, black and stark before my eyes on ticker tape. "I suppose," she said simply, "I suppose you know that Jack has been dating Jane Rady again?" She knew I hadn't known; she knew, but how else could it be said?

For over a week, she told me. Ever since that time I had gone out with Tony. Almost every night since then. To the weiner roast and to Pete's and to shows by themselves. Jane Rady had told all the girls she was going with Jack again. Jane

Rady had told everyone. After all, it had been well over a week.

I was glad Margie kept talking for I wasn't sure of my own voice then. Those minutes on the phone were so long I couldn't even remember ever having talked before.

"Honestly, Angie," she went on in a very confidential, sister-to-sister tone, "I can't see why you had to go out with a boy like Tony when you were dating someone as swell as Jack Duluth."

"Why? But why, Margie? I had fun with Tony. It was nice. What do you mean 'a boy like Tony'? He's a friend of Jack's. Jack introduced me to him. Don't the fellows like him or what?"

"Boys *like* him," she explained with elaborate patience, "and girls like him too — but, well, they don't *go out* with him . . . unless they're *that kind*."

I had been staring at the rug pattern on the dining-room floor till it rose and blurred before my eyes. I was so surprised that what Margie was saying seemed faraway and unreal, like something that wasn't meant for me to hear at all. And after she had said it I wanted her to hang up and let me think my own thoughts.

"That's why everyone was so surprised, and especially Jack, because no one thought you were the kind to go out with a fast boy like that, Angie!"

For the rest of the day the words resounded in my head. But he hadn't been when he was with me, so how was I to know that Tony was a fast boy!

My mother brought home some newly shelled peas they had bought up at a vinery on the highway coming from Sheboygan. I picked out the small, round thistleheads that are always mixed with vinery peas and put the peas on to cook.

"We passed Jack in the bakery truck headed for the lake just as we turned into the street," my mother said conversationally, tying on a clean apron. "He must have been going out to look at his boat."

Since morning my thoughts were so numbed that now I could look at her and nod in answer without my face showing anything.

Late the next afternoon all the ominous, heavy gloom I felt inside of me seemed to come out in the weather. I had been in the kitchen most of the day ironing Kitty's dresses and the clothes had the clean, fresh smell of having blown in the sun, but the steam came up hot from the ironing board and the air was damp and muggy. My hair was sticking in fuzzy curls on my neck, and from the radio in the living room I could hear the monotonous, inarticulate drone of the baseball game. It was the sort of day that made you wish you could go to bed right away and not have to wake up till tomorrow.

The weather was bound to break and finally in the late afternoon a storm rode in from the lake on a low wind that smelled of fish and the dark, troubled water of Winnebago. Over to the north the sky grew heavy and sullen, a dark gray-green, the color of old bruises, and the wind snaked its way through the grass and pushed the bushes flat against the house. Outside, neighbor women came to their doors calling to the children to come in before the rain came, and in our living room my mother switched off the radio, grumbling with sudden static, and came into the kitchen.

"Angeline," she suggested, "let's have a cup of tea and finish those macaroons in the cookie jar."

She set out the cups, but just as the steam began to whistle from the nose of the kettle she said, "Or perhaps it's too near suppertime," and put the cups and teapot away again.

The smell of the lake was so strong the waves might well have been licking the back door step and the trees on the lawn tossed fitfully, as if they were worried beyond bearing. Kitty came in with her hair blown about saying, "Got to close the upstairs windows. It's going to rain." The sky was so dark that the air was gray-green and birds swooped low from the trees, uneasy about the coming storm. As I went to shut the kitchen window the wind blew the first rain against the pane in spiteful gusts, and out in the north, over the lake, lightning crooked a long, bright finger across the sky. It was a storm that would last the night.

"What shall we have for supper?" my mother asked. "It's the sort of night the children will be hungry."

"Pancakes and cocoa with marshmallows?" Kitty suggested hopefully. That is her stock menu for anything from picnics to birthday parties.

"All right," Mom agreed. "And, Angie, if you'll melt up some butter with brown sugar it will save us having to go to the store for syrup in the rain." Kitty hovered close to the stove with comments and suggestions till the syrup was done and I gave her the sweet, sticky pan to scrape.

Later, at supper, she sat bobbing the marshmallow in her cocoa cup up and down, saying every few moments, "Isn't this good, children? Isn't this good?" She always calls my other sisters and me "children" because my mother does and usually I laugh but tonight I didn't care.

Lorraine's hair was damp and uncurled from the rain and hung limp around her face. Every few minutes the lights in the chandelier dimmed as outside the lightning crackled, and we all held our conversations poised for a moment, waiting for the thunder to pass. The house had the warm, oppressive stillness in the air that comes from the tension of a storm and not having the windows open. For a moment I thought I couldn't stand it — all the pleasant, protected smugness that kept making me pretend and pretend. They all sat around the table, enjoying the luxurious taste of syrup and melted butter, with their lips soft and smiling and their faces happy as if they were eating slices of contentment. I had a sudden stifled feeling, as if the house were too small and the cream-colored dining-room walls were crowding in close, so close that it made my very ribs ache.

My mother filled Kitty's cocoa cup again, smiling to herself. "Isn't this a good night to be all home, cozy and inside?" she questioned, and her voice was quiet and warm with sheer satisfaction. Outside, the wind pelted the rain in sheets against the window and went keening through the trees, its sad wail trailing behind.

We spent the whole miserable evening in the living room with the radio off because the air was static-filled with storm. Lorraine had pinned her wet hair into a scraggly knot at the back of her head like a neat washwoman and sat leafing through a pile of old magazines. My mother had picked apart a worn tweed suit of Margaret's to make over for me for college, and I slipped it on, tacked together, over my slacks while she made rough calculations with pins. "There," she said with satisfaction, "look, children. If that won't look smart with a long yellow sweater!" I inched around slowly to give her the whole effect while she said with her head cocked, chewing a bit of thread, "But you must stand straighter, Angie," and she gave me a motherly poke between the shoulder blades with her thimbled finger. "You've been slumping for over a week."

Margaret sat with a magazine and note paper on her knee writing to Art and smiling to herself, while the pen made a steady scratch-scratch in the quietness of the room.

I took a book from the shelf and lay down on the rug to read. There is nothing like filling your mind with new thoughts to crowd the old ones out, but somehow it didn't work. It was like taking caster oil with orange juice. When you drink through the sweet juice floating on the top everything seems all right but you inevitably come to the thick, sickening castor oil, heavy at the bottom.

Lorraine was chipping the nail polish off the nails of one hand with the other hand as she read, making a small, insistent noise as irritating as the screak of chalk on the blackboard. Martin had called just before the rain began for the first time this week. I had answered.

"Hi, there, Angeline," he had said.

And I was so surprised to hear his voice I blurted out, "Hello, Martin! I'm so glad you called!" That was wrong. Martin always laughs at anyone who is glad about anything.

"Yeah?" His voice twisted into a question and I could almost see his face with one eyebrow raised and a half-smile making his mouth sarcastically amused. "Your sister 'round?" he asked.

"Why, no. No, she isn't home from work yet," I explained, "but she'll be here in just a little while — "

"All right," he answered abruptly. "Thanks, Angie."

"What shall I tell her?" I insisted. "Was there anything special you wanted?"

"No, just tell her I called."

"Shall I tell her you'll call back, Martin?"

"If you want. Yeah, tell her I'll call back later," and he hung up.

When Lorraine came home from work I told her and I had watched her waiting as we ate supper, but the phone never rang. She kept looking at the clock every few minutes till the hand ticked its way past seven. Then she didn't look anymore.

Now, in the living room, it made me feel worse to see her so I turned over and put my head on my arms on the rug. I know now how a balloon feels when it bursts. The rough scratch of the pile was almost comforting against my face and my head ached with the effort of trying to hold back my thoughts, so I just closed my eyes and let them come. One sharp thought needled into my brain till I felt like squirming. Maybe right now they're out there, Jack and Jane Rady, listening to the music from the nickel machine at Pete's and laughing together every time the storm dimmed the lights, while outside the lake is tossing its waves high up on the back lawn. Or maybe they're at the movie, in the darkness and quiet, not knowing there is a storm at all. Her hair would be shining and hanging soft and straight. Maybe he had even touched her hair.

I wanted so badly to cry. Not with big, loud sobs, but just to sit by myself without making any noise and let the tears trickle slowly and silently without my having to stop them. I tried to force my mind back, back to the time before I knew

Jack; but it kept puttering with little memories on the way and I couldn't get past that first night in the boat. Pictures kept see-sawing before my eyes till I was sick with unhappiness and my heart felt sore as a bruise.

The worst of the storm was clearing now and a fork of lightning did one last quick dance across the sky while low thunder applauded in the distance. But the rain was still steady on the window panes and runneled noisily in the eaves trough, and the wind was still worrying the tired trees. My mother shifted her sewing on her knee and said again with warm contentment, "Isn't this the best night to be all home, cozy and inside?"

I can't even tell you quite how it happened. I mean, it was the sort of thing that happens so fast that you can't even piece it together again afterward. It was late Saturday afternoon and I had walked down to Paine's drugstore to buy some turpentine to take the paint off Kitty's new sailor slacks. She had spent the morning in the garage refinishing her bicycle.

Paine's is a very plain drugstore with a bare, shiny front window all neatly arranged with well-dusted boxes of tooth paste, a special milk of magnesia display, and a small barrel of horehound drops spilled artistically in one corner. It is the reliable sort of drugstore which does a large prescription business and even the few Cokes they serve have a slightly medicinal tang. I was sitting in a front booth all by myself. The sides of those booths are high and the table tops of cold speckled marble give the back of the drugstore a dusky gloom in the daytime. I was sitting not thinking of anything, just being glad that the Saturday housework was done and noticing distastefully how white and puffy my hands looked from having scrubbed the kitchen linoleum. My mind was so tired of wondering and worrying that I just let my thoughts wander in and out as they wanted to.

And all of a sudden there was Jack. When I think it over now we must have looked very silly to anyone watching — as if we were in a play and both overacting. He came in the door, whispering to himself and was swinging onto a high stool before the soda fountain when he saw me. Something happened to me then — a funny tingling feeling started right at the top of my head and went down over me in a quick wave leaving me suddenly very cold and wide-awake. I remember putting my hand on the bottle of turpentine wrapped in green paper on the seat beside me, thinking vaguely that if he should come over to talk to me it would be nice to have something to hold on to.

"Hello," he said, gruffly, as though he were clearing his throat. "Didn't see you at first."

"Hello, Jack." My face had a tight feeling as if I had washed it with too much soap.

I had always thought it was something like voting, that you weren't really supposed to start feeling with your heart till you were at least twenty-one. And here I was looking at him so hard I could almost *feel* myself seeing the clean, wet look of his crew cut and the familiar coarse knit of his football sweater, while my heart was pounding till it made my voice sound quavery.

"How've you been, Angie?" he asked, sliding into the booth across from me.

"Fine," I said quickly. "Fine, Jack. How have you been?" and I tried to look past him till I could be more sure of myself, till I could put my thoughts out of my eyes.

"I've just been down at the Y," he told me. "Swede too. We had a swim and a shower. I always take an hour off on Saturday afternoon. We're rushed down at the bakery on Saturday night."

And then suddenly we were all out of conversation. There was a long, awkward silence with our thoughts very busy in it and I looked at him with a small smile anxious on my lips. I had the feeling that I wasn't really I at all but another person sitting in the booth across the aisle, looking over and watching.

"What you been doing, Angie?" He urged his voice to sound interested and I caught the cue.

"Nothing. What have *you* been doing? I haven't even seen Swede around lately." It wasn't the right thing to say. He knew I hadn't seen Swede. It didn't mean anything. Here I was with just a few minutes and I wasn't saying anything; nothing that mattered. Jack's hand was on the table and I felt my own close tight on the turpentine bottle; I wanted so much to touch it. Sometimes my hands seem to have minds of their own. I wanted so much to touch him that for a moment there didn't even seem to be a table between us. He looked at me then, straight at me, and I felt my eyes go soft.

"I've got to go, Angie," he said quickly. "I've got to get back right away because Saturday's so busy at the bakery." He said it but he never moved and it was as if he had never spoken at all.

Something had to be said and the words were suddenly on my lips, without any thoughts behind them, tingling to be said. "Jack, Margie told me what Fitz said you thought about that night with Tony...."

But he wouldn't look at me then. "Did she?" and his tone was dull and uninterested. "Yeah," he added. I didn't know how to go on. I couldn't say that what he thought wasn't true when I didn't even know what he thought.

"I guess I was kinda surprised," he said with a half-smile, never raising his eyes.

"Surprised at what?"

"To hear that you went out with Tony."

"Why?"

"Why!" He looked at me in an exasperated way, running his hand through his hair, only his hair was clipped so short he really just smoothed over it. His voice was tight and quick as if he were angry.

"Gee, Angie, I take you out. Everything goes like it did that night at the dance and then at the cottage and everything. And I start feeling : . . well, how I did . . . and then one morning Tony walks into the bakery and says he's got a date with you!"

And there was nothing I could say.

"Just when I start thinking, well, maybe it's all right, Fitz calls up and tells me that Margie just called him to tell him that you'd called her and said that you've got a date with Becker and you're even *proud* of it!"

He looked at me in a puzzled, hurt sort of way and his voice was almost pleading. "Gee, Angie!"

"But, Jack," I said, "Jack, how was I to know? I didn't know a thing about it!" I sat twisting a curl of hair round and round my finger because I was trying so hard to find the right words that I couldn't even keep my hands still.

"Honestly, Jack, I didn't know a thing about it until Margie told me."

"Couldn't you *tell*?"

"No, no, how could I tell?"

"Just by the way he looks at you. And you even danced with him at the Country Club dance!"

"But you were the one that arranged to exchange dances. I thought he was a friend of yours."

"Sure, he's a friend of mine. And he's a good guy too, but he's just that way. And any girl that I go with that would go out with Tony and — "

"And what?"

He looked up at me and his voice was quiet. "Didn't you, Angie?"

"Well, Jack! Honestly!" It was my turn to sound exasperated, but inside my head words were bumping together so fast that I didn't know what to say.

"How was I to know, Angie? I didn't think so at first, but then I talked to Swede and we both know Becker, and well, when you called up Margie to tell her about it and everything . . . how was I to know, Angie?" For a moment neither of us moved or spoke; but when I am very, very old I hope I can look back and remember all the wonderful things that went on in that silence.

"I've got the truck outside," he said huskily, nodding toward the door, "if I can take you home."

We took the longest way, the way that goes through the park and along the edge of the lake where the small boats moored at the shore dip in rhythm with the waves and the blue water is spangled with sunlight. And down the long, thin highway toward the country, passing cars with their windows glinting with sun, to the curved gravel road with scum-covered water in its ditches, growing with tall heavy-headed cattails and slim purple irises. Farther on the air is honeyed with the clean, sweet smell of clover and the willow trees shake their varnished leaves till they glitter in the sunlight.

Jack drove with both hands tight on the wheel and I sat close beside him till we came to the place where the Virginia creeper stretches heavy on the fences and the trees beside the road grow thick and gnarled, reaching up muscled arms, and the fields, all wild with mustard plants, are yellow as sunshine. Jack slowed the car while we held our breath and listened to the whole air singing with the sound of insects and wind in the grass and the warm steady hum that is summer. And along the ditches the weeds were gray with the dry dust that rose in a cloud from the gravel road as we stopped. Behind us lay the town, lost beyond the fences and ditches, and ahead the whole country lay stretching, yellow-green in the sunlight.

And the thought in my mind was as warm and mellow as the sunlight. How odd, I thought. How wonderfully, wonderfully odd to be kissed in the middle of the afternoon.

JULY

IT WAS HOT. It was hot with the steady beating heat that comes from a bare sky and a high sun, still and glaring, that covers the whole ground without a shadow. It was the kind of weather in which high school girls go about with their long silk hair pinned in knots on the top of their heads like scrubwomen, and little children splash in tubs of shallow water in their back yards and older people drag mattresses out onto airing porches to wait for a breeze in the still, quiet heat of the evening.

We were all hot. All of us. The soil in the garden was parched and hard, crisscrossed with wide cracks, and big brown grasshoppers, their wings dusty, were heavy on the bean plants and bared the green stems with their nibblings. Kitty pinned her braids on top of her head so the little ends stuck up like horns and rolled her slacks above her knees while new brown-dot freckles popped out on her nose. All afternoon the dog lay panting under the basement stairs where the heat brought the moisture out of the cement in damp patches like sweat that ran in slow trickles down the stone walls.

"Tomorrow we'll just pack a lunch, shut the house, and go away for the day," my mother said at suppertime. It was so warm that her thin dress stuck to the back of her chair every time she moved. "In all this heat I don't know as I could stand the noise and the firecrackers for a whole day," she went on, fanning herself gently with a napkin.

Art was there too, having driven up from Milwaukee with my father earlier in the afternoon — neither of them wanted to get mixed up with the Fourth-of-July traffic. "If one of us goes we'll all go," my mother added. She was irritated with the heat and talked with her lips in a thin, strained line. Even Kitty had noticed it and was being carefully quiet and polite. "All this worry of accidents and death tolls in the paper takes all the fun out of holidays for me," and she went on buttering her bread with thoughtful annoyance.

"Angie," my mother said, turning to me, "after we finish supper I wish you would hard-boil some eggs and put them in the icebox for the potato salad tomorrow. I don't want to have a single thing to do in the heat of the day.

"And Kitty, run downstairs and bring up the picnic baskets from the canning cupboard and put the dishes in them tonight." She was fanning herself with her napkin again. "Dad," she said to my father, "I wish you would take me for a short ride in the car — this heat is almost too much for me tonight."

Lorraine had been eating quietly but now she put down her fork and ventured, "You know, I don't know as I'll be able to go with you tomorrow — "

"Why not?" my father demanded sharply.

"I have a date with Martie," she went on, explaining carefully, as if it were all very clear and logical, "and Martie suggested that it be sort of an all-day date." (She had been calling him "Martie" for the last week.)

"Well," answered my mother benevolently, "I don't see as that makes much difference. Having no folks of his own in town to spend the holiday with, he might as well come along with us. He'll probably find it a pleasant change, too, after so much restaurant food."

Lorraine was silent for a moment, feeling for the words in her mind. "It would be nice, of course." She was toying with her fork, her eyes on her plate, and I remember asking quickly for someone to pass me the bread, just to edge over that silence. "But if you don't mind," she said, "I'd rather he and I didn't go on the picnic."

My father looked at my mother and she raised her eyebrows back at him, but it was Art who spoke up. "Lorraine, if we get home early enough we can all go out somewhere in the evening, you and Marg and Martin and I."

"We'll have no one rushing home from one place to get to another or spoiling the day for the rest of us. We'll all go or no one at all!" my father said severely and left the table, thinking the matter settled.

Usually I agree with Lorraine about everything, but this time I *did* think she could have been more tactful. She knew that we all knew how Martin treated her. After all, he had just called at the last minute and her voice had been all eager over the phone when she said, "Yes, yes, I would like to go very much!" No matter how much she wanted to, even if she had to sit home alone all day when everyone else in Fond du Lac had dates, just once it would have been better to say she was busy.

"Call him up, Lorraine, and ask him if he wouldn't like to go," Margaret urged. "You don't want to spend the whole day sitting around in stuffy old . . . well . . . places. On the Fourth of July everyone likes to do outdoor things!"

"Really," my mother put in, "it used to be that we could arrange things here without having to worry about individual plans."

Lorraine put down her fork and burst out suddenly, "Honestly, I just can't see what all the fuss is about." Her voice was high and small with a quaver in it. Ever since Lorraine was a little girl she has cried easily and now we all looked the other way and pretended not to notice that her eyes were tear-shiny and that her lip trembled. "If he doesn't want to go," she quavered, "he certainly doesn't have to, does he? . . . Martin just isn't the kind of boy who *likes* picnics!"

My mother rose and began to clear the plates into the kitchen. "I suppose," she said stiffly to no one in particular, "I suppose you'll be wanting your breakfast in bed next!"

Lorraine pushed back her chair and went upstairs through the living room, being careful not to look at my father.

I was very glad then that Jack and I had only made plans to go to the parade.

All the town turns out for that Fourth-of-July parade, lining the Main Street from the lakeside park right out to the fairgrounds in a colorful, jabbering crowd. Kitty stood beside Jack and me, jumping with excitement and making cautious little ventures into the street, peering squint-eyed toward the park against the morning sun, and then running back to report on the parade's progress. Big bass drums vibrated deeply in the distance with a steady, rhythmic throb, and traffic policemen, their silver badges shiny in the sunlight, cruised importantly up and down the street with small flags fluttering from the handlebars of their motorcycles, waving the crowds back closer to the curb. The red, white, and blue bunting on the lampposts was lazy in warm breeze, and shop windows were ribboned with crepe paper and draped in flags.

Lorraine had come to the parade with Martin after all and stood just across the street from us looking very pretty at a distance. Martin looked warm and kept shifting his coat from arm to arm and brushing his hair back from his forehead with his free hand. He hadn't wanted to come. Earlier in the morning I had heard Lorraine say to him on the phone, "But, Martin, you just can't live in Fond du Lac if you don't go to the parade!" Her voice had that bright, brittle sound that always reminded me of Christmas tree ornaments.

I was glad Jack was the kind of boy who looked best in the bright sunlight. His skin was very tan, and the hot, damp weather made his short hair crinkly-curled, and his shirt always seemed clean when other fellows' were warm and wrinkled. Or maybe it was just because I liked him so well that he looked so nice to me.

From across the street Lorraine yoo-hooed and waved, pointing us out to Martin. He nodded and smiled at us with his cigarette still in his mouth. "Cheerful guy," Jack said to me.

When the mayor's car at the head of the parade came into sight, Kitty was so excited that she

tugged Jack's hand instead of mine and then, realizing her mistake, stood very close to me, giggling
with embarrassment. The mayor was followed by
the firemen's band, and the heavy dum-dum of the
bass drum was so loud that my whole chest seemed
to swell and be beating time with it. After the
drums came the firemen with their arms held high,
tootling on their fifes, while between their shoulders their heavy blue shirts were stained dark with
perspiration.

The air was full of the warm smell of buttered
popcorn, the hot asphalt of the street stretched
basking in the sun, and the pungent, exciting smell
of firecrackers. Floats went by with slow grace, like
huge decorated elephants, fluttering with crepe
paper and hung with flags, and Kitty studied each
one with open-mouthed amazement and then
turned to me in bewilderment asking, "Angie!
Where's the man that drives them?" and promptly
lost herself in the excitement of the string of small
ponies that came next.

Each summer holiday a traveling concession
comes to our town, stakes off a wide circle on the
green of the park lawn, rings it in with rope, and
tethers its patient little ponies in a line, waiting for
the children to come with their dimes to pay for
three slow exciting turns around the ring. In the
morning the ponies were part of the parade, walking in a prim straight line, their hoofbeats neat
and dainty on the hot pavement, and jaunty red
and blue pompons stuck behind their ears. They
always reminded me of genteel old ladies who, for
some reason, had to work for a living but never
quite forgot that they had known better things.
"Angie, make Daddy take me to the park afterward," Kitty pleaded. "I want to ride the black

one with the little face," and her voice went soft and her lips were all pouted up with love just looking at the demure ladylike pony.

"If he can't take you, I will," Jack promised and it made my cheeks tingle to hear him say it. I couldn't have been more proud if he had promised to buy her the whole horse.

A drum majorette with a high, pouter-pigeon figure did a fancy goosestep past us, the thin satin of her skirt clinging to her legs. Someone shrilled a sharp whistle through his teeth. A titter went through the crowd and the man next to me guffawed loudly to himself, then looked about him quickly, trying to pretend he had just been clearing his throat. I looked away so I wouldn't have to meet Jack's eyes, and he was squinting very hard at something down the street in the opposite direction. Then the rest of the parade went by.

Almost every business in town contributes something to our parades and a long line of milk trucks, freshly washed and spruced with their wheels twisted patriotically with red, white, and blue paper, drove by; and after them came a string of ice wagons with slow, plodding horses that kept their heads down and their dull eyes on the pavement, while their ribbon-braided tails flicked patiently at the flies. Little boys with smoking punk in their hands rode in and out of the parade, tossing firecrackers at the horses' feet.

It was getting on toward noon and the heat rose shimmering from the pavement and the clear blue sky was as dazzling as the sun. Women in sheer print dresses stood along the curb, fanning themselves with handkerchiefs or folded newspapers, the powder white in the fat creases of their faces. Across the street from us a little boy stood in bare feet, shifting from one leg to the other to keep them off the hot cement, his eyes still intent on the parade. Men took off their ties and rolled up their shirt sleeves, while the sweat ran down their faces and their shirts stuck to their backs and Kitty put her hands to her hair, feeling the heat. Everyone stood around, talking and pointing and calling to one another across the street, with their clothes limp and their faces hot and shining, but no one even thought of going home.

Part of the local American Legion marched past with little flags stuck in their hatbands, swinging striped canes and hailing their friends along the curb. Jack's father went by and waved to us. I knew it was the first time he had ever seen me and I felt self-conscious, wishing suddenly that I had worn a better dress. One of the Legionnaires walked past on wobbly knees, swinging a yellow feather bird on a stick that made a high, shrill twee-twee noise when it went through the air. Kitty squealed with delight.

The parade wound up with a few stragglers and little boys on bicycles twisted with ribbons of crepe paper, and the crowd surged out from the curbs, pushing toward their cars. Bits of red and green paper from the firecrackers littered the sidewalks and the hot air was tinged with the smell of gunpowder. Everyone was smiling broadly with the holiday excitement that takes over on the Fourth of July and with the round, exciting thoughts of a whole long, warm day of shining cars, smooth highways, laziness, and full picnic baskets. Jack took Kitty's hand and together we pushed with the crowd toward the side street where my mother and father were parked.

It may have been the sunny brightness of the

day or it might have been the exhilaration of the band music, but suddenly I was almost giddily glad just to have Jack beside me and I felt that I should walk with my head very high and my shoulders straight. It was the sort of a day when just being able to *look* at people seems wonderful.

But it turned out to be an all-wrong sort of day when Kitty was bound to skin her knee, fat houseflies came buzzing in the hole in the backdoor screen and no one could find the lemon squeezer anywhere. After the parade Lorraine had said, "If we're not back by four, just go without me — I don't know just what Martie's plans are."

And at four-thirty my mother, fresh from her afternoon nap, had lifted the picnic basket from the kitchen table and gone out to the car saying with finality and a "humph" in her voice, "We're not waiting around here all night for anyone."

Art muttered to Margaret under his breath, "What a fellow like him can find to do to pass the time in broad daylight . . ."

So we had gone on without Lorraine.

Even the air coming in the car window was warm as we drove, and the hot, white highway before us shimmered like running water. My mother and father sat in the front seat and the rest of us were crowded in the back seat with the picnic baskets. I tried to sit carefully, so my bare legs didn't have to touch Kitty's small, hot brown ones, and we drove for miles that tailed on miles along the highways and dusty country roads looking for old familiar picnic grounds; and soon the car was filled with the nauseating smell of hard-boiled eggs from the potato salad, so that I had to close my eyes to keep from feeling uneasily giddy.

143

Each picnic ground we passed was lined with cars and milling with men in loose-knit golf shirts and with little, loud-lunged children in sunsuits so scanty that their thin, narrow ribs showed. "Perhaps if we just drive out in the country just a bit farther we can find a nice place with running water which no one knows about," my mother suggested. She was the only one in the car who wasn't warm and her voice was calm and cool.

Cars rushed by with short, whizzing noises and even out in the country the highways were crowded. Every available woods had a car or two pulled up to the ditch and people had even spread their tablecloths outside the fences where the grass was dusty near the roadside. Art, who loves picnics, kept urging that we find a place secluded and well in off the road — "a place with shade but no people," he said.

Beside me Kitty was restless, squirming because the rough upholstery scratched her bare legs. Farther out from the city the fields of corn stood motionless in the still air, the leaves shiny as silk in the sunlight, and the trees were clumped green on the hillsides like huge bunches of parsley. Wild corn flowers grew scattered on their thin, sprawled stems making a low, blue haze along the roadside. Once a flock of black birds rose noisy from a field as we passed, very black against the bright sky, and the whole country was stewing in a slow, heavy heat.

My father drove with one hand on the wheel and the other arm out the window, as if he were dragging it through cool water. We passed car after car and woods after woods till the sun slid westward in the sky and a long, lopsided shadow of the car trailed after us on the highway. The heat filled the air with a steady, pulsing warmth that fanned our faces and made our eyelids heavy until even my mother looked hot and tired. "I think," she said, "that there is no better place for a picnic on a day like this than our own back garden," and it was so warm that no one even bothered to answer.

Once more we slowed up at a group of trees a little way from a farmhouse, but a long, lean dog ran toward us, yapping, and an irate farmer in a damp blue shirt looked curiously from around the barn, so my father, without a word, accelerated the motor and turned toward town.

Back at home Margaret and I spread the lunch out on the back lawn while Kitty amused herself mournfully by pulling the yellow butterflies with torn shreds of wings off the radiator of the car and laying them out side by side on hollyhock leaves.

It was almost five-thirty by then and my mother sat down on a garden chair and balanced her paper picnic plate on her knee. The sun was still as warm as noon, but shadows were beginning to stretch their lengths on the ground and the leaves of the trees were restless with small breezes. "Wouldn't you think," she said, "that Lorraine would have the niceness to *call* and say that she wasn't coming home for supper either? I don't know why it is that no one can make plans here anymore."

Art was lying on a car robe with his full paper plate on the grass and a Coke bottle propped up beside it. It was at times like this that I was glad he was going to be part of our family. He would do anything at all to prevent friction or unpleasantness and he said now in his odd, warm voice that always reminded me of soft suede, "Oh, I don't know, Mom. You know how it is when you're out. You just forget what time it is." Margaret passed him a sandwich just then and brushed her hand with the long bright nails against his, very gently.

My father had never said anything about Martin. In the beginning we were all so glad, and a little surprised, that Lorraine had someone to go out with that no one thought of criticizing. It isn't that she couldn't get along with fellows if she wanted to, I guess, but because she has gone to college and everything she just doesn't like "ordinary" boys. Until now my mother had never criticized Martin, either. "But you would think," she said, "that a boy who has his meals in a restaurant three times a day would be glad to have a nice, home-made picnic!"

Sorrow over the dead butterflies had completely left Kitty by now and she piped up, "Ah, him! He's so old he doesn't like anything. He never wants to catch my baseball or play with Kinkee or anything. I'll bet he doesn't even like ice cream!" and the edges of her voice were curled with scorn.

After we had finished eating I gathered the leftover bits of sandwiches and the half-eaten curves of watermelon that looked like broad, empty grins onto a paper plate, and then we all sat on the lawn, relieved that the heat of the day was passing and the cool of the evening was creeping in low over the grass. Kitty brought out my mother's knitting from the house, all wrapped in a clean towel, but she left it untouched while birds twittered in the garden hedge and a light wind stirred in the trees. Everything was so pleasant that my thoughts just floated, light and elusive, in my head.

When Jack came up the sidewalk the dog gave a short, gruff bark almost as if it were clearing its throat. I was sitting with my back turned and I hadn't known he was coming but yet I knew it was Jack. Without even turning my head I knew it was he and I knew exactly how he looked. My mother smiled at him and asked him to sit down with us while she nodded to me to clear the picnic things away.

My hands felt awkward and unaccustomed as I shooed the flies from the uncovered watermelon rinds and gathered up the paper plates. I stood uncertain for a moment, wondering if I should bring the things into the kitchen or dump them vulgarly into the garbage can at the end of the garden right then. Kinkee nosed politely around my bare legs, sniffing anxiously for scraps, so I decided to take the sandwich leavings into the kitchen and fill her bowl. Jack jumped to his feet to hold open the back door for me and I mumbled a "thank you" that somehow didn't come out at all.

It all seemed too strange to me. Inside, scraping bits of sandwiches and potato salad into the dog's dish, my hands shook and my cheeks had a hot prickly feeling. It didn't seem right to go outside again and sit there on the cool grass, liking Jack so well, right in front of my family! This was the sort of thing that belonged at Pete's or out near the boathouses, but not on my own back lawn with Kitty and Kinkee and everyone watching! It just didn't seem right. The dog sat up on her hind legs, begging with petulant squeaks, till I set her bowl on the floor.

From the back lawn I could hear my father's deep voice, Art's soft one, and the boy-voice that was Jack's, with polite pauses when I knew my mother was speaking. In the half-darkness of the kitchen I curled a few strands of hair around my fingers and held my hands tight to my face, just for a moment, to get my thoughts straight and to wait for that fast, excited beating to stop in my heart. Then I filled the dog's empty bowl with water from the kitchen faucet, set it on the floor, and went outside.

My father was talking in a formal tone, a tone he saves and puts on like a necktie for just such special occasions as this.

"Of course," he was saying, "it depends on what you want to do with your life. But for the girls here, I always feel that college is the best way to start."

"You're right, sir," Jack answered. "I really think you're right but with me it's different. I'm the only one and my dad needs me 'round the bakery. I figure maybe I can get some extra education through extension courses and just reading by myself — but my dad needs me 'round right now." Jack was sprawled on the grass, talking very fast and earnestly, his eyebrows knit together.

"But it seems to me the thing to do would be to try to get the education first," my father explained and my mind quickly jumped to Jack's defense. Maybe there was a mortgage or something. Maybe there was a whole family of poor first cousins that had to be supported. There were dozens of reasons why some people can't afford to go to college. After all, my father shouldn't talk that way to a boy he had met only twice before!

"I understand what you mean, sir," insisted Jack, talking carefully so it wouldn't sound as if he were contradicting. "If I had a son I would want him to go to college. But you see, we had a pretty good bakery business down in Oklahoma, but my mother wanted to move back here to be near her folks and now we have to build it up all over again. And it isn't so good — too many people in this town still bake their own bread and things."

"Where is your mother from, Jack?" my mother asked, her voice pleasant.

"After they were married she and Dad lived in Oklahoma till just a couple years ago, but she is originally from out near Rosendale," he said, turning toward her. "I have an aunt out there who says she knows you because you did some work together at a church bazaar once — her name is Alberts."

So Jack had been talking about my family to his aunt! And he must have been talking about me too. Perhaps, to tease him, his father had said, "Jack's got a new girl," and his aunt had looked up in surprise, asked what her name was, where she lived, and what she looked like, or maybe she had heard him talking to me on the phone or maybe after the parade today his father had said to him casually, "Who was that girl I saw you with this morning, son?" To think of anyone calling him "son" made me shiver a little — it seemed such a daringly personal thought — and I looked up quickly to see if anyone had been watching me. But Jack was chewing a bit of grass, looking off toward the lake, and my mother had her eyes on her knitting.

We sat outside for a long time while the sky grew dark and small new stars popped out and a thin crescent of moon made a bright curve in the sky. We talked of everyday things and my father and mother addressed most of their remarks to Jack because he was company, and when he didn't understand he would question them with a quizzical "Please?" instead of the "Pardon me?" that we always used, and even in the darkness I could imagine his eyebrows knitted together in thought. Art slapped at the mosquitoes that kept up a steady murmur around our heads, but after the heat of the day the coolness of the evening was so pleasant that no one wanted to go into the house.

I found my mind following the conversation with the same back-and-forth movement with which one's eyes follow the ball in watching a ping-pong game. Each time anyone spoke to Jack I waited a little breathless to hear what answer he would toss back. At Pete's and in McKnight's I was sure of him but with my family I had been anxious. After all, it is quite a test for a boy to have to talk with six people at once.

Later on, much later, when the sky was very dark and the stars were sprinkled across it, hard and bright, Kitty decided it was time to go through her Fourth-of-July ritual of lighting her box of sparklers. We all sat, watching and making the right, appreciative comments, while she stood with each sparkler at arm's length, shooting off a wraith of quick stars. As each one burned near the end she tossed it over her head so it fell in a bright arc to the ground, lying in the grass till the hot wire had glowed itself out. Kitty's teeth chittered with excitement and ecstasy, and having Jack and Art as audience added to the thrill. She had taken off her shoes and short socks to enjoy the coolness of the grass, and my mother warned, "Be careful of those hot wires in the darkness with your bare feet, Kitty dear." After the last sparkler had arched through the air and sputtered out in the grass, she gave a breathy little sigh and sat down beside me, all tired from the happiness of it. After the brightness of the sparklers the sky seemed even darker than before.

Somewhere off in the distance an ambulance siren sounded, faint at first with an eerie questioning, the sound swelling as it passed the corner of our street, going down Park Avenue and headed out toward the highway that runs along the lake. It sped on its way, leaving a long, thin wail of sound trailing behind it, while my mother stopped in her conversation, listening. All of us sat with our minds snapped in alterness, knowing what she was thinking. If we are all away from home and hear a fire siren, my mother is certain it is our house that is burning; if one of us is away and we hear an ambulance, she is sure it is one of us stretched out somewhere on the highway. We knew now she was thinking of Lorraine and we all began talking very fast and very animatedly to drown out the weird tail of sound that still lingered in the night. With sudden enthusiasm Jack burst out, "Mrs. Morrow, have you ever been sailboating?" and then petered out in a less eager account of the fun he and Swede had had that afternoon. It made my lips feel soft just hearing him then. How quickly, without even a word said, he had understood and become one of us!

Out in the dark sky just a few blocks from us the annual fireworks display was being set off over the lake. Explosions, like dull thuds, preceded a thin whistle as the rockets shot into the air, bursting into a million bright-pointed stars, showering down into the night. Kitty let out little breathless exclamations of awe, and the dog, frightened by the light, whimpered and lay down close to Art with her head meekly on her paws. For a long time no one said anything. Fireworks should be watched in silence. Above us some of the rockets exploded in circles, echoing outward in diminishing rings of color while others burst into showers, hanging in midair for a moment like bright flower sprays, and one shot high, high above the others, like a brilliant comet and then plummeted to the earth, dragging a long scarlet tail down the sky. Jack whistled between his teeth and Kitty gave a little gasp of wonder. Above us the whole darkness seemed shot through with light and shattered with bursts of color that sent out a melting rain of stars. It seemed as if one could almost hear the brightness. The whole night tingled with it.

"I hope Lorraine and Martin don't miss this — wherever they are," my mother said quietly.

Jack was sitting, propped on his hands, with his head back looking at the sky and he moved his hand just a little so it barely touched mine. A tingling ran up my arm and I felt my face flush in the darkness. As a finale a series of rockets was set off in rapid succession till everything was a dazzle of quick-tailed shooting stars, fiery comets, and huge chrysanthemums of colored light. Long after the display had ceased the spectacle was bright before our eyes and the night sky was suddenly gentle and demure with the coy twinkle of pale stars. All of us felt the strange, silent natural beauty of it. The hushed night seemed so real, so lovely that I felt almost ashamed of the gaudy efforts of the faded rockets.

I wondered for a moment what my mother would think if she knew that I was sitting there in the darkness with Jack's hand on mine. And all those strange thoughts. I wondered if it were just me or if they all felt this night so mysterious, so pulsing with something unspoken. My whole body felt uneasy with it. Suddenly I had an almost uncontrollable impulse to reach out and touch Jack's bare throat gently, lightly with one finger, at the

V of his shirt. And it was just then that he said politely to my mother, "Well, if you don't mind, Mrs. Morrow, I think I'd better be going now. I've got to be out on the route early tomorrow." He stood for a moment not knowing what else to say.

My mother rose from her chair too, saying, "I'm glad you came, Jack, and come again any time. It's nice having you." Her words sang in my ears as I walked to the front sidewalk with him. Kitty walked with us.

It was late and we all went into the house then and the others went straight upstairs while my mother turned back to call to me, "Angeline, be sure to see that the front door is unlocked for Lorraine."

"I will," I called back.

In the living room the window shades were still drawn as they had been against the heat of the afternoon and a few tired flies buzzed behind them against the windowpane. The air was hot and still and had the oppressive weight of not being lived in all day. There was something heavily, depressingly quiet about the whole room, and outside, somewhere in the city, the sound of an occasional late firecracker echoed. On the corner table was a vase of yellow flowers, limp and wilted, and in the heat of the afternoon the broad, smooth petals had dropped to the floor like tired butterflies. The night seemed suddenly husked of its beauty.

Quietly I turned the key in the lock and tried the knob of the front door. It was open. Lorraine would have no trouble getting in.

Of the days that followed I remember almost nothing definitely. Nothing seemed to stand out by itself but all flowed together into a stream of pleasantness like warm, thick honey. Every mo-

153

ment was full of it. Every night there was the lonely, ecstatic wonder of thinking about Jack while I lay in bed alone; outside, the stars just pin-pricked the sky and the wind was gentle in the trees, and in the morning there was the slow luxury of waking with the first sun on the wall and knowing that a whole long day of thinking lay ahead. It was the sort of happiness that almost makes you sad it is so wonderful. Everything seemed different to me — everything.

Sometimes after I had been with Jack, I would go upstairs into my own room and my thoughts seemed as clear and steady as crystal, and I would look at my wrists all traced with thin, blue veins and somehow I almost expected to see them pulsing, all throbbing with the strange new urge that was beating through me. Sometimes I went for walks by myself far out into the big field and my legs felt strong and thin and clean. Touching things sent a new pleasure through my hands that filled my whole body with satisfaction. The rough bark of trees was good, hard, and I thrilled to the soft, silken curve of the dog's head as I stroked it. Words came out of my mouth like bubbles. Standing in our garden, watching fat bumblebees blunder against the broad faces of the sunflowers, I almost laughed aloud, and there was a new fascination about yellow-furred caterpillars, tufted like toothbrushes, inching along the hollyhock stems in the bright morning sun.

Sometimes I felt that my feet just wouldn't stay on the ground. I wanted to pick the leaves from the raspberry bushes with their smooth surfaces and the greenish-white fuzz underneath, and touch the softness to my lips. The lake breeze blew in warm and soft, and black and yellow spiders rocked in webs that glinted in the sun and the whole air shimmered with July heat. Everything, everything was wonderful. Sometimes the world seemed so full of the luxurious lushness and warmth of summer that one could almost reach out and eat it with a spoon.

In the evenings we went for walks, Jack and I — long, silent walks not talking at all, not having to talk. Or we would go out to Pete's with Fitz and Margie or to the movies by ourselves. Sometimes when we sat in the movies Jack would hold my hand. It wasn't silly. We did it because it was good to sit so close together in the darkness and, somehow, by holding hands you can carry on a conversation without talking.

When my mother and I were home alone in the morning, doing the housework, I found myself telling her little, noncommittal things about him, anything just so I could say his name aloud. "Mom, Jack says that his father says that more people are buying regular bakery bread and that the fad for sliced bread is going out. . . ." Often when Kitty and I were together I talked to her about him — Kitty will listen to anything. I told her how he had been the star of the basketball team at high school, how well he drove a car, and I once asked her if she had noticed how clean his shirts always looked. I talked and talked about things that made no difference to Kitty at all but just gave me the chance to think of him and say his name.

One afternoon Margie and I walked down to McKnight's to meet him. It was wonderful sitting there. Fitz stopped in and other fellows and girls came in, together and alone, and called "Hi!" or came over to talk with Jack and Fitz while Margie talked steadily and smiled broad smiles at everyone. She smiled so broadly that I noticed she had got lipstick on her teeth and I thought to tell her about it — but Fitz wasn't looking at her anyway. Occasionally a woman who had been shopping would come in with a little boy or girl and they both would have a quick ice-cream cone or a pine-apple soda, and the child would eat slowly, staring at the older fellows and girls making so much noise, while the ice cream dribbled down his chin. Older people and very young didn't seem to belong here. No one belonged here but the "crowd," those who were "in." Until I met Jack I hadn't belonged here, either. I remembered once in early spring having come in with Kitty and having had a small Coke with her, sitting at the fountain, while from the back booths came the sound of laughing and talking. But no one had talked to me. I wasn't one of the crowd then. I remember I had told Kitty to hurry up and made her leave before the Coke was half finished. I couldn't stand being so out of things. But it was different now.

Fitz was working in a fruit store for the summer and said that he had to get right back, for he had just sneaked out for a few minutes and he didn't want them to miss him. After a while Jack said that he really should get back to the bakery too, for his father didn't know he had gone, either. But I knew he wouldn't leave. After Fitz had gone out the door Jack still sat with Margie and me, finger-ing his bent straws and waiting, as if he wanted to say something.

"How's this hot weather affecting business, Jack?" Margie asked in a professionally conversa-tional tone. She always talks with an up-and-down movement, as if she were chewing gum. And she likes to be a special friend to all the boys, even if she is going steady.

156

"It isn't so bad," he answered. "People have to eat no matter what the weather does." He looked at her and then at me and the three of us just sat saying nothing. "Doughnuts and things will *always* sell," he added lamely.

Margie craned her neck to look over the booth to see if anyone she knew might be coming in the front door. There was no one.

"Angie," Jack said, "unless you've got to get home right away, would you like to go for a little ride with me? I've got the truck and I don't have to be back to the bakery for about twenty minutes or so. . . ."

"Go right ahead," Margie said to me indulgently. "I'll just sit here and talk to the kids and wait till you get back. Some one of the fellows is bound to come in," and she gave me one of her "I know how it is" smiles. I almost resented her thinking she knew all about Jack and me — even if she did.

He had the bakery truck parked just around the corner; the afternoon sun glinted on the windshield and the black leather seats were hot to touch. Jack got in beside me, started the motor, and swung the truck around in the opposite direction, away from the bakery, just in case he might run into his father. He drove out from the heat of the town to the coolness of the lake and pulled the truck up at the water's edge. The breeze was moist and cool and the water was blue and rollicking, teased with sunlight. A sand dredge was laboring in the harbor, its engines making a steady grunt-grunt and the whistle on its bridge giving out short, periodic snorts, as if it were blowing through its nose. We laughed, both of us, hearing it.

Jack reached into the shelves in the back of the truck and picked out four sugar cookies with raisins for us to eat. We sat munching them and laughing at the noises of the sand dredge and feeling the sun coming through the windshield, falling warm on our arms and legs. After a long time we went back to town.

Margie was still waiting in McKnight's when I came back. She had ordered another Coke and was being dainty about lighting her cigarette when I came in. "Where did you leave Jack?" she asked.

"He let me off in front and went on back to work," I explained, trying hard not to look straight at her. "His father won't like it that he's been gone as long as it is."

She took a long, leisurely draw on her cigarette and we both watched the slow smoke curling. Then, leaning across the table, Margie said to me in a low, confidential voice, "You know, Angie, that show's when a boy really likes a girl — when he wants to kiss her in the daytime!"

The very next Sunday Jack's aunt from Oklahoma passed through Chicago and his mother and father drove down to see her. But he stayed home. I wish now he had gone. He stayed to attend to the bakery and to see that the restaurants in town got their orders of hot rolls at eleven o'clock on Sunday morning. I would never have dared to mention it myself — in fact, I never even thought of it — but it was my mother who suggested that Jack come over for Sunday dinner.

"If his mother is going to be away I'm sure he won't want to prepare anything for himself," she said.

So I called him on Saturday evening while he was still at the bakery. My heart was pounding as I talked to him. Even if I did know him well, it seemed such a forward step to ask a boy to have dinner with your family! I could hear the sound of people moving about and the ring of the cash register behind his voice as we talked.

"Jack, my mother would like to know if you would like to come over for dinner tomorrow, seeing your mother and dad won't be home. . . ."

"You'll have to talk louder, Angie," he said. "We're pretty busy here and I can't hear you."

"I said," I repeated, articulating carefully, "would you like to come over for dinner tomorrow?"

"Gee, Angie, that's swell. That's really swell!" and his voice dropped low. "What time?"

"What are you whispering for?" I could tell he was talking with his mouth close to the phone.

"I just don't want my dad to hear," he said.

"Why?" I made my voice sound very surprised and a little insulted, though I knew very well what he meant. I had thought of it myself before I called.

"It's all right, of course," he assured me, hastily. "It's just that I don't know if my dad would like it so well . . . me, having dinner with girls, I mean. You know how it is. . . ."

"Of course," I said abruptly. "We'll expect you about noon, Jack," and I hung up. It wasn't nice of me at all, for I knew just what my father would think if I had been asked to have dinner at *Jack's* house. But I knew that Jack would worry all night. He would want to call back and ask me if I was angry with him, but the bakery would be rushed with last-minute Saturday night customers and he wouldn't have time. After the bakery had closed it would be too late and he would be afraid my mother would be annoyed with him for calling at such an hour. So he wouldn't know until tomorrow if I were angry with him or not and would spend

159

all the rest of the evening thinking about it, while he waited on customers, and making up ways of explaining to me why he couldn't tell his father. Of course, I *knew* why and I wasn't angry at all. Only sometimes, even if you like a boy so much, it is almost fun to know he is worrying about you.

Sunday morning in the summer is almost too good, almost sensuously pleasant. All the windows were wide open and the sun lay in bright patches on the living-room rug and the hollyhocks grew straight and high around the back door and everywhere there was a feeling of warmth and oneness — as if there was no difference between inside the house and outside. Everywhere it was summer. My father spent the morning in the garden, straightening out vegetable rows with a hoe and piling up a heap of pulled weeds in an empty bushel basket, stopping now and then to wipe the sweat from his forehead. In the kitchen my mother tied on a frilled Sunday apron and began cutting the string beans for dinner. She kept looking out the window at my father, humming as she worked.

Even if the day was hot we were having roast pork and mashed potatoes for dinner because, as my mother said, "If your father has to eat out all week he deserves a good dinner at the weekend."

Upstairs Margaret and Lorraine were making the bed together and Kitty was reading the funny papers on the back lawn. Everyone knew that Jack was coming. They had known ever since my mother had suggested asking him, but somehow I shied away from talking about it. It didn't seem quite safe to talk about him anymore. I knew they didn't quite understand about Jack and me and I had a vague, uneasy feeling that if they did they wouldn't like it at all. My mind was always on the alert for the first word of disapproval. After all, what would my mother say if she knew that I, who had just been out of high school six weeks, was feeling the way I was? Families just don't understand about such things.

Kitty came into the kitchen to help peel the apples for the applesauce and then gathered up the long curls of peelings and went out to eat them on the lawn, sitting in the sun. Kinkee came over, wagging her tail and wiggling her nose in anticipation. Kitty held out a curl of apple skin and the dog sniffed it gently and then let it drop to the ground untouched.

My heart felt lumped inside me, warm with satisfaction. Everything seemed too wonderful. I had set the table in the dining room on one of the best white tablecloths and the bright sunshine streamed in the windows and glinted through the tall glasses onto the silverware, sending off sprays of light. In the center Lorraine had put a low bowl of pink cosmos from the garden with their feathery, fernlike leaves. A small green bug dropped onto the tablecloth and began inching its way toward a plate. I lifted it carefully on the corner of the Sunday funny paper and shook it out the front door. Outside the whole world seemed yellow-green and sunny. Even the way the trees shook their leaves seemed different.

Later I went upstairs and put two little pink guest towels in the bathroom. It seemed impossible to think that Jack would even be seeing what our upstairs looked like! From the kitchen rose the pleasant Sunday smell of roast pork and fresh garden peas, and outside I could hear the sound of neighbors laughing together as they sat on their front porches, and just across the street a man stood in his shirtsleeves with a pail of water and a chamois, shining his car. Everything seemed suddenly too wonderful. The clean sunshine, the good dinner in the oven, and just a few minutes to wait until Jack would be here! It couldn't be that good! It seemed as if I were drinking in the almost tangible pleasure of the morning like a rich, heavy malted milk that comes slow and thick through the straws.

My whole head sang with warm, summer-Sunday thoughts, till my hands tingled with the sheer joy of it. "O God," I thought, "O God, O God — stop making me be so glad! I can't stand being so happy!"

I was still sitting at my bedroom window when he came up the front sidewalk, and I waited there until I heard my mother open the front door for him and then the mumble of voices as my father came in from the garden to get cleaned for dinner. In the living room someone turned on the radio. I knew that Jack would be sitting in the chair near the front door where he always sat and I waited till I knew my face was calm enough to face him without looking too happy. Then I went downstairs.

I don't know just what went wrong at dinner. It wasn't Jack's fault. It wasn't his table manners that were poor — it wasn't that at all. He sat very straight just as he should; kept his left hand in his lap while he ate and broke his roll into four little pieces just like it says in etiquette books. So it wasn't that.

We had all sat down at the table, my mother and father at the heads and Jack across from me.

My Mother had passed him the butter and the cut-glass dish of applesauce with her usual cool care and talked with him while my father was carving the roast. Art and Lorraine added little comments here and there. Martin had called Lorraine right after church to ask her to go out with him that night and she was in a soft-mouthed, benevolent mood. I thought then that everything was going to be all right.

Jack was just saying to my mother, "This aunt of mine that's stopping in Chicago is the one who used to live next to us in Oklahoma." My father should have seen that Jack was busy talking. But he didn't. He had just finished carving the roast and wanted to make room for the serving plates so he passed him the salad, thrusting it right into his hands, and Jack was so startled that he knocked against his water glass, steadying it just in time with his free hand while the salad bowl wavered in the other. He was across the table from me and no one else offered to help. It was agonizing to watch. The salad bowl was large and the table crowded so he balanced it on one hand, trying to serve himself with the double servers with the other and keep up the conversation at the same time. Art kept talking too, attempting to cover up his awkwardness and pretending not to notice. My own fingers were anxious for Jack's as they fumbled.

And after that everything that happened was Lorraine's fault. She knew Jack had only graduated from high school. She knew that I had never said he was a smart boy. She knew it and yet she kept talking to him as if he were one of the boys she had known at college. Lorraine is like that sometimes. If I had been sitting at the table at the beginning I might have stopped it but I was in the kitchen just then.

Kitty had been quietly toying with her glass and one long-stemmed cosmos that leaned out from the rest until she knocked pollen from it into her milk and I left the table to go to the kitchen for a fresh glass. Someone had mentioned that the flies weren't bad at all for this time of the summer. It was just a casual remark but when I came back with Kitty's milk Lorraine had begun. She was saying. in her schoolteacher voice, "Perhaps it's like in that book. About us being like flies that the gods crush — only this time they got the flies." She laughed pleasantly but no one knew quite what she was talking about.

Jack was buttering his roll, not even listening, but she turned to him abruptly, "You've read that book, of course, haven't you, Jack?"

"What book?" He was startled.

The Bridge of San Luis Rey," she explained kindly. "By Thornton Wilder . . . you know, the same man who won the Pulitzer Prize with *Our Town. . . ?*"

Jack gave her a half-smile of acknowledgment but his face remained blank. Lorraine should have stopped there. right there. Art broke in heartily to ask if anyone would like to go for a good swim later in the afternoon, but Lorraine went on with enthusiasm. "I hear," she said, looking first at my mother and then sweeping her eyes around the table back to Jack, "that William Saroyan writes his short stories in only three hours! Imagine!"

"It seems to me that worthwhile things should take more time than that," my mother commented mildly.

"Of course," Lorraine went on with pointed

condescension, "that depends on whether you're a genius or not. Have you read his *My Name is Aram,* Jack. . . ?" and her voice trailed off into a question.

Leave him alone, my mind snapped at her. Leave him alone, why don't you? You wouldn't have read it, either, if you hadn't been to college and if you weren't as old as you are! He's only young. You can't expect him to know everything about everything. . . .

Jack looked at her in embarrassment and his lips were awkward with his words. "I don't read much," he confessed and my heart slipped down a little. "I don't read at all as much as I'd like to," he went on, "but, gee, with school and everything . . ." He looked at her in apology and then at me, adding feebly, "I played a lot of basketball and things. . . ."

Lorraine gave him a bright, understanding smile and let him go back to his eating. It wasn't that Lorraine is a mean girl. She didn't talk like that just to make Jack seem like a dull boy, she just wanted to make herself seem smarter. But he didn't know that and from that moment on everything went wrong. Each forkful of food seemed to be a separate problem to him. I saw him look at each piece of roast pork, lift it a little from his plate as if he were wondering whether or not he could make it, and then raise it quickly to his mouth with a jerky, forward movement of his body. He was so scared that someone would start to talk to him again that he ate too fast and kept his eyes glued to his plate in apprehension. Once my mother asked if he would care to help himself to more buttered peas and he stopped eating suddenly and looked at her with a startled "Ma'am?"

The day was suddenly unbearably hot and the

knife in my fingers was cold and slippery. When I moved, the cloth of my thin dress stuck to the back of my chair and I had to keep my eyes busy with the salt and pepper shakers and the empty cut-glass applesauce dish to avoid meeting Jack's across the table. It seemed even worse because my mother had tried to make everything as nice as she could. In front of my whole family he had to act like that!

How were they to know that out at Pete's he was different? How were they to know that he had been president of his class at school for two years in a row, or that he had come in second in the state in the basketball free-throw contest? How did they know that he could dance to any kind of music at all, fast or slow, and that any girl in town would be glad to wear his basketball sweater even for one night? All they would remember was that he hadn't even been able to serve himself with double salad servers and that he filled his mouth too full when he ate. In our house where we had never been allowed to eat untidily, even when we sat in high chairs! It all seemed so suddenly and sickeningly clear — I could just see his father in shirtsleeves, folding food onto his fork with his knife and never using napkins except when there was company. And probably they brought the coffee pot right in and set it on the table. My whole mind was filled with a growing disdain and loathing. His family probably didn't even own a butter knife! No girl has to stand all that. Never. If a boy gets red in the face, sputters salad dressing on the tablecloth, and hasn't even read a single book to talk about when you ask him over for dinner, you don't have to be nice to him — even if he has kissed you and said things to you that no one has ever said before!

Even now it is hard to talk about what happened

next. It was too awful. It was the kind of thing you read about but can't believe could ever happen to you. It sent the tears nipping at my eyes and made a tight ache in my throat till I almost thought I would have to leave the table. You see, we were having ice cream for dessert. Everyone was eating nicely and quietly and Lorraine, just at the moment it happened, was being dainty about selecting a cookie from the plate. I have heard *old men* making noise eating soup and other things but that's different, and I don't care because they are *old* and they perhaps have something wrong with their teeth. But eating such a simple thing as ice cream and with my family sitting there and everything, Jack clicked his spoon against his teeth! He looked up in surprise, as if he was wondering who could have done it, and then went on eating hastily. Lorraine cleared her throat and gave a little ho-hum sound to herself. And then it happened again! Quite by mistake but a definite, neat click, like knocking two water tumblers together. No one said anything — my family are too polite to say anything with their mouths but I knew what they were saying in their heads.

I saw my mother raise her eyebrow just a little. Just a little, as if a quick thought has passed through her mind and my heart shrank up into a tight ball of loathing till I felt that my whole insides would rattle around like a hard, brown peanut in a shell. In my mouth was a bitter taste as if I had been sucking a penny and I couldn't even raise my eyes to look at anyone. Twice! Twice in a house where no one ever forgets to say "Pardon me," or gets indigestion, or neglects to have a clean handkerchief! The utter shame of it sucked the whole hot, bright afternoon dry of happiness and I felt myself slowly begin to hate Jack.

167

And later on it was the same. My mother suggested pleasantly that we leave the dishes till the cool of the evening and that Jack take our car and drive Kitty and her to the movies. My father had to work on his business reports for the week and the others had plans of their own.

Sitting beside him, I never said a word. There was nothing to say. We dropped my mother and Kitty at the theater and then Jack turned the car north on Main Street toward the park. Any other afernoon it would have been different. Ordinarily we would both have thought of Pete's where Swede and some of the fellows were bound to be playing poker in the dark coolness of a back booth, or we would have thought of having a Coke in McKnight's with its air-conditioned brightness, or even of looking for Margie and Fitz who were bound to be parked out along a country road somewhere. But today was different. I wasn't thinking that kind of thoughts any more. I sat very still beside Jack but my mind squirmed with repulsion and my lips curled with distaste as I thought of it. Any boy who couldn't even eat ice cream without making noise! Along the street people were walking leisurely, men in their shirt sleeves with the cuffs turned back and girls in summer dresses. A strong tar smell rose from the sun-baked streets and little glints of light shot out from the chromium radiator cap on the car. But I didn't care any more about anything . . . just sat with my eyes straight ahead.

My hand lay beside me on the plush of the car seat. I was conscious of its being there. I felt Jack turn his head to look at me. Then he looked down at my hand. One move would have done it. If I had turned my head or even moved my hand just a little his fingers would have been on mine and we would have held our hands tight while we drove out along the lake shore and then out toward Pete's and everything would have been as wonderful as before. I knew that but somehow I just didn't care. There was one. small breathless moment, as quick as a thought. But I didn't move and Jack swung the car off Main Street and headed straight home with the afternoon sun glinting on the windshield and the warm air soothing in through the window. We drove straight home and Jack pulled the car into the driveway and opened my door for me. We walked to the front steps and, being very careful to avert my eyes, "Good-bye, Jack," I said.

He said good-bye and then stood looking at me. "Well," he began again, pursing his lips and then stopped. "Well . . . good-bye, I guess," and I turned to go into the house.

And he hadn't even touched my hand!

And it was foolish of me. I know that now, and I knew then that in the bottom of my mind I wasn't angry, it was only in the very top. It is self-pampering, a sensuous luxury, to let yourself pretend to be angry, if only for a little while, with someone you really like With summer so short and with college looming up large in September, I don't know why I did it. It was foolish when each day went so fast and each night was only a quick, breathless moment with not nearly enough time for seeing and thinking and wishing.

The next morning as I hung the clean clothes that smelled of soap and hot starch on the rope line, I thought it all over carefully. In the freshness of the new morning with the air warm and shimmering with summer and singing with the sound of the children playing and laundry trucks and my mother busy in the kitchen, I felt oddly ashamed. Jack must have been thinking funny thoughts that morning. He probably hadn't even known what I was angry about!

Margaret, who had the last two weeks of July for her vacation, had left the night before to spend it in Milwaukee with Art and his family. Even though she was engaged, my mother had disapproved at first with halfhearted, habitual disapproval. But she had gone and now the house was very quiet, especially at mealtime, but it gave Lorraine and me a chance to talk together. Lorraine always has to talk to someone and when Margaret is gone she talks to me. Of course, she doesn't say quite the same things and skips a lot she would tell Margaret but we *do* talk some things over.

I didn't see Jack all day Monday, but on Tuesday he called to ask if I would go to the movies with him that night. All day I had a shy, expectant feeling — as if I were going to meet him for the first time all over again and I had to keep crowding the thought of kissing him out of my mind. It isn't good to keep thinking about things like that. You get to look starry-eyed even in the daytime. It was swelteringly hot and we kept the living room shades drawn all day and Kitty left the kitchen wet and sticky with her several watery attempts at lemonade. My mother was in the basement canning a bushel of early peaches and I went down casually to tell her it was Jack who had just called. She was sitting on one of Kitty's little doll chairs, slipping the skins from the peaches dipped in boiling water, and the air was clammy with a sweet steam, and moisture ran oozing from the cement walls. Bits of the wet skins stuck to the floor where they had dropped and plastered against the side of the big aluminum canning kettle. There were shiny canning jars set in a row, collared with red rubber rings, waiting to be filled. I told my mother about Jack and she pushed her hair back wearily from her forehead and said noncommittally, "I'm glad he called, Angeline. Will you run upstairs and bring me down the sack of sugar from the third shelf in the kitchen?"

Later in the afternoon Kitty went to the store for a pint of ice cream and the three of us ate it off saucers, sitting on the back lawn in the slanting shade of the house. Around us the afternoon was humming with the steady beat of the heat and the sonorous drone of the bees in the hollyhocks and the small, quick wasps with black and yellow bodies that zigzagged low over the short cloverheads. My mother sighed. "You know," she said, "I almost wish this summer was over with heat and rush, and you and Lorraine were packed off to school. There is still so much to do to your clothes and getting curtains and a bedspread for your room. . . . Here it is almost the last week of July. . . ." And she left the thought in midair.

She is a little sad sometimes. I think it is because we are growing up — my sisters and I. Things that used to be so important aren't the same any more. We are all beginning to care about separate things now. My heart beat faster with a sense of caution. Perhaps my mother was going to mention Jack. I felt sure that any day someone would find out and begin to ask questions. I don't know just what they would find out or how they would know what was going on in my head but they would guess somehow. They would ask — Were Jack and I going steady? Why did I see him so much? Wasn't I a little young to be *liking* a boy? I didn't want to have to answer things like that.

The grass on the side lawn was parched brown with irregular scallops of green where the shade of the trees shadowed the ground. Kinkee lay stretched in the sun, watching the little mud-colored grasshoppers that skipped in the dry stubble. Out in the garden the flowers were heavy-headed and tired in the steady heat and even the sparrows in the hedge were quiet. "I think," my mother went on quietly, "that I'll just finish up the rest of those peaches tomorrow. I'm not up to canning them in this heat!"

A sudden thought struck me. Wouldn't it be odd if my mother got old! After so long. After so many summers of picnics and parades and long walks around the park in the peace of the afternoon, to be suddenly tired. It is only natural that when your children are big you must be older but somehow I had never thought of its happening to my mother. It made me feel queerly conscious-stricken and there was a strange stiffness around my lips. What a peculiar thing to think of in the bright sunshine of the afternoon!

We went swimming later in the afternoon, Jack and I. He came just after four o'clock and pulled the truck up to the curb, honking the horn sharply twice. He couldn't come in, he explained, for he was in his swimming trunks and a sweat shirt — just finished work and was going out to Pete's for a swim and wanted to know if I would like to go with him.

I hurried upstairs for my suit and a bath towel while he carried on a loud conversation with my mother who was sitting in the late afternoon shade on the side lawn. As I came out the front door, Kitty was sitting on the front steps, fresh from her bath with her braids pinned up and a clean blue playsuit on. She was being very nonchalant about picking the leaves off a bit of twig broken from the bushes, careful not to look at Jack or me. "She wants to go with us," I thought. "She's been so hot all day and she wants to go with us but doesn't want to ask." Her whole attitude was tense with hoping and I knew it but shut my mind against the thought.

"Please, God," I said quickly to myself. "I haven't seen Jack since Sunday and I have so much I want to say to him. Just this once let me be selfish. Kitty can go swimming tomorrow or any other time but not now. Not with us."

Jack and I pulled away from the curb and I waved back at them, but Kitty's face was puckered with disappointment and I knew she was trying not to cry and my conscience turned over within me. As we turned onto the highway toward Pete's, Jack said lightly, "Maybe your little sister might have liked to come along, huh, Angie?"

Someday, I thought to myself, when she is very much older — say eighteen or so — I will explain to her and she won't be angry with me at all.

For the first few minutes I kept my eyes straight ahead, busying myself with the yellow and green summer scenery. Jack was whistling softly through his teeth. Out of the corner of my eye I saw his legs, as tan and smooth as a girl's, and I imagined suddenly how strong and clean he must have looked playing basketball in short khaki trunks. When he pushed down on the clutch, the ligaments moved under the smooth brown skin of his leg. All the antagonism and disgust of Sunday afternoon melted when we were alone together. Jack reached over to my side of the car to get a package of cigarettes from the glove compartment. His arm was very close to me and the consciousness of it made both our thoughts stand still for a moment. I laughed, a little self-conscious laugh, and turned my face toward him. He looked at me too, just then and I felt my eyes go soft, and his face was so close that I could have touched it with my cheek; and suddenly everything was just as it had been and I didn't even remember what day it was — that just two days ago had been that Sunday.

Someday when Kitty is very much older I will explain to her and I know she won't be angry with me. She won't be angry at all.

The lake behind Pete's lay flat and glassy in the sunlight. The lawn was green and lush near the water's edge, but farther from the shore it was littered with cigarette stubs, small bits of bottle glass, and faded scraps of red and green fire-cracker paper left from the Fourth of July. Sometimes people have weiner roasts here and on one side there was a patch of burnt litter where someone had made a fire, and around it lay bits of charred wood and a blackened beer can and the grass was burnt short like curly black hair.

Jack had pulled the truck over into the shade and had gone into Pete's while I put on my swimming suit. Finally I stepped carefully out onto the grass and slammed the truck door loudly to let him know I was ready. His steps crunched across the gravel as he came out and I was almost afraid to look at him. I wasn't sure just what he would look like without his sweatshirt on. I put a big bath towel carefully around my own shoulders and went down to the water's edge, waiting while he pulled the white sweatshirt off over his head and came up beside me. Then he gave a little run to the end of the short pier and took a shallow surface dive that brought him up laughing and shaking the water from his hair while his teeth shone white in the sunlight. His shoulders above the water were smooth and brown, shiny with the wet, and when he moved, the muscles in his arms made a barely perceptible ripple. He swam out a short distance and then signaled for me to jump in.

Why is it there is always that self-conscious feeling about looking at a boy in swimming trunks? I think I was afraid that because I had only seen him in clean white shirts or sweatshirts or in his heavy basketball sweater that he might suddenly be thin and scrawny underneath and I would never have known it. Or his skin might be pale and soft like the underside of a frog and I might want to turn away and not look at him till he had pulled on his clothes again. Or maybe it was because my mother had always been careful about things like hanging the underclothes on the inside of the clotheslines, away from the street, and had always told us to pull our window shades down before going to bed at night.

The little wooden pier was slippery from the constant wash of the waves that slipped over the old boards, rotting open-faced in the sun. A long, green slime clung to the piles and moved slowly with the water. The lake was warm near the surface and chill near the bottom from the shifting, underwater springs that make Lake Winnebago treacherous. Jack was far out now and the water between us was smooth and limpid. Very near the shore where the trees hung low, a school of quick-tailed minnows glinted in the sun and were gone.

I began to walk out with the easy, languid grace one has in water, and beneath my feet the sand was

175

hard and cold, ridged into regular little ripples. The far Oshkosh shore lay opposite, almost lost in the shimmer of sunshine and a low haze of smoke. When I reached swimming depth the water was warm and caressing on my shoulders and my arms looked very white and shapeless through the water. Jack and I swam side by side, leisurely, until we hit the first sand bar. When we stood up the water was only up to our waists and Jack looked at me with a surprised laugh, "Gee, Angie, you look pretty in the sunlight. Your eyes look like water!"

All around us the lake was flat and motionless, reflecting the sun and the puffs of clouds in the sky, without a movement or a ripple, as if the fish were down, down close to the sand and we were the only moving things in it. We seemed all alone in the smooth, unspoiled loveliness of the water. The sun was warm on our backs and Jack stood with water drops running from his hair and glistening on his face. I had a sudden impulse to reach out and run my finger lightly over the even, dark arch of his eyebrows as he stood looking at me. But there was an odd look in his eyes, an odd, warm look that made my lips tingle as his eyes met mine, and I knew it would be better not to touch him, not even to talk to him, just then.

Instead I turned away from him just a little, trailing my arm gently, slowly through the warm, green water till the ripples made slim, silver bracelets round my wrist.

Later we pulled ourselves onto the slimy little pier and then lay on the grass in the late sun where the trees began to stretch their large shadows lengthwise on the ground. The air was warm and a slight breeze just stirred the surface of the sun-glazed water. Jack looked up at the sky and sighed with contentment.

"Say, Angie — your sister still hear from that Martin fellow?" he queried.

"She sees him sometimes three times a week," I answered, unconsciously coming to her defense. "Why?"

"No reason. Just wondered."

"But why did you ask then?"

"No reason, Angie. Really. I just happened to think of it."

"Does he still come into the bakery for rolls in the morning?"

"Sometimes he does. Sometimes he eats at Walgreen's drugstore when the weather is so hot."

"He's nice, I think," I ventured slowly. I always had a feeling that Jack knew something about Martin that he didn't want to mention.

"Yeah, he's a good guy," he answered laconically and rolled over on his back, covering his eyes against the sun.

"Jack," I persisted, not wanting to let the matter drop. "Do you think he is too *old* for Lorraine?"

"No, no," he said, reassuringly. "He dates lots, lots younger ones sometimes."

"What do you mean?"

Jack sat up suddenly and ran his hand over his hair in irritation. "Gee, Angie, don't keep asking me questions about a guy I don't even know. All I see him is when he buys rolls or maybe I might meet him out some night. How do I know what he does or who he dates or anything. . . ?" He pulled a long grass stem and sat chewing the end, looking out over the lake, pretending to squint at something on the opposite shore. I knew he didn't want to talk about it anymore so I didn't probe him further.

177

Pete's is very quiet in the afternoon. There was only the occasional sound of a delivery truck with beer or Coca-Cola as it swung off the highway onto the gravel parking lot. The sun was sinking low in the west, making hot glass of the water, and a dragonfly as large as a humming bird, with shiny gauze wings, darted toward us and then zigzagged back toward the sun. Here and there on the lawn late dandelions were yellow and bits of broken glass caught the light. I put the towel around my shoulders and lay in almost sensuous warmth with the sky bright and the grass rough on my bare arms. There was a long silence with thoughts going on in it.

Jack sat flicking bits of stick toward the water and without looking at me he said, "You know, Angie, I've known you over a month and a half now...."

I lay still, not saying anything, pretending to be watching the sun that was turning to pink in the water.

"That's the longest I've ever gone with any girl ... at one time."

Something below the lake moved, making wide, silent rings on the smooth surface. The silence of the afternoon seemed suddenly loud with the rustle of the trees and the soft, sucking sound that even calm water makes against the shore. Something in me was suddenly alive. It was something new, something I had felt only in the last few days. It was warm, strange, and beating, and I wasn't even sure what the feeling meant. And somehow I was afraid to know. My lips felt hot and my cheeks were tense with waiting. Without lifting my eyes to look at him I knew his hand was close to mine on the grass and I could sense his groping for the right words to say.

"We'd better go, Jack," I said quietly. "Please. We'd better go right away." And I tried to keep my thoughts out of my words as I said it.

I had been so happy myself for the past few weeks that I hadn't had time to notice. But that night I realized Lorraine had changed. I wasn't sure just how, but she was different. While she waited for Martin we sat in our bedroom talking. It was close and hot and the night air was like warm velvet. The fluffy curtains at the window puffed out slowly and rhythmically with the summer breeze as if they, too, were panting in the heat. Lorraine's hair was pinned up in a tight roll around her head and she carried a small powder puff in a hankie so she could powder her shiny nose without being noticed. Martin was late and she was restless.

She began cleaning out her purse, arranging the things on the bed. We aren't supposed to smoke in our house, but I knew she did for there were tobacco crumbs on everything. "You know," she said and her voice was tight with agitation, "I almost wish school would start right away. You and I are going to have so much fun, Angie. I'll see that you get started with the right crowd of freshmen from the beginning and we'll really have fun together this year.

"I'd like to get away from all this," she went on.

"From what?" I asked. "From what? Don't you *like* summer?"

"Oh, no, it isn't that . . . it's just . . . well, everything."

"I don't know what you mean," I told her. "I think this has been one of the most wonderful summers we've ever had," and my heart beat faster as I said it.

179

"It's the sameness of it," she explained. "It's the same every morning," and she then went on in a mock singsong, "You get up and it's hot, you get dressed and it's hot, you go to work and it's hot. . . . I'm so sick of potato salad and cold meat and silly old ice cream and flies coming in the hole in the backdoor screen and having to wash out my slips every night that I could just die! I don't know — " She broke off with a little laugh.

We were silent for a moment and outside I could hear the faint sound of cars going by on Park Avenue and the early evening noise of the summer crickets. "If you and Martin aren't doing anything special tonight, why don't you come to the show with Jack and me?" I ventured. "It will be cooler there and it's nice to have somewhere definite to go."

"No, I think we'd rather not," and her superior tone was back again. "Martin and I never *plan* what we are going to do. Besides, if you are with someone interesting you don't have to *go* any place. That's what I mean is wrong with people in this town. They always have to *go* somewhere and never think how it is to just sit and talk about worthwhile things. It isn't like in cities where . . . well, you know what I mean . . ." and she let the sentence trail off, not bothering to finish it.

She sat thinking hard, mulling over her thoughts. "Do you know," she said unexpectedly, "I think Martin really likes me. . . ."

"Did he *tell* you?" I asked cautiously. I wasn't sure if that was too private a question or not.

"No," she answered laconically.

"How do you know then?"

"I just know. There are ways . . . I can just tell."

But somehow her voice sounded tired as she said it.

The last two weeks of July melted away like brown sugar into nothing but warm, crowded memories. I let the inevitable imminence of college ride on the top of my thoughts, never really admitting to myself that it was there. Fitz and Margie and Jack and I went swimming together twice on the hottest days and one night when there was a moon — full and lush with that overripe look — we went sailing with Swede. And one afternoon Jack brought over a quart of ice cream and we all sat eating it on the back lawn. Jane Rady called Jack and asked him to go to a weiner roast with her that night, but he told her that he had a date with me. Margie told me about it later and I couldn't help feeling contentedly smug inside.

I tried to keep myself from seeing that summer was slipping by though everything about me sang with it — the full, warm swell of the July breezes and the full-blown poppies that turned heavy-headed and scattered their petals to the ground. In the garden the corn was ripe and the leaves were satin-shiny in the sunlight, and when I broke open the ears, the rows of even kernels showed through like teeth, in a sudden yellow grin. The tomatoes lay open to the sun, ripe and tight in their skins and crickets burrowed into them from the ground side, nibbling ragged holes in the firm red fruit. The squash vine that trailed between the corn put out a yellow trumpet of a blossom and little green warted cucumbers lay on the hot earth. There was no more small pink and white clover scattered on the lawn and no damp, hidden corners, close to the house, with fresh, new shoots coming through. The air was heavy and sultry and the earth rich and full with growing. Summer was in its heyday.

Late one afternoon Jack and I went out for a ride along the old creek road. On the bridge over the stream he parked the truck and we got out to lean over the rail and look at the water. The long, hot days had shrunk the creek into a narrow trickle, leaving the green water reeds high and dry in a muck of red clay. As we stood there a farmer with a team of horses clop-clopped over the bridge with a straggling load of alfalfa with tiny purple flowers, and he stared at us in silence as he passed. Long after he had gone, a low, yellow dust from the wagon wheels hung over the road.

"I guess he thinks we're crazy," Jack said.

"Uhuh. I guess he does."

In from the fields came the silken hush of the wind in the tall weeds and the air was honey-sweet with clover. Along the creek, small willows shuddered and showed the white side of their leaves to the breeze and an occasional fat frog plopped into the water, dislodging patches of green-brown scum that lazied along with the current to catch against water reeds farther down the stream. Jack kicked a sprinkle of gravel over the bridge with the toe of his shoe and it splashed with a tinkling sound like small bells. The sun was warm on our heads and shoulders.

"It's getting on so that summer's almost over," he said, musing. "And it seems just like yesterday that school let out."

"It isn't nearly over," I told him. "It isn't much more than half gone."

"Sure it is," he insisted. "About four more weeks and you'll be going away to school. After July is gone, summer is gone."

"Four weeks is a long time, though, Jack, and maybe you can come down to see me at school once in a while — and then I'll always come home for holidays and things. . . ." I tried to make my voice sound reassuring.

182

"Sure, I know it," he said. "But it's just that it won't be summer anymore and it won't be quite the same."

A bit of bleached wood floated slowly beneath us, bobbing gently, and we watched it till it passed under the bridge and was gone. The coffee-brown water was shot through with sunlight. Jack turned to look me full in the face, squinting a little against the sun. "Gee, Angie," he said in a puzzled voice, "I don't know what it's going to be like around here when you're gone!"

My father had some business in Minaqua in far northern Wisconsin and my mother, Kitty, and I drove with him and spent the weekend. We drove for miles over long, cool highways lined with silent pine woods, strange and dark. All Saturday my mother and I shopped. We bought a playsuit for Kitty with Swiss embroidery and some bright, striped chintz for drapes and a bedspread for my room at college. "Something cheery is good when you're away from home," my mother said.

That night I tried to write Jack a note on hotel stationery but tore it up because the pen scratched and I couldn't think of anything to say anyway. I bought a colored postcard in the lobby with a picture of a tall, stratified rock with an Indian standing on it and wrote, "Dear Jack — You wouldn't believe how beautiful it is up here. The pines are wonderful. Be good and I'll see you soon." The next morning I was sorry I had sent it. It didn't say what I meant. But you can't put on a postcard how much you miss a boy.

I never expected to meet Lorraine and Martin there that night. Except for the few moments at the Fourth-of-July parade I had never seen them out together. Jack and I went down to the Rathskeller by ourselves and met Fitz and Margie there. The Rathskeller is a night club; a dark, down-a-flight-of-stairs sort of place where it is necessary to keep the lights on even in the daytime. There are imitation windows set with leaded-colored glass and arranged with a glow of light behind them to give a touch of reality, but they are really set in the wall below street level. The walls are paneled in heavy wood and the tables and chairs are thick and brown so that the whole room seems to be in a yellow-brown haze all the time. It gave me a dark, excited feeling just to be there.

It was a hot, muggy night and even the breeze was warm, but in here the floors and walls gave off a dusky coolness. The four of us sat at a small table in the corner and I let Margie take the chair on the outside — I felt uneasy to be seen in a place like this. There had been bars in Pete's and Chet's but this place was different. It had such a dark, night-time look. A waiter in a short, white coat and a pencil stuck behind his ear came to take our order and they all asked for beer except me. Even Margie asked for beer and when it came she poured it herself, tapping the glass with the bottle to keep the white foam from topping the edge of the glass. Then Fitz filled his glass, raised it, and touched Jack's. Then he touched Margie's and they all said something in a chorus that sounded to me like "Roast it!" and took the first swallow. I just sipped my Coke and pretended to know what they were doing. I meant to ask Jack about it later.

Over in one corner was an ornate jukebox with lights inside that made its decorated front shine like murky, colored water flowing upward in a steady stream, twisting and turning until the colors seemed to be braided together. It was a gaudy thing, like a woman with too much rouge on, and the glow it made in the corner of the room was almost warm and tangible enough to touch and the bright, twisting colors added a strange color to the music that came out of the box. There was something oddly sensuous about it. Even when I was talking to Jack I could see it out of the corner of my eye, the slow, blurred turnings of the lights, quietly insistent.

Fitz and Margie left the table to dance and we watched them. There were others dancing, people who were older than we were. Most of the fellows had slick, wet-looking hair that still showed the comb marks — the kind of boy who wears a navy-blue suit with a narrow stripe for Sundays and for best occasions even in the heat of summertime. I remember noticing two girls sitting together at one of the tables. They wore thin blue satin blouses that caught the colored shine of the light of the jukebox, making them seem to move beneath the shiny material even when they were sitting perfectly still. I seemed to remember vaguely having seen them somewhere before. When they danced they stood first very close to their partners and then far away, moving with short, jerky steps and flat, expressionless faces. They never talked when they danced. Fitz danced with his chin on Margie's head and held her hand down far, near her hip. She closed her eyes and they didn't talk when they danced either, but that was different. Jack and I watched them till the glow of the jukebox and the warm dusk of the room mingled together and swam before my eyes in a low-light murkiness as exciting as wine.

We had doubled with Fitz and Margie so often that I had learned not to seem surprised at anything they did. When they came back to the table both had another bottle of beer and we talked together for a short while before Fitz glanced nervously at his wrist watch, saying, "I hate to break this up but we'd better leave you kids and shove off. Margie's mother don't want her going out so much lately so we got to be cautious."

Margie opened her purse and patted her hair in the mirror, remarking coyly, "I know you two aren't going to mind being left alone. . . ."

Fitz looked at his watch again and stammered apologetically, "It's just a little after nine o'clock now but she has to be in early and if you kids don't care . . . well . . . you know how it is. We want a little time."

"That's all right, fella," Jack answered. "Go ahead."

After they left we moved to a table nearer the big grand piano that was set in the middle of the floor. "They've got a wonderful colored pianist for the floor show," Jack told me. "He doesn't come on till ten o'clock but I want to sit where we can see him as well as hear him. I don't know much about music myself but they say that fellow's got magic fingers.

"He's from Chicago," he explained. "Used to play at the Three Deuces there."

I drew my eyebrows together, trying to look interested, but I couldn't remember ever having heard of the Three Deuces before. And I had only been in Chicago twice.

"You know, that 'home of swing' place that everyone used to talk about," he went on, explaining with his hands as if he were blowing on a trumpet. "That place where they had big jive sessions and stuff — regular Bix Beiderbecke. It burned down a couple of New Year's Eves ago."

He sat thinking, making wet rings on the brown table top with his beer glass. "Used to play there before it burned down," he commented absently.

Just then Martin and Lorraine came in. She was squinting a little to get used to the duskiness of the place and didn't see me at first. I was as surprised to see her as she was to see me, though I had often wondered where she and Martin went at night. Jack stood up as they came over to our table. "Hello there, Angie," Martin said heartily and, "Hi there, fellow, long time no see!" to Jack, pumping his hand and slapping him on the back. Jack looked surprised.

"Won't you two pull up a couple of chairs and have a glass of beer with us?" he asked politely.

But Lorraine put in hastily. "Thanks anyway, Jack. I don't think we'll bother. We were on our way somewhere else and just stopped in for — "

"Sure. 'Course we will," Martin interrupted, and pulled over two chairs from the next table. "We got a little time to spare — especially when I haven't seen this cute young sister of yours for such a long time," and he gave me an exaggerated wink. I had never seen him act the way he did that night.

When the waiter came to our table he said benevolently, "We'll have the same as before for these two and a couple of Scotch and seltzers here," pointing to Lorraine and himself.

"No, thank you," Lorraine interrupted again. "I'll have a Coke if you don't mind."

Martin looked at her. "A Coke . . ." he began incredulously and then looked at me. "Oh. Oh, all right. Sure. Waiter make that one Scotch here and one Coke."

We were sitting near the jukebox and had to talk above the music. "You know, I'm beginning to like this little town of yours." He looked at Jack and me as if expecting an answer. "Yes, sir, it's a pretty good little town when you get to know the people. It's not like the big city, of course, and you can't have the fun you can in some towns, but it's like I always say — if you want fun, you've got to make it yourself."

"You're right there," Jack assented. "I know I've always had a good time here."

"I met an old fraternity brother of mine the other day in Waupun and I said to him, 'You know, if I had a wife and six kids and nowhere else to go there is nowhere I would rather live than Fond du Lac,'" and Martin guffawed loudly. But Jack didn't laugh with him and neither did I. Talking about your home town is like talking about your own mother.

Lorraine was restless and excused herself, going into the powder room. Martin turned to me, "That sister of yours is the greatest one for fixing up. Everytime you look at her it's prink, prink. I tell her sometimes she's going to wear her face right off with that powder puff. Another beer, Jack?" He was trying hard to be pleasant now. I almost liked him.

When Lorraine came back she was freshly lipsticked, with her hair fluffed out, and her heels clicked sharply on the floor. "Come on, Martin, let's go now."

He turned in his chair and looked her squarely in the face, saying very deliberately and a little too loudly, "Let's go! We just got here, didn't we? We've got about twenty minutes to wait until the floor show starts and you want to go already!"

"I know, Martie," she answered coyly, her lips pouted, "I know we just got here, but I want to go. Come on!" and she smiled at him. Sometimes Lorraine talks as if she were sucking sugar lumps.

He drank down the rest of his drink and looked at us, sighing in mock exasperation. "It's like that all the time. Just when we get where there is people and fun it's 'Let's go! Let's go!'" and he squeaked out an imitation of Lorraine. "To hear her talk you'd think she *had* somewhere to go!"

Jack and I sat in an uncomfortable silence after they had gone. I noticed that Martin had nodded to the two girls in the thin satin blouses as he went out the door. We both knew that he hadn't been trying to be funny, and it made me curl up inside because it had been my own sister he had been talking to. Jack lit a cigarette, trying to think of something to say.

"Say, why don't you try a bottle of beer with me, Angie?" he suggested.

"Oh, no! No, thank you, really. I never drink beer."

"Come on," he urged. "Just for fun. One bottle won't hurt you."

"It would look so awful, though — me sitting here with a beer bottle in front of me. I'd look like a witch or something."

"All right," he assented. "I wouldn't want you to have to have one if you didn't want to but I just thought you might like it — this once."

"I'll tell you what," I suggested. "You order me a bottle and if I don't like it you can finish it. Will that be all right?"

"Well, if you want to, Angie . . . but don't do it just on account of me."

"No, no, I really want it. It will be sort of fun, I think."

"Waiter," he called. "Make that two bottles of beer this time. And bring us some potato chips to go with it."

He put his hand very close to mine on the table and looked at me with a warm gratitude in his eyes. It made my cheeks tingling hot and for a moment I forgot what I had been saying. When the waiter brought the beer Jack poured both our glasses. I took a cautious sip and screwed up my face at the flat bitterness. Jack winked at me and I laughed back at him — so much fuss over one bottle of beer. But when he wasn't looking I pushed the bottle over a little toward his side of the table. A girl can't feel like a lady with a bottle of beer before her.

When it was time for the floor show even the dim wall lights were switched off and the spotlight tossed a bright lariat of light around the baby grand piano in the middle of the floor. There was a moment's pause and the pianist came out of the darkness while a spatter of applause from the tables greeted him as he slid onto the bench. I had never seen a colored pianist before.

He sat for a moment, very still, with his head back and his eyes closed, poised and waiting, and then began running his hands up and down the keyboard. His fingers were chocolate-brown against the white keys and his foot kept up a dull beat-beat on the floor; his head bobbed. Jack looked at me and winked approval. This wasn't small-town music at all. With his eyes still closed, the colored man leaned back on the bench, way back, one hand limp at his side and the other like a dark spider on the high notes at the end of the keyboard, quick and supple, tingling the keys in a rippling, tantalizing way until it made my scalp prickle to hear him. Suddenly he swung back into position, both hands playing the whole keyboard, and let out a queer, wild cry that sounded like "Oh, rock the baby!" A laugh went round the room, from table to table, and everyone relaxed. He played on and on, rocking back and forth on the piano bench, rolling his eyes and shaking his head till his white teeth shone like dice against the black of his face. He played "St. Louis Blues" and then "Honeysuckle Rose," singing as his fingers ran over the keys, with his eyes turning up wildly in his head, drawing out the first words of the song long, sweet, and high, with a sensuously slow half-smile on his lips, holding it till I felt myself looking at Jack and laughing uneasily and almost breathing with relief when he swung off the high note into the rest of the piece. He played on and on, sitting in the bright circle of light, his fingers flashing, and after each number he paused, wiping his forehead, while people at the surrounding tables tossed in their requests like pennies.

"Like it, Angie?" Jack asked.

I nodded, sipping my beer slowly, almost enjoying the bitter, unpleasant taste. Jack ordered another bottle for himself. All around us the room was dark and cool with the underground coolness of wet stone, but the piano, its dark wood shining in the spotlight glare, set the air warm and throbbing with its music. The glass of beer made me cozy inside.

Jack leaned over and said quietly, "Gee, this is fun, Angie. Each night seems to be more fun because it's getting near the end. We've only got a few more weeks before you go back to school. . . ."

I didn't notice Jack order again and I didn't notice the waiter come to our table, but soon there was another full bottle of beer before me. The pianist had launched out with a fast piece, singing as he played, his foot on the pedal of the piano and his shoulders keeping rapid time to the beat of the music. Jack put his hand on mine and together we drummed time. At other tables people were knocking their glasses together in a clinking rhythm. I don't know how long he played. I can't remember that. I don't know how long we sat there sipping beer. I can't remember that, either. The table top felt like a cushion under my hand. Before long the music of the piano and the sound of the clapping of the audience seemed to come to me as from another room, floating in soft, gentle waves, and the effect struck me as so funny that I giggled!

Jack leaned over to touch my cheek with the back of his hand and I think he was laughing at me. "You're a honey, Angie. I like you so much tonight!"

I said something to him then — I must have said something. But talking was a queer feeling. I felt as if the thoughts came out of my mouth in bright bubbles and floated over to Jack before they burst into words and the sound of them came back to me. Everything seemed to be at a distance. I looked at the beer in my glass, clear as amber, and even to look at it made me feel mellow.

The colored man was playing again with his head thrown back; quick, sharp notes that seemed to trip over each other. His fingers kept up a rapid sparkle over the keys.

"Look, Jack," I remember saying, and the thought first puzzled and then amazed me. "He has red nail polish on! Isn't that funny — for a man?"

"Yeh," he answered laconically, playing with his beer glass. "It's pretty funny." It struck me as so amazing that I wanted to talk about it but Jack looked the other way. And that was all he said.

The whole room was cool with the smell of beer and blue with cigarette smoke. The piano tinkled through my brain in a steady stream and my thoughts seemed to run out with the note sounds.

There was a tingle in my head like the sparkle of ginger ale. I could hear myself talking and talking to Jack, the words all mixed up with laughing, and he smiled back at me and I hummed to the music and we laughed and laughed again and I don't remember all the funny things he said. My brain was in a singsong. It was such a hot night outside that he had worn no necktie; just a white sport shirt, open at the throat, and I had a blurred thought about how much he looked like the picture of Lord Byron that had hung on the wall of my English room at school.

In the corner the face of the jukebox still shone with light and the twisting of the colors made me giddy. My cheeks were too hot now and I thought how nice it would be to feel for a moment the coolness of the night wind off the lake. "You must drive me down to look at the water before you take me home, Jack," I murmured to him. At least I think I did.

He finished his beer and the pianist played one last piece, hunched over the piano, his forehead shining, while he fretted the lower keys in a grumbling boogie-woogie that rumbled out to the very corners of the room, and then slid his long, dark fingers up the keyboard in a flourishing finish. He slid off the piano bench, gave the audience a quick black-and-white grin, and disappeared into a back room.

The bright spotlight was snapped off and the dim wall lights glowed on. The room was filled with an almost pleasant gloom, very quiet and cool, with its damp-stone smell. "We'd better go," I said. "We'd really better go home because I'm so sleepy now."

After that I never drank beer again. It had really been a wonderful evening — but no evening can be that wonderful by itself. That's how I know. I didn't realize it then and I hate to admit it now, but I must have been a little tight that night!

After that evening at the Rathskeller, Lorraine talked and talked about Martin even more than before. She told me about the smooth girls whom he used to date when he was at the university — long-haired, pretty girls who belonged to the best sororities; she told my mother how particular he was about everything he ate — never touched salads and didn't like butter on anything but toast; she even asked my father if he knew some man who lived out near Campbellsport who owned a big garage and to whom Martin had sold insurance at the beginning of the summer. Anything just to say his name. I was surprised at her. In fact, she talked about him so much that my mother began to give my father alarmed, raised-eyebrow looks at the dinner table.

She even asked Jack what kind of rolls Martin bought for his breakfast each morning, and how many, and whether he came every morning or bought a two days' supply at once. Jack told me later that he had charged the rolls for two weeks now and owed a little over a dollar and a half at the bakery. Martin phoned for three nights in a row, just before supper, and one night he and Lorraine went out for a Coke together, coming home much later, when we had all gone to bed. She borrowed three university annuals from a fellow who lives down our street — she wasn't just sure what year he had graduated — and looked up his picture. We lay on the living-room rug one evening, she and I, to look at the books together. We found his graduation picture on a back page and under it a list of the activities in which he had participated and Lorraine pointed out with pride that he had as many as any other boy on the page. He looked much younger than he did now, with a high, white collar and a shiny look — like a man in a brilliantine ad. We found another picture of him standing before his fraternity house with the rest of the committee for arrangements for the Junior Prom, but only half his face showed for there was another boy standing almost directly in front of him. Quite by accident Lorraine found the picture of the girl he used to date and on whom he had hung his fraternity pin when he was a sophomore.

"Where is his pin now?" I asked her.

"I really don't know. Maybe that little bonde still has it," she said. "Some girls are like that, you know, Angie. Never want to give a fellow up even when he doesn't like her anymore."

Margaret and Art drove up from Milwaukee late that Saturday afternoon — Margaret had to be back at work the following Monday morning — and Lorraine showed Martin's picture to them. At suppertime she announced that maybe he was even going to come to Chicago to work in November; he was writing to the main offices to see about a transfer. "You know, he is the kind of man who would be good in any territory," she commented. "And then if he is down that way he can come to the dances at school next year and he probably will be able to get blind dates for Angie too. That would be good," she added significantly, "because it takes some girls a long time to get started." I wondered what had made her change so suddenly; what had made her so sure of herself.

She even said that Martin might drive her back to Chicago when college classes began in the fall.

Art looked at Margaret, winked and said, "Hey, hey, what goes on here? We've been away too long, Maggie."

Jack went out with Swede and Fitz and some of the other fellows that night and Lorraine asked me to walk up to McKnight's for a Coke with her. "It's all right for me to be seen without a date," she explained lightly, "when everyone knows I'm practically going steady anyway. . . ." Martin had called just after supper to say that he wouldn't see her that weekend — he was driving up to Eagle River and wouldn't be back until late on Tuesday. He asked her then to go out with him the following Sunday.

"That's his birthday," she told us happily when he had hung up. "I don't know just how old he will be, but it certainly is something to have him ask me out for that night when he knows other cuter girls in town and everything, isn't it? We'll probably do something very special and have dinner somewhere first. I don't know what I should wear. Either I will have to get something new or borrow something of Margaret's. . . ." She was giddy with excitement.

Under his breath my father muttered, "Just lucky you're going back to school in a month, young lady!" and went huffily back to his paper.

I have never known a hotter July. There was a soft, hazy, constant heat that hung over everything and never let up — only seemed to turn dark with evening. In our garden the black earth dried and crumbled brown, shrinking away till the twisted tomato roots showed above the ground. Out in the country the fields were a parched patchwork and only the trees were still green against the dust-yellow roll of the hills.

One afternoon after work, Lorraine walked uptown to pick out a birthday present for Martin. She had thought of giving him a year's subscription to *Time* magazine but came home with a wallet instead. "I think he'll like this," she explained, "because it is such a 'mannish' sort of gift." It was brown pigskin with a long zipper in it and special compartments for driver's license and personal papers. On one inside corner she had had his initials "M.K." stamped in gilt. That was Tuesday night and after supper she wrapped it in white tissue paper and I held my finger on the red ribbon while she tied three small bows. "Maybe I should think of something clever to put on a little card to go with it," she suggested. "I won't give it to him till Sunday though."

Jack came over about nine o'clock and we went for a walk around the park that night. Even the wind off the water was warm. When we came home Lorraine was still up, curled in a chair by the front window. "I just thought I'd sit here and read a bit," she yawned, "in case Martin calls when he gets back to town. He is supposed to get in tonight. It's too hot to sleep anyway."

On Wednesday he didn't call either and Lorraine puzzled over it all evening. "He must have been delayed in Eagle River," she explained to me. "That must be it. There wasn't a postcard for me in the noon mail or anything, was there, Angie?" No, I told her. There hadn't been a postcard or a letter. Nothing at all.

Kitty and I went for a ride with Jack the next afternoon. It was so hot that he pulled up near the water's edge at the park and opened the doors of the truck to let the breeze blow through. The sand dredge in the harbor was still at work, its engines rhythmic in the stillness, and the lake was almost

197

perfectly calm, greenish near the shore and deep blue farther out. Here and there ominous shadows lay on the surface where silent undercurrents shifted beneath. Along the breakwater small waves lipped over the rocks, spreading their foam in quiet frills, then slipping back into the stiller water.

"Your sister and Martin figure out what they're going to do to celebrate Sunday?" Jack asked, casually making conversation.

"No," I told him. "He didn't get back yet."

"Oh, didn't he?" his voice pricked up in surprise. "I thought he was supposed to come back on Tuesday night."

"He was, but he evidently didn't make it," I explained. A quick suspicion shot through my brain. "Why, what made you ask?"

"Nothing. I just wondered what they were going to do, that's all."

"But I mean, what made you think that he was going to get back on Tuesday night?"

"Because you told me he was," he answered.

"I know that," I insisted. "But why did you use that tone of voice when you said you thought he was supposed to come back Tuesday?"

"Don't be silly, Angie," he said, looking down at his hands. "I didn't use any tone of voice."

"You sound so queer. Why don't you look at me?" I demanded. "You talk as if you saw him. You talk as if he *did* get back — did he?"

"You're the one who ought to know that," he answered and started the motor of the car. I was certain then that something was going to happen.

Thursday and Friday limped by. On Friday night my father came home for the weekend and Lorraine took Martin's birthday wallet from the corner of her dressing-table drawer, unwrapping it carefully to show to him. "Look, Dad," she said. "Tell me honestly, if you were a fellow would you like this?"

He turned it over and over in his hand, looking into all the special compartments and trying the zipper. Then he looked at my mother and winked, "I'm still a fellow," he answered, "and I *do* like it so I guess that makes it all right." My father is always in a good mood when he comes home from work. He must have been trying to sell an order at a new house under construction, for I noticed there was red clay on the soles of his shoes.

Lorraine stayed at home all Saturday afternoon and all Saturday evening in case Martin might call. On Sunday she sat out on the back lawn where she could hear the phone easily if it should ring. No one mentioned him to her. Once she said to me, as if I had been arguing with her, "But, Angie, he wouldn't have asked me if he hadn't wanted me to go!" I knew what an empty, aching feeling she must have inside her. If only she hadn't talked about Martin so much earlier in the week!

In the later afternoon I brought out a deck of cards and she and Mother and I tried to play bridge on the grass of the back lawn; but the wind kept flipping the cards about and Lorraine wasn't interested anyway. So we just sat, not talking at all, and let the late sun fall warm across our legs. The breeze was sweet with the hay smell of grass long burned by the sun. A flock of wild canaries had flown in from the fields, flitting quickly in and out the trees, and bobbing like fat yellow blossoms on the topmost branches.

Each moment dragged by, trailing suspense behind it. I couldn't make myself believe that he really wasn't going to call at all! We had our supper on the back lawn as usual and Kitty had to close Kinkee in the garage because she kept sniffing at the plate of sandwiches on the grass. It had been a long, warm day and the sun went down slowly and shadows were low on the ground, while the clouds above were still light and the trees were silhouetted black against the soft pink of the sky. The seconds were as slow as minutes. There was still no word, and watching Lorraine sitting, waiting, my heart felt as raw as cubed steak.

In the last glow of early evening sphinx moths came out, with their soft, furred bodies like small birds, blundering from flower to flower with their wings whirring and setting the tall honeysuckle rocking in the dusk. Mosquitoes hummed in the garden hedge and a meadowlark called, perched on the handle of a spade stuck in the earth at the far end of the garden path. Art was lying on his back on the cool grass, his head in Margaret's lap, looking at the first new stars that were just twinkling yellow in the pale of the evening sky. Lorraine gave a short sigh and then went into the house and up to her bedroom.

After a long time my mother said to me, "Angeline, you'd better go up and speak to her."

I waited for a moment in the living room, trying to decide what would be the best words to say. Lorraine was sitting on the rug in her bedroom with the little dresser lamp beside her, its pink shade off, and the bare bulb glaring bright. She was sitting with a long darning needle in her hand, carefully picking at the gilt initials inside Martin's wallet. Neither of us spoke.

"See, Angie!" she said triumphantly, holding it up. "Look, I've got it all off now but one little part of the M. Probably Dad can use it or something. . . ."

I looked at her closely. She hadn't even been crying. I took the wallet and turned it over in my hand, holding it to the light. "That's nice, Lorraine," I said quietly, "You'd hardly ever know." That's what I said but there were needle pricks in the leather and I could still see where the initials had been.

That night, lying in bed, I could not help wishing that there wasn't so much sadness in growing up. It was all so confused in my mind. There had been the long, long days of being young and not wondering about tomorrow at all and thinking in a strange, forgotten child's world. There were days when my thoughts were as mild as feathers and even an hour seemed like a long time. Then suddenly it was like turning a sharp corner — you were older and the things that counted when you were young didn't count anymore at all and, looking back, you couldn't even see them. Growing up crowds your mind with new thoughts and new feelings so that you forget how you used to think and feel.

When Lorraine was a little girl she didn't know about people like Martin — none of us did. Nothing she had ever done had prepared her to feel the way she felt that night. We had never known about anything unpleasant. Our whole lives had been little-girl lives, crowded first with thoughts of kindergarten and going for exciting walks with the class in the early gray of spring to gather pussy willows along the creek banks, and eating oranges on the school playground at recess, oranges with skins so thick that they gave off a fine spray of fragrant oil when they were peeled. Somewhere in the years, Kitty was born and we seemed bigger because she was so little. Quiet memories of her slid into my mind. I could remember putting her into her crib on warm summer nights, her skin cool and baby-soft through the thin cotton of her nightgown; and then before long she was sitting by herself on the living-room rug and the floor was always strewn with painted-eyed dolls and scribbled-up color books. On the piano stool there is still a white mark where she set her wet box of water colors. After Kitty the days went faster, merging into long Wisconsin winters with snowdrifts piled almost up to the living-room windows, and hot, still summers with the sunlight pouring through the trees like yellow honey. Lorraine and Margaret and I were changing. Things that had once been so important didn't matter any more. Carnivals still came to town and set up their Ferris wheels in bright wheels of light against the night sky and pitched little striped tents all stained brown with rain, but we no longer felt the same ecstatic thrills. And we didn't go out barefoot in the wet grass hunting for tiny, green-brown toads that came out after the rain. Our thoughts were on different things.

When Margaret was seventeen she had her first date with a Western Union messenger boy, and then one day I found a tube of lipstick hidden in the pocket of Lorraine's coat and shortly after that my mother bought her special Castile soap to use because her complexion wasn't good. Finally Lorraine went away to college, Margaret met Art, and we all began to live our lives separately. And no one said anything or seemed to think it odd.

I had seen it happen to both of my sisters and here was I, letting it happen to me. Every moment I was awake I was thinking of Jack, letting him into my house and into my days. Everything had changed. Until this summer telephones had never been important to me and now, always, I was waiting for it to ring. Growing up is like taking down the sides of your house and letting strangers walk in.

Lorraine lay beside me in bed sleeping — I think she was sleeping. We had both gone to bed early and quietly, not mentioning Martin. I had lain awake, waiting for her to say something, but she didn't; she hadn't even moved or turned her head on the pillow once. The night air made a light whistle through the screens and blew warm over the thin top sheet, and the trees on the front lawn seemed to be crowding their leaves stiflingly close to the windows. Somewhere, far off in the sky, heat lightning winked.

And I lay there wondering sadly how long — how many days and nights — it would take Lorraine to forget about Martin. How long before she could listen to soft music on the radio, see cars shining in the sun, or blue smoke rings floating without some thought of him coming into her mind. It would take a very long time. And for her there would be no more summer.

In the morning the sky was a dazzling blue with clean, white puffs of clouds scattered high over it. There was something brightly expectant about the morning — as if the sun had been up for hours and hours just waiting for the rest of the world to wake. Even before breakfast the air was hot and sparrows were bobbing in the hedges and the plants in the garden were drooping. There were big, dry cracks in the earth as wide as my wrist. "Looks like another scorcher," my mother remarked cheerfully. "Fine weather for the last day of July!" The house was buzzing with hurried, Monday morning noises, with my father talking through his coffee and his paper and Kitty keeping up a steady excited chatter that no one bothered to listen to, while Margaret click-clacked about the kitchen in a pair of flat, wooden-soled sandals she had bought in Milwaukee. My mother had got up earlier than the rest of us and the sonorous hum-hum of the washing machine in the basement came up to us as we ate breakfast.

But the brightness of the morning didn't last long. We had just got the first clothes hung on the line when a light wind came up and a few dark clouds floated into the sky out of the west; and by noon they had gathered together, dark and sullen, heavy and sagging with rain. The hot, dry air changed to an oppressive mugginess but still the rain didn't fall. The clouds were lined up, gray and sulky, as if they were waiting for something, and the day dragged sluggishly by in a tiresome, clammy heat. The clothes took a long time to dry and I spent the afternoon ironing while my mother sat at the kitchen table sewing on buttons and mending little tears in Kitty's playsuits. It was so quiet that all my thoughts seemed to have a yawn in them.

At five o'clock Jack came. I had seen the black truck pull up at the curb and had run to open the door even before he knocked. I was wide-awake again the minute I saw him and the house no longer seemed hot. The storm had finally broken and the first rain fell in slow, round drops that spotted the sidewalks dark, drying up almost at once on the warm cement.

"Hello there, Mrs. Morrow," Jack said to Mother. "They've got you pretty busy, I see!"

"I like to get these things put away mended right away," she explained, snapping off a bit of thread with her teeth. "Angie's been ironing all afternoon and we'll be all through in about half an hour."

"We send our washing out," he said, but added hastily, "but that's because my mother helps down at the bakery sometimes and just doesn't have time to do it herself." Jack is always very careful not to hurt people's feelings; very careful not to pretend about anything.

He was restless that afternoon, seemed worried about something. He was sitting on a kitchen chair opposite my mother while I finished the shirt I had been ironing. I noticed he hardly heard what I said when I spoke to him. He took a cigarette and lit it at the kitchen stove — we were out of matches — and I took a saucer from the dish cupboard for the ashes. He just nodded at me and in a moment crushed the cigarette out. I had never seen him nervous before and it puzzled me to know what he was thinking. He shouldn't even have been away from the bakery so early in the afternoon.

"Mrs. Morrow," he said suddenly, "mind if I take Angie for a short ride?"

"No, of course I don't," she answered, "but it's almost suppertime."

"Oh, I'm sorry," and his tone was crestfallen, "I didn't realize that. I wasn't even thinking what time of day it was."

He looked at me to say something and my mind worked quickly. "Mom," I asked hopefully, "we could be back almost right away?"

"You may go if you like, Angeline. I don't mind at all, only I don't want you to miss your supper. Just be back by six." She gathered up a pile of clean, ironed clothes in her arm. "I'll get these things put away before Lorraine and Margaret get home."

I pulled the iron cord out of the wall socket and fluffed my fingers through my hair. Just as we were going out the front door my mother called after us, "Bring home some lemons, will you, Angie? It won't take you a minute to stop at the store and I think the children might like iced tea for supper."

"We will," I called back.

The rain was coming down harder now and together we ran for the car. The storm seemed to be rolling toward us high above the dark clouds, rumbling like a bowling ball. In the trees the sparrows cheep-cheeped in excitement and fluttered among the leaves.

The moment we were in the car Jack said impatiently, "I've got to talk to you, Angie. Where shall we go?"

"Out to the park maybe?"

"No, not there," he said, shaking his head. "I don't want to run into Swede right now. I talked to him a little while ago and he said he was going out to put an extra rope on the boat. This looks like a pretty bad squall coming up and that water gets plenty choppy."

We both thought a moment. "How about down past the creek on Willow Road," he suggested.

But I didn't want to go there. "That's not a — a 'daytime' place," I explained.

He started the car. "Let's just make it Pete's then. I could stand a Coke anyway."

The rain was falling at an angle, blown by the wind and dashing slantwise against the car windows. As we turned onto the highway the storm wind swept low in from the lake, making furrows in the waving grass along the fields. We passed a farmyard where a little boy was driving a team of horses into the barn and the chickens ran across the yard squawking, the wind parachuting their tail feathers and pushing them from behind.

"Have a cigarette?" Jack said, pulling out his package. It was a standing joke between us for he knew I never smoked, but he took one himself and I held the steering wheel for him while he rummaged through his pockets for a match.

"The farmers can really use this rain," I remarked. "This has been the hottest, driest July I can ever remember." It was falling so hard that the drops splashed back off the highway and the bushes at the roadside bent beneath its weight.

There were already puddles in the gravel lot as we pulled in behind Pete's. Jack shut off the motor and was silent for a moment. "Aren't we going in?" I asked.

"No," he answered. "Let's just stay here." The rain made a noisy pit-pat on the car roof and with the windshield wipers shut off, the water ran down the windows in a steady sheet.

"I thought you said you wanted a Coke?"

"I do. But we'll get that later. I want to talk to you alone, Angie."

All the way out to Pete's I had been wondering what it was he had to tell me; what it was that made his forehead all wrinkled with thought. As often as I had seen Jack and as much as I liked him I still felt almost afraid to be alone with him. I still had the self-conscious feeling that I should have worn a better dress and that I should have brushed my hair again before I had gone out with him. When he looked at me directly I almost felt that I knew what he must be thinking — he had gone out with so many girls who were prettier than I.

Now he started the motor again and pulled the truck to the very edge of the gravel lot as far from

Pete's as we could get, very close to the water. The sky hung low, dark, and forbidding, and the lake was gray-green, choppy with waves, angry in the wind and lashed by the gray rain. Lake and sky were storming at each other in almost visible argument.

Jack shifted toward me and sat for a moment, absently picking at the cracked leather of the car seat. His face was thoughtful. His hands were as brown as his face and there was a white ring on one finger where he had changed his class ring from the left hand to the right. He was as ill at ease as I was and kept moistening his lips as if he were trying to work up the courage to say something.

I looked back at the wooden shelves in the truck behind us. They were still lined with several boxes of doughnuts and a gooey lemon meringue left from the day's sales and the air was sickeningly sweet, smelling like melted marshmallows. The front seat of the truck was suddenly very small and close.

"Jack," I said, "It's awfully hot in here!" The still, hesitant tension of waiting made me giddy with excitement.

He rolled down the car window on his side. "There. That better?" With the window open the storm seemed even nearer. Cool, wet air blew across my face and the tall old trees on the lawn bent low, twisting and moaning, wrenching at their trunks and writhing in a strange sympathy with the tormented water. Gray waves rolled crashing toward the shore and thrashed against the wooden pier, slapping like bare hands against the flat rocks. High sprays of foam tossed into the air and the wind was heavy with the damp, suggestive smell of fish. It gave me a strange, wild feeling, restless and lonesome. From the gray-green tumult of the water and the weird twistings of the trees we might have been miles and miles away from everything. Long, sharp lightning tore at the clouds and angry thunder snarled after it, loud above the noise of the lake. I had almost forgotten about Jack for a moment.

"Angie, look at me, will you?"

I turned toward him, my heart pounding in my throat. And as always when I looked straight into his eyes my clear, practical thoughts began to slip away from me as if they were buttered.

"I wanted to come out here where there was no one else so I could talk to you, Angie. Something's happened that I want to tell you."

The thoughts in my head were beating with my heart and I found myself watching his lips for the next words rather than waiting to hear them. Outside the wilder waves were leaping the rock barrier of the shore, puddling the grass beyond, and occasionally far-flung foam dashed itself against the windshield of the car. Jack's hand on mine was warm and insistent but his voice was strangely stiff and scared. I had never seen him like this before.

"I don't know quite how to tell you this, Angie. I wasn't going to tell you at all — at least for a while. But last night I talked it over with Swede and we talked and talked and he said what else was there to do?"

He paused again, not knowing how to go on. Taking another cigarette from the package in the pocket of his shirt, he lit it and flipped the match out the window. The damp breeze ran clean, soft fingers through my hair and laid its cool touch on my neck.

Jack took my hand again and began in a hurried, determined voice, "See, Angie, I don't mean that I'm a fast boy or anything but — I've been around a little. Not like Swede and Fitz maybe — I mean, well. I've dated a lot of girls though . . . and I've kissed a lot of them." He wasn't looking at me now.

"I know that, Jack," I answered quietly.

"I even went steady with Jane Rady for about two weeks last year. And I let her wear my class ring for a while. . . ."

I didn't know what he was going to say; or what he wanted to say. It might mean that after today I was just going to be one of the other girls with him, but somehow I couldn't believe that. Early in June I might have believed it. Even last week I could have imagined what it would be like not to see Jack any more, but not now. Not after everything.

The inside of the car was suddenly very small and secret with the storm outside thrashing around us and the rain pelting on the car roof. The whole wildness of it was pounding inside of me and there was a throbbing ache in the palms of my hands. The suspense in Jack's words, the warm slowness of his voice, made my throat dry with anxiety.

At last the words broke from him so quickly that he sounded almost as if he were going to cry. His forehead was puckered up with earnestness. "Gee, Angie, honey," he said, "I don't know what goes on in your head or what you feel, but I like you so much I think about you all the time! Nothing like this ever happened to me before. All the time — at work, when I'm with the fellows, and when I'm alone at night — all the time I think about you and wonder what you're doing and what you're thinking. When I first went out with you I just liked you a little bit but now it's getting worse and worse. I like you so much that I don't know what to do about it!"

210

The car was so quiet that the drumming of the rain on the roof was deafening. Everything else was breathlessly still. I wanted to reach over to touch the smooth, pulsing brownness of Jack's wrist as it rested on the steering wheel and to feel the warmth of his cheek, but my hands stayed open and empty in my lap.

His voice was strangely low and calm now. "I've thought about this for a long time and I know what I'm saying . . . I'm in love with you, Angie!"

Words tingled at my lips and I felt my hands trembling but there was nothing I could say. I didn't even know what I was thinking. Love is such a big word. And no one had ever said it to me before.

After a long time Jack started the car, the wheels crunched on the wet gravel, and we turned back toward town. Along the highway, lights showed blurred through the rain and the storm sky was dark with the darkness of night. Turning down my own street I saw that the light was on in our dining room and that my family was sitting around the table at supper.

It wasn't until I was inside the front door and Jack had pulled away from the curb that I remembered we hadn't stopped to get lemons for the iced tea!

AUGUST

IN A MOVIE it might have ended there. In fact, I almost thought it would for I didn't know myself what could come next. I was so bewildered and mixed up in my head about the whole thing that my first thought was to call Jack on the phone in the morning, just to hear his voice and to make sure that I hadn't been dreaming.

But I didn't, for that morning my mother wasn't feeling well. She was still in bed when I woke, the pillow wrinkled and the top sheet rumpled from her tossing, so I went downstairs softly to make fresh coffee, bringing it up hot and steaming, but she couldn't touch it. I knew then that she was really ill. I woke Margaret and Lorraine and they got ready for work in careful quietness, opening and closing doors gently, their faces worried and their lips pursed in silence. Each tiptoed in cautiously to say good-bye before she left, easing the bedroom door shut behind her. The whole house was filled with soft, whispery stillness.

Kitty slept late while I straightened my mother's bed, drawing the window shades carefully to keep them from squeaking on the rollers and slipping a clean pillowcase on the pillow, cool and smooth beneath her head. It was alarming to have my mother ill. It was like having the clock stop. Her cheeks were flushed and she complained that her head was throbbing, like hammers beating at the back of her neck; so I brought a cloth wrung out in vinegar and an ice pack, setting it gently on her forehead. Then I waited a moment, helplessly. There seemed to be nothing more I could do. She looked so quiet lying there with her eyes shut and her hands palms upward on the sheet. Already the warm air of the room was sharp with vinegar.

"Mom," I whispered, "anything else you would like?" but her lips didn't move though her hand gestured wearily on the sheet. The door closed quietly behind me. I realized then with guilt that I had noticed her being tired often lately, in little, quiet ways. . . .

Kitty had just waked and, sensing from the stillness of the house that something was wrong, she came tiptoeing out in her nightgown, her eyes round with questions and her braids fuzzy with sleeping. I explained in whispers that Mom didn't feel well and that she should dress quietly and come downstairs quietly, without her shoes. And to be very careful about slamming doors. She nodded solemnly and padded back to her room on feather-soft feet, turning back to me with a cautious finger on her lips. Kitty can make a game out of anything.

Downstairs the sun lay in bright squares on the kitchen floor as I cleared away the earlier breakfast and set Kitty's toast and milk on a napkin on the end of the table. Even running the hot water into the dishpan made too much noise and I had to wash each piece of table silver separately, sliding each clean plate carefully onto the pile on the kitchen shelf. The vacuum cleaner raised such a quick banshee wail that I shut it off at once and just dusted the front room, plumping up cushions with soft fists and straightening the pictures on the wall. After that there was nothing to do.

Kitty had to be kept quiet and away from the house so I brought out her old straw sun hat and a basket and sent her to pull weeds at the far end of the garden. I watched her as she inched along the rows, bent over so her playsuit pulled short, showing her small, round legs brown in the sun. Once I went upstairs softly, opening the door just a little. My mother was lying quiet, with the ice bag slipped down over her eyes. She was breathing as if she were asleep, evenly, with an odd weariness.

By noontime Kitty had grown long-faced and mournful from playing by herself, so I packed a quick lunch of bread and butter and three small round tomatoes and sent her out to the creek to have a picnic. The tomatoes were still warm-skinned from lying in the garden sun and she took salt and pepper in a twist of wax paper to sprinkle on them, skipping off toward the Field with the dog behind her.

Shadows squatted short in the noon sun, so I set a tray very carefully with a clean linen napkin — crisp toast and canned chicken soup, steaming hot. I carried it upstairs hoping that by now my mother would be feeling well enough to eat something, but she was still asleep and her breathing was tired and regular, so I tiptoed back to the kitchen with the tray. I had never known her to sleep so late into the day before.

The house was so still that every step I took seemed to make the floor creak and the clock in the dining room ticked loudly through the whole downstairs. It was as annoying and sharp as fingers snapping. During her lunch hour Margaret called to see how Mom was feeling and I hurried to the phone, picking up the receiver before it could ring twice.

I wasn't used to having so much quiet time to myself and somehow I didn't like it. With no one else's thoughts about, it was necessary to think my own — and yesterday afternoon at Pete's was too disturbing to mull over by myself. It only made me more restless, for each thought was like tickling my heart with a feather. Sitting in a chair by the living-room window, I tried to read; but the trees outside sent in mottled leaf shadows that moved restlessly on the square of sunlight on the rug and I couldn't keep my mind on the print. My mind was drumming its fingers. The afternoon lagged by in a slow haze of heat and quiet till I began to think lazy, ho-hum thoughts that made my eyelids heavy. Then I realized suddenly what was wrong with me — I was lonesome. Between twelve o'clock noon when Kitty had gone on her picnic and four o'clock while the house was still quiet and noiseless, I had used up all my own thoughts, all the comfortable ones, and now I was just lonesome. And I realized, too, what an empty place our house would be if my mother weren't in it. Thinking of it, I felt uneasily as if I were going to cry. I almost wanted to go upstairs to turn the water faucet on loudly in the bathroom or rattle a window shade just to wake her up. . . . A house is no use at all if there are no noises of living going on in it.

My mind was so turned inward with thinking that I didn't hear the truck pull up at the curb; didn't even know Jack was there till I heard his footsteps pounding up the front steps.

Hurrying to the front door with my finger on

my lips I whispered at him, "Shhhh, Jack. Not such big feet! My mother doesn't feel well!"

He whispered back a loud apology and stepped in, closing the door behind him. "Angie, I've got something to tell you!" His voice was different from yesterday, quick and eager, and there was a bright, excited look on his face. He stayed standing as he talked.

"We're going back to Oklahoma!"

His words snapped my mind into alertness. "Jack . . !" Why?"

He went on in a hoarse whisper, as loud as his natural voice, "We're all going, my mother and Dad and me. I've known for a long time that we might, but I never mentioned it because I always thought the plans would fall through!"

My heart slipped down inside me. "When did you find out for sure?"

"Just at breakfast this morning — my mother and Dad decided. You remember that time when that aunt of mine was in Chicago and they went down to see her? That time I had dinner at your house?" I remembered, I told him. "Well, they all talked it over that day and yesterday my father had a letter from her and this morning my mother and he decided that we would go back — definitely."

The whole idea was so new, so unexpected, that I couldn't jar myself into comprehending. I had thought of college. I had thought of Jane Rady or of a new girl but never of something like this! "But why, Jack?" I asked in a small voice. "I thought your mother and father *liked* it here. All your friends are here."

"But it's just five years since we moved away, Angie. We have friends down there too, and my dad has two brothers and my mother has a sister there. It isn't as if we were going down to strangers."

"But why go at all?" I insisted. "You have your house here and everything. I don't see why. . . ." It was such a radical step, moving hundreds and hundreds of miles. Our family had never moved at all ever since I was born. People who live in our town stay there. It might be all right to go away for a vacation or to move a few blocks, but hundreds of miles!

Jack's voice was very earnest as he explained, as if he wanted to convince me that it was necessary to move, that it wasn't his idea, but I could tell he was just repeating what he had heard at home. "You see," he said, frowning, "the bakery business isn't so good here. There is a lot of competition and we're just a small place. Down in Oklahoma my dad figures he can go in with his two brothers and really make a go of it. He's been thinking about this for a long time. They didn't want to while I was in school because that would break up things for me, but now I'm graduated there really is nothing to keep us here." His last words limped out lamely.

The significance of what he had said seeped into my mind slowly, word by word, each bursting like a bubble into an inkling of realization as I stood staring at him. We had never talked about things beyond Pete's or Chicago at the very farthest and now — Oklahoma! The idea was too big to fit into my head all at once.

He fumbled with the doorknob. "Well . . . I've got to get back," he said. "I just brought some things home to my mother from downtown and I was supposed to take the truck right back to the bakery but I just thought I'd stop over. We aren't going till next month though, Angie."

He waited. I knew he expected me to say something; that I was sorry he was going, that I hoped something would happen to change the plans, anything at all. But I couldn't. I couldn't break down the shyness that always kept me from saying what I really thought and felt. It was, somehow, too embarrassing to be affectionate in the daytime and I couldn't even make myself touch his hand.

His voice was hesitant. "I could have called you, Angie, but I wanted to see you anyway."

"I'm really glad you came, Jack, but it's just that I'm so surprised I can't talk for a minute." Upstairs the bedsprings creaked as if my mother had waked and was tossing. Jack heard it too, and whispered, "I'd better go, but is it all right if I see you tonight?" I nodded stiffly and he laughed. "Angie, don't look so scared! There are still trains and buses and besides I haven't gone yet." He shook me a little. "We'll talk about it tonight."

Upstairs my mother asked for a glass of ice water, and when I brought it I had to hold the glass with both hands to keep the ice from rattling. The bedroom was hotly stuffy and sour with the smell of vinegar, the bedclothes tossed and twisted. "I so hate to be a bother to you children, being ill this way," she fretted, half to herself. "But I do think I will feel better by tomorrow. It's just the heat, I think."

My lips trembled with soft words but we aren't the kind of a family who loves each other out loud. "Wouldn't you like to change rooms, Mom?" I suggested quietly. "The shade of the trees has been on Kitty's room all afternoon and it's so much cooler than this. I could put on clean sheets in a minute. . . ?"

"No," she answered weakly. "Perhaps before

218

supper, but I just don't want to right now. I'm a little tired, Angie." Her hands lay limp on the sheet and her head was heavy on the pillow, as if her neck was too weary to hold it up.

"Perhaps I can sleep again for a little while."

"Are you sure there's nothing I can get," I urged, "nothing you would like to eat?"

"In a little while I'd like a cup of strong tea but not now . . . Did I hear someone downstairs a few minutes ago?" she asked, her eyes still shut.

"Yes, that was Jack."

"Did he want you to go out for a drive? Go if you like, Angie, I'll be all right lying here."

"He's gone now," I told her. "But that's all right — he didn't want anything — special." There was no need to talk about it now. Later, when she was feeling better, and when I had had time to realize it myself, there would be opportunity enough. Jack was going away and there would be weeks to talk about it.

"That shade could go down just a little lower and then I'll try to sleep again. Make whatever you like for the children's supper, will you?" and her voice trailed off. Quietly I fixed the window shade and smoothed the pillow under her head.

Downstairs again I kept hoping that Kitty would play out at the creek until suppertime. There was so much to think about, I wanted the quietness now. All I had ever known about Oklahoma was vague stories I had heard about people striking oil down there and a few scenes of desert, spiky cactus, and milling cattle that I remembered from Western movies. None that seemed to fit in with Jack. Certainly cowboys didn't want bakery goods! Jack belonged in drugstores, swimming behind Pete's, or playing basketball in a school gym somewhere. I couldn't imagine him anywhere else. It struck me then that he hadn't said *where* in Oklahoma he was going to live, but I felt sure it would be way down near the southern border; probably almost into Texas. There was an old geography book in Kitty's bedroom, I knew, but I didn't want to look the state up; I didn't want to know how many miles there were between Wisconsin and Oklahoma.

Jack came over early that night and dried the supper dishes for me. After that we sat out on the front steps. I needed to talk to him alone, even if I didn't know what I wanted to say. The night air was warm and filmy, hanging loose around us like thin, black chiffon. Beside the front steps the pine trees were fragrant with the same cool spicy smell that lingers over pine forests. Yet there was a quiet lonesomeness about that night, a poignant stillness that made my voice sound small and hushed, hardly like my own.

"Jack, I forgot to ask you where you are going to live in Oklahoma." He was sitting two steps below, resting on his elbows with his head back and his hair almost touching my hand.

"We're going right back to where we came from," he explained without turning. "It's a pretty big place called Shawnee — about third largest in the state next to Tulsa. I went all through grade school there."

I remembered then that earlier in the summer his cousin had mentioned a little girl in a white house who used to live near Jack; a little girl Jack had liked. It was a white house with pine trees in front of it, his cousin had said. And probably it had green shutters and a broad back lawn, the kind of house a pretty girl would live in. I wondered vaguely, not really caring, if she were still there.

220

It would be a different life without him: I could feel it already. Probably I would slip back and back into the old self-consciousness that made even walking into McKnight's an agony. But it wouldn't do to have him know what I was thinking. "What are you going to do down there?" I asked. After all, we still had almost a month left.

"Well, I'll still be with my dad, of course. My uncle has a bakery there and we'll all work together. Dad thinks he can make a go of it." And suddenly his tone was casually defensive. "I suppose you wish I were going to school some more, don't you, Angie?"

All summer long he had talked as if I were ashamed of his not going to college; as if he were ashamed of it himself. He went on now in the same half-apologetic voice, "I'd like to, Angie — you know that. But I've got to stick with my dad. I guess I'll have to get educated my own way."

. . . Without Jack there would be no more Swede or Fitz and no more nights at Pete's. All the summer days would slip by as they had in other years, not meaning anything. There would be no reason for sunshine or the tangy, fishy wind off the lake. It made my throat ache with lonesomeness even when he was sitting so close to me that I could smell the clean soapiness of him and could have touched his hair with my hand.

He lit a cigarette and I could smell the blue smoke I couldn't even see in the darkness.

"Angie," he said, turning to me, "I think I'm growing out of the bakery business. I can't tell my dad that — not yet — but it's not what I want to do all my life. He gets sort of a happiness out of it but I am tired of it already. I'm tired of sweet sugar smells." He pondered a moment, with his lips puckered in thought. "There's something . . . disgusting about eating anyway."

Just as he couldn't tell his dad, so I hadn't been able to mention it to him, but I had never liked it, either — his being a baker. It didn't seem right that a tall boy with such a fuzzy crew cut and smooth sunburned skin should wear a big white baker's hat and work with vanilla and powdered sugar all day.

"Have you decided what you would like to do instead, Jack?"

"I don't just know, Angie. But I like to do 'hard' things. Sometimes I think I would even like to be a farmer. I still have some relatives out in Rosendale who farm — it's good, clean work. Last summer I spent about two weeks with them and I loved it. I talked to the fellows about jobs to see what they wanted to be and that, but Swede doesn't care much what he does and Fitz thinks he'd like to work in a men's store — he *cares* a lot about neckties and things."

He puffed at his cigarette. "I wouldn't like that because I like to do things that make me feel big. I like to row a boat; I like to lift heavy boxes down at the bakery — things that make you feel as if you have muscles." His voice grew louder as he talked about it. "I don't know if you know what I mean, Angie."

"I do, I do," I exclaimed, surprised to realize I knew exactly what he meant. "I know what you mean, Jack — it's like shaking rugs out of an upstairs window on a spring day. You can *feel* things — the air is cool and it's good to have a grip on something. The feeling comes to you through your hands, you can feel it on your cheek — you can almost *see* what you feel, it is so wonderful. Is that what you mean, Jack?"

222

"That's just it, Angie! You've got it," he said in excitement. "I never knew that anyone else felt like that. I'd like to do work that made me feel all the time the way I feel when I'm swimming — as if my legs are long and hard. I *feel* the way they *look* in the water." He was talking fast and holding my hand so tightly that my knuckles hurt. He realized what he was doing then and both of us laughed.

"Gee, Angie, it's a relief to talk to a girl who knows what a fellow's talking about."

He stuck his legs out in front of him, stretching and leaning back, looking up at the sky. The night was so pricked bright with stars, like a page from an astronomy book, it hardly looked real. His voice went on in a dream singsong. "What I'd really like to be is a transport pilot, Angie. I'd like to take a ship up at night when it was as black as this and you wouldn't even be able to see me. The tail light and the wing lights would look like stars and no one would know there had even been a plane up there at all till they noticed there were three stars gone."

He was leaning back so that my hand touched the warm brownness of his neck and his crewcut felt fuzzy against my bare knees like the fur of a teddy bear. "Way, way up," he whispered to himself, "so the moon would shine on the wings."

After a little while Lorraine came out. She had spent all evening in the bathroom combing and recombing her hair, parting it first on one side and then the other, critically. Now it was twisted up in tight curlers and knotted in a big red kerchief. Her face looked very small and pinched with no soft hair fluffed around it.

"Hear you're going to Oklahoma, Jack," she commented sharply, as she sat down on the steps

223

beside us. "You're lucky. Wish I were getting away from this town myself."

"He won't be going away for a month though," I told her. "He won't leave until I leave for school," and I felt suddenly reassured for having said it. If I could actually talk about it I mustn't care so much myself!

Jack didn't stay long after that — he and I couldn't really talk with Lorraine there — but after he had gone we stayed out on the steps, thinking in silence. It was a night for thinking. I sat with my hand around my knees trying to urge myself into a belief that everything I had heard that day was true. Lorraine was picking apart a sprig of fir tree with her sharp fingernails.

I don't know how long we stayed there, without saying a word, and I didn't even hear her speak until she repeated loudly, "Angie, did you or didn't you?"

"Did I or didn't I what, Lorraine?"

"I said," she repeated with slow sarcasm, "None of you ever liked Martin very well from the beginning, *did you?*"

His absence had been brooding silently over the whole house ever since the Sunday of his birthday when he had broken the date with Lorraine, and I knew the tension would have to crack sometime. He was the kind of boy that a whole family remembers and, often, wholly unrelated things would make me think suddenly of his hands and the odd habit he had of slowly flexing and unflexing his fingers as he looked at them and the perpetual soft sarcasm around his mouth. But Lorraine was waiting for me to answer.

"We liked him — of course, we did, Lorraine. Mom asked him to come with us on the Fourth of

July picnic, didn't she? And we always were nice to him when he came over. . . ."

She had been so quietly thoughtful all evening that I was almost afraid to hear what she was going to say next.

"You weren't nice to him, Angie. You weren't rude to him but you weren't nice to him, either, none of you. But none of you ever understood him, that was all." There was no resentment, no bitterness. It was just something she wanted to say and she was saying it.

"You know, you didn't like him because he was different from us. He cared about different things and thought that other things mattered. That's why I liked him. He is a big-city boy all the way through."

Her words were hurrying out now, one after another and I could tell it was almost a relief to her to be talking. "I learned things from him that I never knew about before," she went on. "Lots of things — I know what it means when people are really happy, when they are really alive. You all feel sorry for me — you and Margaret and Art — but I don't care. I saw him lots of times when none of you even knew I was out with him!" she added triumphantly. "I can't even count how many times I've been with him, it's been so many. You will never know all the things we talked about and all the things he said. I know everything about him. I know what he likes to drink and how he smokes a cigarette and what kind of clothes he likes a girl to wear and how he looks when he's angry — you all thought I just dated him like any other boy. You didn't know he *liked* me, did you?

"And no matter what ever happens," she said defiantly, "no matter what ever, ever happens; no

225

matter what anyone thinks and no matter whether I ever see him again — I'm not sorry!"

She was no longer talking to me. She was only saying out loud the things that had been pounding in her head for days and days and the words came out now, cold and calm, as if she knew very well what each one meant but didn't care anymore. Sitting there, I felt oddly that I had never even known the girl; that she wasn't my sister at all. Not now.

The moments were long and tense as if both of us were waiting for something, somewhere, to answer, to make her take back what she had said. And suddenly her hands were limp on her knee and her voice was slow and heavy, "Angeline, I don't know why I'm pretending when it isn't true. This isn't how I meant to grow up. I've heard of other girls . . . but that isn't how I meant to be. I don't want to pretend . . . but nothing will ever be the same anymore!"

She sighed with a little tired sound and I kept looking up at the stars, not wanting to see her face just then. And when she spoke again her tone was as dull, as flat as milk of magnesia, "Oh well, Angie. I guess it doesn't make much difference anyway."

We stayed there a long, long time for there was a soothing kindness in the wind and in the restful silence of the night and it was I who moved to go into the house first. Lorraine followed. My mother had been asleep for hours and the house was quiet with the breathing quiet of sleeping people.

My heart felt so hard it hurt inside me and as we tiptoed upstairs Lorraine touched my arm, whispering, "Angie, don't tell any one I mentioned him, will you? Everything will be all right. I guess the night just . . . got me." She laughed to herself. "Don't worry. I won't ever mention him again."

It seemed only moments until morning and I woke with the sound of my mother's voice calling. The fever flush was still in her cheeks as I brought her a drink of ice water and her voice was still incredibly tired. It gave me an odd chill in the early aloneness of the morning. The hem of the sky was just faintly pink as I pulled her shades against the rising sun and, shutting the door softly, I went down into the half-light of the living room. Sleepy-eyed and curious, the dog came up from the basement, her tail wagging slowly in a contented stupor.

Once up I hated to go back to bed, so I made fresh coffee in the kitchen, deciding to wait up until the others waked. Kinkee nosed companionably around my bare ankles and then, lying down in the corner, went back to sleep. Except for the intermittent hiccup of the coffee pot percolating on the stove the house was quiet, breathlessly quiet. I opened the window wide to look out at the garden, fresh, green, and awake in the early morning with the clean smell of growing things. The air was like crystal and slowly the sun came up, sending streaks of apricot light across the blue of the sky. The cool air seemed to go straight down to the tips of my fingers as I breathed.

Is is odd how one can feel like someone else early in the morning — bigger, cleaner, so much more alive. The dew on the back lawn, caught with sunlight, the quick twittering of the sparrows in the hedges — all seemed to be happening especially for me. It was going to be another August day, mellowed with sun; another day for thinking and feeling everything. It was wonderful and even the thought of Oklahoma didn't seem so gray in the freshness of the morning. We still had a month between us.

The strong smell of the coffee, the wind coming in from the lake, and the very fact that it was morning, filled me with a new exhilaration so that I dared to let myself play with a thought that I had shooed from my mind for the last two days. Such adult boldness is almost sinful, but ever since Jack told me in the truck behind Pete's I had wondered. But no matter how hard I tried to imagine, my lips wouldn't say it. Love is such a big word.

Later that day I brought the stepladder from the garage into the house to get the two big trunks for school out of the attic. Carefully I eased them, one at a time, out of the trap door in the roof, while Kitty stood below holding the ladder and chattering directions up at me. Both locks had to be fixed and I cleaned the trunks out carefully before sending them away with the repairman. In one was an old blue gym suit and a pair of gray rubber tennis shoes that made the inside of the trunk smell like old balloons. In the other were some papers of Lorraine's from school — an incomplete chemistry notebook, a sheaf of English themes, and a dance program with a browned gardenia stuck between the covers. The gym suit I threw into the clothes hamper and put the tennis shoes in the garbage can, but the other things I saved for Lorraine.

When she came home that afternoon I asked her what should be done with them.

"What did you find, Angie?"

"Just some old papers, a dance program, and a withered gardenia that looked as if it might have been a souvenir," I explained. She looked them over curiously, leafing through the papers, and then picked up the dance program. "This is from the spring dance of my sophomore year. So is the flower," she mused, and then suddenly gathered them all together in a crumpled heap.

"Just burn them, Angie," she said. "I'm not going to save anything anymore."

By evening my mother was feeling well enough to sit on the back lawn in a garden chair, still weak and thin-voiced but her cheeks had cooled. I asked her if she would mind my going out for a little while that night and she answered, "Of course not, dear. You go. Lorraine and Margaret will be here with me, and besides I think I will only sit up for a little while anyway." It worried me to hear her, for I knew she was patient and soft-voiced like that only when she was very tired. She is more gentle then because she hates to bother anyone by being ill. There is always a sadness about her.

Jack had asked me to go for a ride that evening and he and Swede came over together to pick me up. He came down the back sidewalk, his face flushed with embarrassment, Swede trailing behind. "I certainly hope you're feeling better, Mrs. Morrow," he faltered. "Angie told me you were in bed yesterday and I thought maybe you would like this." He had been balancing a pie very carefully between two cardboard pie plates and he held it out to her.

"I asked my mother," he explained, "and she said that even if you weren't feeling well this would be all right to eat because it's lemon and there's only simple things in the filling."

My mother was surprised into silence but Margaret, sitting beside her, spoke up quickly saying,

"Why, Jack, you honey! If that isn't nice. I just hope there's enough for a piece for all of us."

He smiled sheepishly and Lorraine took the pie from his clumsy hands, bringing it into the house. I heard her open the icebox door to slip it in.

"Really, Jack I can't tell you when I've been so pleasantly surprised." My mother's voice quavered a little. I couldn't tell if she were going to laugh or cry — sometimes she cries at the most surprising things. "Are you sure you and your friend wouldn't like to have a piece with us now!"

"Oh, I'm sorry," I interrupted, "I didn't introduce you, did I? Mom, this is Swede Vincent, and Swede, these are my sisters, Lorraine and Margaret, and the little one, Kitty, is out playing along the block somewhere."

They exchanged hellos, Swede jerking his head forward to each in turn, and then there was an awkward silence. "Swede is the one who sails the boat so well," I ventured.

"Of course, I remember," and my mother took it up smoothly. "You graduated in June with Jack, didn't you?"

Swede answered with a few embarrassed nods and a few mumbled words, smiling as if his face were starched. No one would ever believe he had been one of the most popular boys in the senior class last year. He seemed so uncomfortable I suggested almost at once that we leave and he sighed audibly, bowing to my mother with a hasty, "Very glad to have met you, ma'am" as he backed down the sidewalk. Jack nudged me and laughed.

Safe in the car, with the motor running, he soon got his confidence back. "Which one of those sisters was which now, Angie," he asked.

I explained that the one who had taken the pie

from Jack was Lorraine and that the other one was Margaret. "That's the one I meant," he exclaimed with relish. "The one with the long hair and the low voice. That's what I call cute," and he licked his lips in mock appreciation. "Boy, that's something!" All his old swagger was back now.

Jack nudged me again quietly and winked.

Swede had a date with Dollie that evening and we had to cross the railroad tracks and drive beyond the river to get to her street. The house was gray and shabby and across the front ran a low wooden porch that sagged down to a mud lawn, pounded hard and flat as if children played on it often. There was a little red wagon across the sidewalk.

"Just honk!" Swede said. "Dollie don't like me to come in after her."

Jack honked the horn sharply twice and someone swung open the front door, bawling, "She'll be right out!" and the door bounced back on its hinges. The top half was made of screening and the lower half was of brown cardboard, stuck in the wooden frame, and on one side of the porch was an old car seat, set up as a couch.

"Dollie's the oldest," Swede explained, half in apology. "There's four kids younger."

Just then an upstairs window screeched in its sash and Dollie stuck her head out and waved, "Be right with you, Swede," and the window slammed down again. A few moments later she ran out, banging the door behind her.

"Hi, there, kids," she said to Jack and me, and "Hello, you big thing" to Swede, snuggling up to him playfully. Her face is so round and her mouth so baby-soft that next to Swede she looked like a doll.

"Is Pete's all right with you?" Jack asked.

And from the back seat Swede shouted, "Don't know where else!"

Long hot days and sudden rains had given Pete's a stuffy, musty smell and shot new, crooked cracks through the plaster. There were still ribbons of red, white, and blue crepe paper twisted in the lattice around the booths, hangovers from the Fourth of July, and the jukebox was blaring out music that rocked to the ceiling. We took a back booth and Swede ordered a Coke for Dollie, lit her cigarette, and went out to the bar. "He always does that," she giggled.

The old parrot in the corner was scrawking to itself, irritated with the heat, and the floor around the cage was littered with broken peanut shells, and the old bird swayed on the perch, breast feathers ruffled. It was cross and so dirty that we always took a booth as far away from the cage as possible.

Jack and I danced together once and then Swede came back from the bar, crowding Dollie into the corner of the booth as he sat down, nudging her with his elbow till she giggled at him to stop. "You old meanie," she pouted. While we had been dancing she had printed her initials and Swede's on the wall with lipstick and was coyly waiting for him to notice. She looked at me and giggled again.

But he finished his cigarette, flipped the butt at the parrot who scrawked and fluttered on the perch, rolling its yellow eyes in anger, and said, rising, "Let's get out of this firetrap. This is the kind of night to be outside," and he winked at Dollie. She drank down the rest of her Coke quickly and followed him, fluffing out her short hair with her fingers, signaling to us to come on. I guess she forgot all about the initials.

"We might as well go too, Angie," Jack suggested. "We can take a ride and, if you like, we can come back here again later."

In the car we turned the four windows down and the night wind came in, gentle and cool as water. Dollie sang as we drove in a soft, round voice as if her lips were pouted, and Swede joined her with a low boy-voice, improvising bass notes and joining in on the chorus. It was a beautiful summer night.

Jack turned off the main highway onto a dry country road that spat up gravel against the sides of the car and sent bits of stone stinging at the windshield. The road twisted before us, taffy-colored in the moonlight, and the moon shifted first from the right side and then to the left as we turned, laying shadows all around us. Dollie's singing dropped off to a quiet hum and then, after a while, stopped altogether. We drove and drove and the landscape was weirdly melancholy in the moonlight, touched with a lonesomeness and mystery that eluded it in the daytime. The trees along the roadside showed a light side to the moon, but secretly shielded the quiet, black shadows that lurked behind them, while on either side the fields lay flat and open. Something about the whole night made me want to whisper.

We were far out in the heart of the country now, lonesome with single barns and dark silos. Jack turned into a narrow, muddy lane, and bushes reaching out along the ditch brushed the car. The wheels caught in the deep, dry ruts and swerved to one side. "Jack," I said, "let's stop here."

Without saying a word, without asking why, he

pulled the car to one side and shut off the motor. Swede and Dollie were silent in the back seat. To the right was a broad field, spotted with dark bushes and rimmed with a line of dark trees. Behind them the moonlight was clear and mellow, sending long, lean shadows across the ground like thin fingers. "Jack, I'd like to go for a walk right now. Not far. Just out to where those bushes are," and I pointed.

Swede sat up straight in the back seat and shouted, "You kids *crazy?* If I'd known you wanted to go walking we could have left you in town to walk round the park!"

"I just want to go as far as those dark bushes, Swede," I explained, turning round to him. "It all looks so odd in the moonlight and I've never walked in a field like that at night before. Don't you and Dollie want to come?"

"No, thanks," he answered, his voice slurring, "Dollie and me can be more comfortable right here in the car!"

Jack leaned over to open my door and the thick roadside weeds brushed as high as the running board. I stepped through them carefully and he took my hand to jump the low ditch at the edge of the road. Puddles from the last rain lay in the hollows, glassy in the moonlight, and the ground on the other side was spongy beneath our feet.

As we ran across the field the ground was bumpy beneath our feet like pastureland and I could hear him breathing hard as we went. Night dew was on the grass, cool and wet about my ankles, and here and there grew clumps of wild field daisies, their petals still open and white in the moonlight. Jack let go my hand and ran ahead. I tried to keep up with him, laughing and panting, stumbling in the

234

darkness while my feet slipped on the wet ground. He didn't stop till he had reached the trees and waited there till I came panting up to him, my shoes heavy with clay. The trees were farther apart than they had seemed at a distance, with broad, squat, half-stumps in between. I sat down on one of these to rest, and the sides were furred with layers of white fungus that crumbled like paper between my fingers, giving the air a damp, mossy smell like wet, brown leaves. Jack sat down beside me.

From where we sat we could just barely see the car, black and shadowy at the edge of the gravel road with a small red wink of a tail light. No one but Jack would have come out here with me, without even asking why. I guess he *knew* why. We were near the dark clump of bushes I had seen from the car and the leaves were cool against my arm, their undersides wet with dew. I was still panting from running and laughing at the same time, a delicious feeling. The trees around us were old and tall, with thin, straight trunks and leaves that rustled high above us. Something quick, probably a rabbit, moved in the bushes.

"I'm glad we came out here," Jack whispered to me. "You can't really see the moon from inside the car." I nodded.

A leaf from the bushes brushed my hand and I recognized the touch. Picking one of them I handed it to Jack. "Feel this," I urged. "Feel how fuzzy it is on the other side. These are probably wild raspberry bushes."

He rubbed it gently against his cheek. "Oh, yeah," and his voice was slow with awe. "It feels just how Dollie looks like *she* feels — from looking at her, I mean." I laughed to myself to hear him.

235

Between the trees thick weeds grew high, black and secret in the moonlight; everything a different shade of darkness. All around us were muted night sounds as if the trees and bushes were whispering among themselves. Both of us sat listening. "Angie," he said suddenly, "did you know there is no such thing as sound!"

"What do you mean — no such thing as 'sound'?"

"Well, I'm not sure if I can explain it to you," he went on, "but it's what our teacher told us in science last year. For instance, if you break a balloon or something there really is no sound. There are sound *waves* sent out but unless there are ears — on people, of course — to pick up the vibrations, there is no sound."

"That hardly sounds right to me," I puzzled . . . "I never heard anything like that before."

"Sure, Angie, and the teacher told us that long ago, in cavemen times, if those big dinosaurs went crashing through the forest, if there was no one there to hear them, there was no noise at all! Do you see now what I mean?" he asked.

"Maybe I do," I told him. "But it still doesn't seem quite right. If the dinosaurs made noise and still it couldn't be heard, I wonder what happened to it?"

He put his arm around my shoulder. "Now look, Angie, it's like this. Listen. Say that right now we aren't here, you and I. Say we're back in the car with Swede and Dollie or that we're still out at Pete's. There's no one here. There isn't a single car on that whole stretch of road. All of a sudden one of these trees cracks in the trunk and falls over. There is vibration but there is no sound at all because there is no one here to hear it. Now do you see?"

I tried to crowd my thoughts into one small space to concentrate. In my mind I could see the bare field in the moonlight with the dark row of trees standing. It was deadly silent. No sound. No one to hear. Suddenly one of the trees sways a little, its top branches heavy. It sways again and then suddenly it topples over and falls full length on the ground. But it made no noise at all. It was like a feather falling on feathers. But the thought of the tall tree so silent in the darkness was eerie, almost terrifying, and I shivered. Jack's arm tightened round my shoulder, "Cold?" he asked. I shook my head.

I knew Swede and Dollie would be wondering where we were, what was taking us so long, but there were things I wanted to talk to Jack about. I had wanted to talk to him for a long time. For months there had been something inside of me, a disturbed, excited feeling as if there was something I should do at once but I was never sure just what it was. I thought Jack would understand. It was such a quick, urgent feeling and yet all very bewildering. I felt that I should learn to dance better; that I should know how to drive a car; that I should read more. It seemed suddenly as if I had never done anything in my life — that everything was still ahead — and I wanted to know if Jack felt some of the same eager restlessness. I wanted to know but I didn't know how to ask.

"Jack," I ventured, "tell me something. Don't you wish sometimes that you had studied more in school? That you hadn't wasted so much time?"

His answer was hesitant. "I don't know as I'd say that, Angie. I had a pretty good time."

He didn't understand what I meant so I tried again. "But, Jack, don't you feel sometimes that you should have read more — that you've wanted your mind to be bigger so you could understand what goes on? You know what I mean. . . ." He was sitting looking out into the darkness, hardly listening.

I wanted him to understand so badly, I almost shook him. "Jack, Jack, listen to me. This is important. I got it figured that I could be a smart girl and a smooth girl if I wasn't scared of so many things — if I didn't spend so much time wondering why I'm not what I'm not. I could be as smooth as Jane Rady if I stopped thinking about myself, don't you know that, Jack?

"You and I could start now to work on ourselves so we would be, maybe, great people when we grow up. I could brush my hair every night and you could read a lot so we would really be something. Do you see what I mean, Jack? Everything can be so wonderful if you work at it. . . ."

Somehow I still hadn't said what I wanted to say and the words tripped over each other, trying to sort out the right ones. "It's just that I feel we are wasting time. I think we are different from Fitz and Margie and Dollie — and even from Swede. Jack, it seems sometimes that I can't ever do things 'enough.' When I eat, everything tastes so good I can't get all the taste out of it; when I look at something — say, the lake — the waves are so green and the foam so white that it seems I can't look at it hard enough; there seems to be something there that I can't get at. And even when I'm with you, I can't seem to be with you . . . enough." That wasn't quite what I had meant to say and I let the words trail off awkwardly.

The night was suddenly very quiet except for the wind in the trees and the sound of the crickets singing — a pulsing chant that hung low to the ground. It was a pregnant, breathing silence and the whole field was throbbing with the still mystery of shadows and moonlight. I realized then that Jack hadn't been listening to me at all. He was watching me and his hand was on mine and his face was very serious in the dim light. His hand was on mine and then I felt the light touch on my wrist that sent a vague stirring through me and then his fingers were warm on my arm. The night seemed to be waiting; too still. "Jack," I whispered. "Jack, whatever is the matter with you!"

His voice was low, almost husky. "You know darn well what's the matter," he said.

But I didn't. I really didn't, and in a few moments I took his hand and we crossed back over the field to the quiet car.

After a while I tried not to count the days. Each night when I went to bed I pretended that I was just going to bed and nothing more; that it didn't mean marking off another day. I tried not to let myself think, "This is Friday and after this weekend we will have three more and that will be all." I fixed my dreams so carefully that I woke each morning almost believing that this was the beginning of the summer and not the end.

But even if it was only August there were already signs of summer's dying everywhere. The poppies in the garden that had been tousled pink blossoms only a few weeks before were now full-blown and hung heavy with bursting seed pods, scattering the seed like little black bugs to the earth. The corn leaves dried in the sunlight and rustled with wind, while the fine, silken hair that hung from the ears shriveled, tobacco-brown. And I knew by the tomatoes that summer was ending. The vines sprawled luxuriantly over the earth still, but the runt tomatoes ripened before they were full-grown, not trusting the sun to shine many weeks longer. Small, white-cocooned webs of spider eggs appeared on the undersides of the clapboards of the house. There was a new ripe lushness about everything; not a fresh, bright greenness as in early summer but a full, heavy maturity that made everything look overripe and basking in the sun.

Jack noticed the change, too, and drove me out to look at the lake one afternoon. Dog days had come and the lake was thick with sea grass, rolling toward us in full, lazy, green swells. Water birds, with white arcs of wings, swooped low, reveling in the warmth of the air. It was almost impossible to feel sad. There was too much hidden excitement in the weather itself.

And something had changed in me too. What in the beginning had been a quick, breathless thrill was now a warm, beating gratitude that bordered on contentment. A strange, bewildering contentment. My feelings toward Jack were different now, fuller, richer. I was no longer afraid to look into his eyes or to touch his hand when I talked to him. I felt much older than I had in June and just being with him made my lips feel softer, smoother.

One night we went to the Fond du Lac County Fair — Fitz, Margie, Jack, and I. The fair is an annual county event and stirs our town for days. Weeks before, black and white banners had been hung low over Main Street, announcing the coming horse races and stock show, and little boys stuck handbills on front porches, printed with splashy ads for the carnival features and sideshows. All the rest of the year the buildings at the fairgrounds stood drab and empty, but for the week of the fair they were sprayed with whitewash and little red and blue flags shot up along the roofs and around the doorways. For several days before, the rutted roads that led from the main highway into the fairgrounds were lined with truck loads of vegetables and noisy livestock, and farmers led in their prize horses, the tails braided stumpy with ribbon and the manes shiny. The whole fairgounds reeked with an earthy, animal smell.

We went to the fair the third night after its opening and it was as crowded as a dance floor with people bumping and jostling, shoving along. Fitz and Margie were waiting for us just inside the gates. It was still early so we decided to leave the Ferris wheel till later and walk by the sideshow tents, looking at the gaudy-colored posters and watching the barkers and come-on girls first. We saw people craning their necks in front of the Hawaiian tent show and we stopped too. It was advertised as the largest show on the grounds and the barker wore a bright-red shirt and a flower *lei* twisted around his neck. There was a bare wooden stage with two hairy-stemmed palm trees on each end and four girls in the center, swaying gently, disinterestedly. Fitz whistled loudly between his teeth and Margie nudged him in the ribs, giggling and whispering. Other people crowded around us, shoving and pushing until we four stood almost at the edge of the platform. The barker shouted and pounded on the ticket box till the crowd grew larger, pressing in a gaping semicircle all around the tent, while the four girls waited, talking among themselves and staring down at the faces staring

241

up at them. When the crowd got large enough one of them brought a ukelele from the tent, plunking at it tunelessly, singing as she played while the others twisted and swayed in a loose-hipped hula, coarse grass skirts swishing noisily as they moved. They all wore flat tennis shoes and no stockings and their legs were red with welts of mosquito bites.

The blond dancer on the end was younger than the rest and she kept watching Jack with a slow, easy smile as she danced. "That one on the end's got a case on you," Fitz remarked, his hand over his mouth. The girl on the stage whispered something to the dancer next to her and they both looked at Jack, laughing and thinking with their eyes.

"Let's get out of here," he said suddenly, pushing his way through the crowd behind him.

But Fitz caught his arm. "Naw, wait, Jack," he urged. "This is good. I want to see what happens."

Just then the girl with the ukelele twanged out a weak finale and the dancers turned to troop in under the flap of the tent. "Only ten cents for each and every one of you. Women and children alike," the barker shouted, slamming down the tickets. "Ten cents for the biggest musical dancing show on the grounds! Show going on inside at once — only ten cents. Get your tickets here!"

Just as she turned to go in the tent, the blonde called back to Jack, "Come on in, boy. For kids like you it's free — all of it." She looked at him a moment with her queer, easy smile and followed the others inside.

"Wow!" Fitz exploded. "You've got it on the ball! I want to see the rest of this!"

"We're not going in," Jack said, tersely.

"Come on," Margie pleaded in a sugar voice.

"This is the first thing we've run across tonight that's really been fun. Come on, Angie, tell him to come on in. This is good."

I looked at Jack but said nothing for I didn't want to go in, either — women like that frighten me. Around us people who had heard the girl call to Jack stood waiting, staring curiously to see what he would do.

His face was dark and angry and he muttered to Fitz, "Shut up and get out of here." Fitz looked at him open-mouthed and then followed us through the crowd.

"Gee, Jack," he said in a puzzled voice when he caught up to him, "I didn't want to get you mad. I didn't think —"

"Let's just forget it," Jack answered abruptly.

"But, gee, Jack, all I said was —"

"Skip it, Fitz, will you?" and Jack turned and walked the other way.

After that the evening was spoiled. Fitz kept trying to explain that he really hadn't meant anything and Jack kept saying that was all right he wasn't angry; and yet all the time he was scowling and walking along stiffly with his hands in his pockets, hardly looking even at me. Just to break the tension, I suggested we go up in the Ferris wheel. In the seat above us, Fitz kept rocking till Margie squealed in fright but Jack just sat beside me, looking down and saying nothing. Beneath us the people were only round, dark heads and the lights were strung in bright necklaces around the booths and tents. We could look out past the fairgrounds to the highway where the car headlights were creeping in a bright line and the whole scene below us looked like a needlework picture in black and yellow.

Back on the ground we walked past a fun house with ugly pasteboard faces stuck on the front of it that let out groans and weird music, while inside the people shrieked and laughed, muffled by the walls. We passed hot-dog stands, and popcorn stands that smelled deliciously of hot butter, and a lemonade booth with lukewarm lemonade in a huge glass barrel, floating with lemon rings; and we stood watching the merry-go-round with bright, dappled horses, shrilling out its loud, up-and-down music. But the fair wasn't fun any more. Jack wasn't enjoying it and he showed it. His hands were still jammed in his pockets and he hardly heard me when I spoke to him.

The crowds, jostling and pushing, were suddenly annoying, while earlier in the evening they had all been part of the fun of the fair. Sometimes large families brushed past, all the children holding hands and gaping, trailing along in a line, their faces solemn with awe. Jack tripped over a taut rope from one of the tents and swore under his breath. I had never heard him swear before.

We were swept with the crowd before a large, open-faced tent where the barker was yelling, "Three balls for a dime, ladies and gentlemen. Three balls for a dime, ten for a quarter. Step right up and try your luck!"

At the back of the tent white wooden milk bottles were pyramided on a box and along the sides of the tent were shelves lined with canes, dolls, and fancy candy boxes for prizes. A fat man was throwing balls when we came, puffing as he threw, and his wife stood beside him, holding his coat and laughing till she shook. She was as fat as he was with cheeks like pink marshmallows.

"Fitz, win me something," Margie cried, in her

petulant, going-steady voice. "You used to play baseball a lot."

"All right, honey. You pick out what you want. Give me three balls," he said to the man. Margie and Jack and I stepped back to give him room.

With the first three balls he tried too hard and his aim was bad. He tipped over one bottle and the other two balls bounced off the canvas back of the tent. "Give me three more," he said, trying to be casual. "I didn't know those balls were so light. But I think I've got the hang now." He took three more and wound up carefully before he threw them. It looked so easy, watching, but this time none of the balls even hit the box. His neck was dull red.

"Gimme ten," he said, sullenly, fishing in his pocket for a quarter.

We all stood waiting while he rolled the ball around in the palm of his hand, winding up slowly, and threw. This time he knocked two of the end bottles down and his face relaxed and with four more balls he knocked down the other six bottles. He was grinning now and Margie was smiling in a sort of relief. "What do I get?" he asked the man.

"Eight bottles with five balls will entitle you to a genuine gold-headed cane," the barker answered pompously, taking a little wooden cane off the shelf and handing it to Margie. It was enameled red with a gilt top tied with a piece of braid and she stuck it under her arm like a drum major, beaming at Fitz.

"What are you going to do with the other five balls?" I asked him.

"Jack, why don't you try throwing," he offered generously. "Get a cane for Angie, too."

"No, thanks," he said. "Not in the mood."

"Go ahead, Jack," Margie urged. "If Fitz can do it you can. . . ."

He took the balls from the man and eyed the milk bottles carefully. His fingers were supple on the ball and he weighed it casually in the palm of his hand before he threw. His aim was sure and easy and three end bottles toppled and with the next ball the center bottle supporting the rear and the last four bottles rolled off the box.

"Well, good for you," Margie said, tonelessly. And Fitz slapped him on the back.

Even the barker looked surprised. "You just shouldn't throw so hard," Jack explained to Fitz. "Those balls are light and so are the bottles."

"I guess you win," the man said and took a doll from the top shelf. Jack handed it to me. It was a kewpie doll with feathers glued on behind so they stuck out around its head like a peacock's tail.

"Maybe Kitty would like it," he said, and "Thanks for the balls," to Fitz. Margie was annoyed now and trying to smile through a pout. She was annoyed because Jack had thrown the balls better than Fitz and because he had won a doll for me with Fitz's balls, and her lower lip stuck out like a sulky baby's.

We turned away from the tent and Fitz went to take her hand but she pulled it away in irritation. "I can walk by myself," she said.

Everyone was so cross by now that I suggested we go home, but Fitz burst out, "We haven't had anything to eat yet! What's the matter with you, Angie? You don't want to eat or go into sideshows or anything."

"Leave her alone," Jack said. "You're in a worse mood than I am, Fitz," and they looked at each other crossly. Suddenly Fitz reached over and gave him a playful punch in the ribs and Jack poked him back and they laughed sheepishly.

"If you two boys don't mind, I wish you would excuse us for a few minutes," Margie said primly. "We'll meet you somewhere, in a little while."

"Sure," Jack assented. "And we'll meet you . . . where, Fitz?"

"Make it in front of that hot-dog stand by the main gate," he answered. "Don't get your faces too painted up," he added teasingly, trying to catch Margie's eye, but she wouldn't look at him.

"Come on, Angie," she said crossly.

I turned back as we went and saw the fellows walking toward the shooting range where little mechanical ducks floated by on a revolving belt as targets, and I wanted secretly to go back to watch to see if Jack was better at rifle shooting too. Margie turned toward the Fine Arts Building where the 4H exhibits were on display. "I didn't really want anything," she explained. "Just wanted to get away for a few minutes." Her mouth was still twisted into a discontented pout and she tossed the gilt-topped cane away under one of the booths. "Too much bother to carry," she said.

We looked with mild interest at the sewing exhibits lined on the walls, pinned with yellow and blue prize ribbons. There were gingham aprons with carefully ironed frills, fancy square-legged pajamas, and gingham dresses with stiff puffed sleeves and sashes of the same material. Margie sniffed in derision. She reached over the railing to look at the ruching around the neck of one of the dresses and a woman with a large, toothy smile came over, saying with elaborate politeness, "Mustn't touch, girls!"

"Who wants to touch her old stuff?" Margie

said under her breath, as we walked away. "Let's get out of here."

We went into the Produce Building next door that was bright with the colors of curved yellow squash, scrubbed brown potatoes, and shiny jars of honey arranged on display. There were shelves lined with boxes of red and green apples arranged in designs and little early pumpkins with skins like orange wax, and the whole room had a sweet, clean smell like summer clover. But neither of us looked at the displays for Margie was thinking about something — I could tell by her restlessness — and she walked along listlessly, her thoughts far away. I had learned to know her so well during the summer that I knew something was wrong. And I knew if I waited patiently she would tell me when she was ready.

And just as I thought, she turned to me in a few moments. "Angie," she said, "I've been thinking about you all day. Fitz was telling me last night about Jack's going to Oklahoma and everything. I knew that you were going away to school, but doesn't this make things different?"

"It makes some difference, Margie, but what can we do? I have to go to school — in fact, I want to very much — and Jack naturally has to go where his family goes, so what *can* we do? I don't know just what you mean at all."

Her voice was irritated. "It's just like I said early this summer — you don't think like other girls and it makes me mad 'cause I can't figure you out. You never seem to 'worry' about Jack and try to do anything about it. . . . It seems to me that if you liked him like he likes you, you'd worry more about his going away."

I couldn't help laughing at her for she was so

cross that her face was screwed up like a Pekingese. "Margie," I said, "why don't you worry about yourself? There's nothing Jack and I can do. How about you and Fitz — you've been going together a long time and this is the first fall that you haven't gone back to school. . . ."

"I'll work somewhere," she answered, feeling suddenly important again and fluffing out her hair with her finger tips. "My dad knows some man in town who's going to get me a job in one of the department stores. . . . I'd tell you about it, but I don't know myself for sure."

"And how about Fitz?"

"He'll work too, I suppose," but her tone was disinterested, as if her thoughts were already on something else. "Maybe he'll just stay on at the fruit store where he is as regular help. I don't know."

There was a short silence before I ventured casually, "What's wrong, Margie?"

She turned on me suddenly, her eyes screwed up. "Honestly, Angie, I'm so mad tonight I could just cry! I should think you'd be able to see it — anyone could see it with any sense! I've been getting just a little tired of a lot of things lately and I think I'm just about through."

"I didn't notice anything," I fibbed politely. "Fitz always seemed to be such a nice boy to me."

She looked at me closely. "I suppose he is nice enough but do you think he has anything else. I mean — personality or ability? Sometimes he seems so dumb — like tonight, not even being able to throw baseballs — that I just hate him. Sometimes I wonder if I haven't spoiled my chances by going steady. . . . I don't even think he's as nice looking as I used to. . . ." She was watching me carefully, to catch any reaction. "What do you think, Angie?"

"The four of us have had so much fun together I thought you liked him real well," I told her, verbally sliding out from under.

"I haven't liked him since one night this July when we went for a walk and we stopped for a while to sit on the swings at a grade school playground. After a while we went on the little merry-go-round and he got so dizzy he had to get off. I don't know why," she said, "but every time I think of him getting dizzy I get so disgusted I can't stand to look at him."

The thought was topmost on my mind, "Why do you go with him then?" but before I could say a word she added, "But a girl has to go out with somebody!"

They had gone steady since the middle of their senior year and she had worn his class ring since March. And they had been out together every night all summer. To realize that the whole thing was a farce was depressing and I didn't know whether to be annoyed with Margie or sorry for her.

"Oh, well," she shrugged, "let's go back and find the fellows anyway," and her voice was brighter now. She is probably relieved now that she has told someone, I thought. She just wanted to get it off her mind.

"Of course," she added, in her old matter-of-fact tone. "You wouldn't mention what I told you to anyone, would you, Angie? I'm not ready to break up yet."

Jack and Fitz were waiting for us and we all sat down on the plain benches at the hot-dog stand and ordered wieners stuck in crisp buttered rolls, oozing with yellow mustard and tomato sauce. Margie ate three and seemed to feel better afterward. She and Fitz smoked a cigarette before we left and I noticed he was holding her hand under the counter. I thought then that everything was as it had been.

They had walked to the fair so we were all driving home in Jack's car. It was parked far over in the grass lot and when we had walked to it, Margie said unexpectedly, "Fitz, why don't you drive instead of Jack?"

"Instead of Jack!" he asked in surprise. "But why — Jack's a good driver!"

"Sure," said Jack. "Don't you trust me, Margie? I've never run you up a post yet!"

"I know it," she answered calmly. "But I want Fitz to drive this time," and she opened the door herself to get into the front seat. Fitz looked hurt but said nothing.

Jack just looked at me, shrugged his shoulders, and he and I got into the back seat. Fitz backed out carefully, then went forward so suddenly the gears shrieked. He was angry now but Margie didn't seem to care. "I'd like to go home first," she said quietly.

He drove into town and went straight down Main Street, turning left and then on toward Margie's street. His face was stiff and sullen. He pulled up at the curb without a word and went round the front of the car to open her door. She turned, said good night to us, and then they both walked up the front sidewalk without saying anything.

"Hey, what goes on there?" Jack asked me, his voice puzzled.

We sat waiting. The porch was screened in and thick with Virginia creeper vines, and the low hum of voices floated out to us. And then the hum died

251

out. We waited a long time and finally Fitz slammed the screen door and bounded down the steps and into the car.

He started the motor, turning toward us as if we had questioned him. "She said to call her tomorrow and she'll let me know. I guess everything will be all right . . . Gee, I don't know what gets into girls some times!"

No month of my life has ever gone so fast. Those last days seemed to slip through my fingers like egg white and I almost wished the end would come, for the waiting was so hopeless and so tantalizing. I did the housework each day as usual, sewed name tags on my clothing for school in the afternoon and tried not to think what would happen when those September days finally came.

Thoughts of September were on Jack's mind too. We had Cokes together in McKnight's one afternoon while my mother was shopping and he told me that his father had already made arrangements to sell most of the bakery equipment to a baker in Waupun. "My uncle has all the equipment we'll need in Oklahoma already."

"I'm going to give some of my things to Swede too, before I go. I've got things in my room I won't want to pack and I won't be needing my ice skates, either."

It was a warm afternoon and quiet. The druggist was dusting the shelves, removing the boxes and bottles, and rearranging them carefully, humming softly to himself. Neither Jack nor I spoke for a few moments but we were both thinking the same kind of thoughts. He had finished his Coke and was sitting sideways, one foot on the bench, smoking. Even the smoke was slow and lazy that afternoon, curling upward quietly.

Jack turned to me unexpectedly and, as if I had spoken first, said, "But, Angie, I couldn't have seen you much when you were away at school anyway!"

He stopped then and grinned, realizing I hadn't said a word. "Just thinking out loud, I guess."

His voice was earnest now. "I just want you to know for sure, Angie, that I don't *really* want to go to Oklahoma. . . ."

"I know it, Jack. It's just . . . well, I don't know . . . something." "Fate" was the word I had been thinking of.

"I can always come up to see you any time and you can come down to see me," he lied pleasantly, laughing at me.

"And over weekends you come up as far as Kansas City and I'll come down to meet you every Saturday night," I answered.

"Yep," he said and his face was serious again. "Honestly, though, Angie, I've got four-fifty already that I started to save toward coming down to Chicago to see you."

I felt my heart beat faster. "Really, have you, Jack? Maybe you *could* come up sometime then!"

"Sure, I could!" and he made his voice bright and confident, so confident that I knew he didn't mean it himself.

"What would your mother and dad say?" I asked, knowing in my heart that he was thinking exactly the same thing.

"What *could* they say, Angie? I'm pretty old now. I do mostly what I want."

"But they would want to know why you wanted to come back. It's so far. What could you ever tell them, Jack?"

"Maybe I could say I want to come back to see Swede and Fitz." He didn't laugh as he spoke and

253

I didn't feel like laughing, either. With the end only two weeks away it was no laughing matter.

Jack crushed his cigarette out with a thoughtful sigh. "Don't worry, Angie. I may not make it right away but I'll get up here again sometime."

Kitty and I worked in the garden for a whole day with the sun hot on our backs, pulling up the rows of overgrown vegetables and piling them in a heap in one corner of the garden to dry. The radishes had blossomed with white flowers and gone to seed, the round red radishes grown into long, gnarled roots, coarse and reedy. The leaves were rough and scratchy. Even the onions' stems were thick and bulbous, topped with purple flower clusters. In the late afteroon we were finished, hands scratched and legs muddy, and we cleaned ourselves while my mother set out tea for us on the back door step. While we sipped at our cups Kitty was lying on the lawn, chewing a bit of grass. "Too bad you have to go away, Angie," she piped up, " 'cause we are really going to have a fine fire when those things are dried."

I tried to pretend I hadn't heard her, but everything I did and saw and heard seemed to bring the days nearer to the end. Along the side of the house, the earlier hollyhocks had dropped their last blossoms and the seeds in the seed pods were like round, green overcoat buttons. The first asters were out, smoky-purple and heavy on the stems.

Lorraine came home from work early, even before I had set the table for supper. "We didn't have much to do this afternoon, so they let us out ahead of time," she explained. "The summer business has slowed up so we aren't very busy any more."

"I'm glad you came home," Mom said. "It

seems as if I've hardly seen you this summer at all — with one thing and another."

"I know it," she answered. "The first part went so fast and this last part is just dragging. At first everything seemed so busy and now it doesn't seem as if it should be summer any more at all." I was busy at the open kitchen window and heard their voices on the back lawn.

Lorraine spoke again and her tone was cautious. "This afternoon I was thinking, Mom, that if all of you don't mind . . . I'd like to go back to Chicago!"

My mother said something I couldn't hear but Lorraine objected, "But she won't have to come. Freshmen don't have to be there till the tenth of the month, but I just *want* to go back early. There are some girl friends I would like to visit — a couple of them asked me to stay with them if I ever got to the city. And besides," she added hastily, "I've got a lot of important reading to get finished before I take my English comprehensive exam this year and I would like to get a head start — before the regular homework gets too heavy."

At supper my mother told us that Lorraine had decided to go back. "Of course, I think you're crazy, but if you want to, go ahead," Margaret shrugged.

"Your father won't like it either," my mother objected, "but I suppose it's all right."

"I'll get a lot of reading done and having worked all summer, this will be like a vacation before starting school again," Lorraine explained. "I'll just take a few things and you can send the rest with Angie when she comes."

"It really seems a little foolish to me. . . ." My mother was still hesitant but it was decided. Lorrain would leave on Sunday.

That night in bed she nudged me, saying softly, "Asleep, Angie?"

"No. I'm awake," I whispered. "What do you want?"

She was lying staring up at the ceiling, her arms behind her head, and she had been silent for so long I had thought she was asleep. "Guess what, Angie — I saw Martin today."

I felt myself instinctively grow cautious and eased my voice into casualness. "Did you really? What did he say, Lorraine?" As far as I knew she hadn't seen him since the Sunday night he had failed to call, and except for the night on the front steps she hadn't mentioned him once.

"He didn't say anything," she answered. "I just saw him driving by in the car." She waited a moment.

"He looked so nice, Angie. He went by quite fast so I just got a quick look but he had on that brown tweed suit of his that I always liked and his hat pushed way back on his head. He looked just like he used to look. . . ."

"Did he see you, Lorraine?"

"Well," and her voice was careful, picking the words thoughtfully, "I was just standing on the corner waiting to cross Park Avenue and he came up a side street and then turned down the Avenue. . . . It was during lunch hour and I think he was hurrying uptown to eat. Angeline, he didn't see me. . . ."

Her voice was very quiet now and very empty, tired with lonesomeness. "He didn't see me," she repeated. "I'm almost sure."

She caught a late afternoon train for Chicago on Sunday. We all went out for a ride right after dinner — so she could say "good-bye" to things for the summer. We took the lake highway out to Pete's and I noticed that already the swamp grass along the road was turning yellow and the glossy leaves of the willow trees were a fading yellow-green. There were birds everywhere, flying low in the bushes and bending the tall grasses with their weight. Lorraine looked out the car window as we drove, not saying anything.

We passed fields of wheat, ripe and heavy-headed, honey-colored in the sunshine, and already long yellow feathers of early goldenrod grew in the ditches. There was a lush heat over everything; a slow, simmering heat that made you warm from the inside out. "We'll go for a turn around the park road. Would you like that, Lorraine?" my father asked and she nodded. I secretly hoped we might see Swede and Jack down by the boats as we passed, but the boat was empty, bobbing quietly by the dock.

Farther out on the lake sails tipped the skyline, matching the white of the clouds. We pulled up along the bank of the lagoon to give Lorraine a last summer look at the park and the water. It was peacefully quiet and water lilies like white wax floated on broad green pads, rocking on the slow current. "I never knew a summer could go so fast," she mused. Near the edge of the lagoon floated a dead white fish, its sides shining like mother-of-pearl, almost beautiful in the sunlight. I heard Lorraine sigh a little.

"Dad, I think it's almost traintime now. Let's just drive down Main Street once more before you take me to the station," she said.

The shops were all closed and the street was calm with Sunday afternoon quiet, but there were a few cars lining the curbs and Lorraine kept looking from side to side, very casually. We went from one end of the street to the other and then my father turned toward the station, saying cheerfully, "Well, Lorraine, there's your last look at Fond du Lac for a while anyway."

"Oh, well," she said.

I carried one bag and Kitty lugged the other with both hands, and we waited with Lorraine at the platform until the train came and stood waving after her as it disappeared smaller, smaller down the track.

Going home we drove down Main Street again and though I looked on both sides of the street, noticing each car, I didn't see Martin's long green coupe that time either.

Fall was coming early that year. There was a queer sadness in the fact that summer should die so quickly, this of all years. Each day the freshness in the garden and the fields faded a little. The morning dews lay chill and frosty and in the evening long, quiet dusks came early, growing dark around the treetops while the birds lingered longer, with a strange melancholy in their songs.

Jack came over every morning, stopping off on his bakery route, and he called me every afternoon just after lunch. Once he remarked, laughing, "Angie, I never knew being in love took so much time!"

Every night we went out somewhere. Once when I was rushing through the supper dishes my mother came into the kitchen, the evening paper in her hand, saying, "Angeline, I hardly think it's . . ." and she paused. "You shouldn't really be seeing . . ."

"What did you say, Mom?" I asked, my heart pounding.

She looked at me a moment and smiled an odd, soft smile. "Oh, well . . ." she said quietly and went back into the living room.

For the last week she had been mending my clothes, tightening snap fasteners on my skirts and sewing buttons on my pajamas for school. Newspapers were spread in one corner of her bedroom and she laid my clothes in neat, careful piles, ready to be packed. The drapes and spread were ready for my room and she was just knitting the last sleeve on a new pale-pink sweater.

"We'll have no last-minute worries at all," she remarked one afternoon and I realized suddenly that she meant what she said. She knew that Jack would be leaving just a few days after I had gone, but she wasn't worrying about that at all. And I realized suddenly too, that she didn't know that that was the only thing on my mind through those last days. But how could she know? To me every moment passed with an awareness that it had slipped by and that time was coming to an end. But to her these last days really meant nothing.

When Jack and I were together neither of us talked about it much — it was a refusing to admit and a refusing to believe that September was only a few days away. But without saying a word, we began to do "last things" together. One night out at Pete's the whole realization swept over me, coming so suddenly, startlingly, that it made my cheeks feel numb. All the same crowd was there that we had seen every night all summer. The air was still full of the damp, cool smell of beer and the musty pleasantness of old wood, and the juke-box in the corner was still blaring out its nickel's worth of music every few minutes. I seemed to see them all separately — the familiar town boys standing at the bar, laughing, and girls with long sweaters pulled over their summer dresses. For them everything was the same. Only one or two of them would be going away. All the rest would be here night after night for nights on end, till outside the lake would be frozen over and the snow white on the ground and the tall bare trees creaking in the wind of winter. This time two weeks from now they would still be here. Two months from now they would still be here when I had counted out my last nights and rationed out my last minutes.

There were memories in everything. They seemed to hover in the corners and hang wispy in the music that came from the jukebox. They were floating like dust motes everywhere I looked. Swede danced with me once and he said softly, under the music, "Jack's going to miss you, Angie. You're a good kid — I'm sorry we didn't get to know you sooner, that's all," and I had to keep my head against his shoulder so he couldn't see my face just then.

Later Jack and I sat in a back booth by ourselves in silence, just being glad to be together, and we could hear the sharp voices of the boys in the front room playing cards and the muffle of feet dancing on the wooden floor, mingled with the music and the ring of beer glasses on the table — all the old, familiar sounds that were part of Pete's. Sitting on its perch, the old parrot was sleeping quietly with its head lolling to one side and its tail feathers drooping.

Jack gave a little laugh, smiling at his own thoughts and, looking up at me, he said, "Remember that first night, Angie?"

I nodded and he laughed again, shaking his head. That's all he said.

We decided to go sailboating one of those last nights and Swede went with us, but when we got to the lake it was dark and choppy, beating angrily against the boat as it rocked against the pier and sending high foam up over the gravel walk. The sky was dark and threatening and there was no moon. "I'd rather be a dead Chinaman than go out on a night like that," Swede muttered, shuddering, so we all got back into the car and drove uptown instead.

The next evening the three of us went out again, going along Willow Road far into the country and then back down the highway that runs along the lake and finally through the rutted roads of the silent, empty fairgrounds with its buildings already shuttered closed, as if they were already asleep for the winter. We even drove out to the narrow gravel road, past the field where the field daisies were still blooming and the thin trees stood still and dark and there was the same breathless mystery; the same strange quiet.

I remember Jack's remarking, "To look at it at night you'd never know anything had changed, would you?"

But it couldn't end as soundlessly and as painlessly as it had begun — that I knew. All the days and nights and warm weeks of sunshine couldn't fade away into nothingness like breathy whispers as soon as they were spoken. They were too full for that. There was too much behind it. Even as I counted those last hours I knew that something had to happen. I didn't know what it would be but I knew it would come — somehow.

And it did. It was the third night before I left. We went on a wiener roast together, about ten of us, as a sort of farewell party for both Jack and me. Jack had his car and we stopped to pick up Swede and Dollie and then Fitz and Margie, crowding all four of them into the back seat with the kindling wood and a picnic basket, while the others went in another car. We drove out to a wooded ledge about five miles from town where the trees grew thick and the woods were as wild and overgrown as a forest preserve.

It was barely dark and the trails were easy to find between the trees as we trailed along in Indian file, each carrying something, while Jack came last with his arms heaped with kindling wood, dragging a car robe behind him. There were clearings in the trees along the path, scattered with bits of charred logs and the dark ashes of other picnic fires. As we went in deeper and deeper, the woods seemed filled with quiet listening, as if it hadn't heard another human sound for long years.

Margie led us to a place she knew of where the ground was flat and there was a heap of blackened stones already arranged for a fireplace. Swede pulled some paper from his pockets, bunching it together and placing kindling sticks carefully over the stones, while the rest of us scattered to look for more wood. The trees grew close together here, thick-trunked box elders with occasional slim birches slipped in between, and the dead branches on the ground were tangled with vines and matted with damp leaves. We broke off what smaller branches we could and kicked at rotten stumps till they rooted out of the earth, sending up a damp, mossy smell. Margie was pushing along beside Jack and Fitz who went in another direction. It was the first time I had seen her for almost two weeks — since the night of the fair — and I was anxious to talk with her. Jack was a little distance away between the trees, breaking sticks sharply over his knees. He couldn't have heard us.

"Margie," I whispered cautiously, "I've meant to call you for almost a week but didn't get around to it. I wanted to ask you how things were going with Fitz and you."

I couldn't see her face clearly in the half-darkness but she shrugged. "We've been going out as always since two days after that night at the fair. I stayed home for one night and then decided I didn't like it so I called him up the next day. I guess he knew I would. Anyway, I'm almost glad I did."

"So am I," I told her. "Otherwise maybe you two wouldn't be here tonight and it wouldn't be the same at all."

"Yeah, you get kind of used to having a boy around," she answered. Jack returned then and we turned back through the woods toward the fire. It was shining through the trees, licking light around the dark trunks and up into the branches.

Margie caught up with me and whispered softly in my ear as we walked. "Thanks a lot for not telling, Angie. I could tell by the way he acted that he really didn't know what went on at all."

Back around the fire the others were sharpening green sticks for the wieners and Dollie was buttering rolls with the handle of a spoon — Jack had brought them from the bakery, fresh and hot. Fitz and I spread the blankets carefully on the ground, watching out for twigs and sharp stones, and then had to fold them up again to look for a jackknife someone had laid down somewhere. We each cooked for ourselves, putting the wieners on sticks and holding them over the flame, turning slowly, carefully till the tight skin burst, sending juice sputtering into the fire. The fragrance was tantalizing and Swede jammed his impatiently between a roll and ate it half-roasted.

"You big, old pig," Dollie laughed at him across the fire. "No wonder you're so fat." The firelight dancing made dimples in her cheeks and a soft, dark fluff of her hair, thick and shiny.

Someone had brought along some bottles of Coke but no one had remembered to bring a bottle opener, so Jack twisted at the tops with the edge of his jackknife till he had to give up in desperation, muttering under his breath. No one wanted to go into town for an opener so the bottles lay untouched on the grass. "Maybe afterwards," Jack said.

At first the fire was so hot that it crackled and snapped, sending twigs sparking out onto the grass till we had to draw our blankets farther back, out of reach. I almost forgot that we were miles from town; miles from anyone else. While we ate, everyone chattered and laughed so loudly that the circle of brightness around the fire seemed to be a room by itself in the middle of the forest darkness, walled with light. I looked furtively behind me once, awed by the silent bushes, dark and lonely, changing shape in the flicker of the firelight. "Something the matter, Angie?" Jack asked, touching my arm. But I shook my head.

As the fire burned lower we toasted marshmallows over the flames and Dollie pulled off the first toasted skin, retoasting the soft white ball that was left on the stick, licking her sticky fingers like a baby. Margie lay back on the blanket, looking up into the darkness, and Fitz crawled over to sit down beside her. She asked him for a cigarette and held his hand to steady it as he brought a match to the tip. Then he tossed the match away and put his hand back in hers, looking into the firelight. I felt almost sorry for Fitz then, he seemed to want to be liked so badly. The others pulled their blankets closer to the fire and tossed the paper bags and bits of wax paper into it, watching them go up in a quick blaze.

One of the boys suggested we sing for a while but the suggestion died away without an answer. We talked quietly and Jack sat close beside me with his knees hunched up, staring at the flames. He had been silent all evening long, and several times I caught him looking at me strangely, as if he were just going to say something and had suddenly changed his mind. Swede came over to sit on our blanket, too, and Dollie curled up beside him with her head on his knee. He bent over to whisper something to her, laughing and tangling his fingers in her hair.

Someone had picked up an old wooden wagon wheel in the woods and laid it over the glowing embers of the fire, and we all sat watching till it burst into slow flame. "Looks like a big Fourth of July pin wheel, doesn't it?" Swede whispered down to Dollie.

The trees stirred restlessly and the night was filled with a sense of uneasiness that made me feel uneasy myself, almost afraid of the darkness around us. The firelight sent shifting shadows onto the bushes and tree trunks so that the whole forest seemed to be full of silent things, watching. I couldn't tell what was wrong with me. It sent a queer panicky beating in my throat and my hands were hot and dry. Above us the sky was a dark velvet with pale small stars. The trees hid the moon.

The night was torn between the comforting

warmth of the fire and the weird, restless shadows beyond the circle of light, but the others didn't seem to notice it. Only Jack was moody. He sat breaking up bits of twig and flipping them into the fire, his eyebrows knit together in thought. Once he looked at me and then ran his hand over his hair with a tired, unhappy gesture. The fire was burning low now and the wooden wheel lay flat in the ashes, the spokes still glowing red. The burned wood crumbled and settled down into the embers with an eerie sound like a soft sigh. As the fire burned low, the darkness closed in silently around us and a night wind blew over the coals, turning the ashes gray. Jack flipped the last twig into the fire.

"Someone want to go look for more wood with me?" Swede suggested.

Jack jumped to his feet. "Let Angie and me go, will you? I feel like a little walk anyway."

"In the darkness?" Something inside me went suddenly alarmed, cautious, and sent a chill around my heart. I didn't know of what I was afraid but there was something there. It seemed almost as if the darkness beyond was listening, waiting. My mind warned again and again with quick, sure thoughts not to go out of the protective circle of the firelight, out past the bushes where the trees grew close. I wanted suddenly to stay very near Swede and the others, away from the gentle, dark sway of the bushes and the quiet shadows that lay beyond. But yet there was something about Jack's voice that made me go.

"You aren't afraid to go with me, Angie," he said insistently, his voice warm with persuasion as he took my hand to help me to my feet.

At the edge of the circle of firelight he turned to call back to the others, "Better put on what wood you have there. This may take us a long time . . . in the dark."

We went out of the clearing and the bushes brushed against me as we passed, stretching out and touching my legs with their cool, damp leaves. Dead leaves were silent beneath our feet and trees leaned together like tall dark pillars, the light between them thin and eerie. I held tight to Jack's hand and stumbled after him. "Jack," I said. "Jack, this is silly. Please, please let's not go!"

He pulled at my hand, almost pleading, "Come on, Angie," he urged. "Oh, come . . . I really want you to!"

So I hurried along with one hand in his and one hand before me to feel for the trees in the darkness, and the bark was dry and rough beneath my touch. Once I tripped over a vine and it coiled around my ankle like a wet rope. "Jack," I cried, "Jack!" I was really frightened now and I didn't know why but I couldn't keep the fear out of my voice.

"I'm with you, Angie," was all he said.

We walked on cautiously, feeling between trees, stubbing against stones and breaking through bushes that scratched against our legs and cracked under our feet. Over our heads was the almost soundless hush of the wind in the heavy foliage, uneasy with the secrets of darkness, and the rest of the night was so quiet we could hear ourselves as we breathed. The firelight was far behind by now and the darkness had closed in around.

Suddenly ahead of us the trees parted, and beyond I could see a flat, rolling field high with wheat. And ahead we could see the moon that had been hidden in the trees and it hung very low, yellow and solemn, as if it were too heavy for the sky. Along the edge of the field ran a low wooden fence and we broke through the woods, leaving the darkness behind us. Jack held apart the last bushes and I stepped through them into the little clearing. The woods behind us was like a black wall. My breath came short and quick from running and I sat down on a fallen fence rail while Jack stood beside me, lighting a cigarette, but neither of us spoke.

Around me the weeds grew tall, almost up to my knees and cool with a night dampness, and reaching down I felt the leaves of one, knowing by the hairy softness and the fine cluster of tiny blossoms that it was wild foxglove. All around the plants grew thick and lush, with a late-summer richness, and I crushed a dark leaf between my fingers. Almost instantly there rose in the air the cool, sharp smell of mint, its fragrance startlingly eerie in the darkness. Jack moved toward me and then stopped.

Along the fence rails vines grew heavy, covered with thick, flat leaves shining broad in the moonlight. "Look, Angie," Jack whispered. "Those are wild grapes." I walked toward him, brushing through the weeds, and we felt through the grape leaves, our fingers quick in the darkness, till we found the hidden grape bunches. They were hard to pluck, and cool dew from the leaves shook down around our legs as we pulled them. Curling vine tendrils touched my arm like cold fingers. Some of the grapes were still green and hard but the earlier ones were ripe and soft to touch, the purple bunches oddly black in the moonlight. They were bitter in our mouths as we ate them, with a strange, wild taste, and the seeds were hard against my teeth. But I plucked them and plucked them till both my hands were full and they fell to the earth and purple stains were dark on my arms. Jack was standing back from the fence now, near the trees, and suddenly I knew he was waiting for me. And all the strength seemed to run out of me and the grapes felt cold and heavy in my hands.

Very quietly I stood. Everything around us was waiting. I could feel the tenseness of the bushes, the hushed expectancy over the grass tops, and behind us the wheat field was still in the moonlight. Great webs of silence seemed to hang, dark and heavy, swung low from tree to tree. The great treetops above leaned together, waiting with hushed whispers. I wanted to speak but the words were dry in my throat.

I could feel Jack's thoughts straining toward me and then I heard his voice, so low, so tense that I wasn't sure for a moment if I heard it at all. "Angie," he said, "Angie, please! Let's get married. . . . I don't want you to go!"

Once it had been said, the night came suddenly alive, pulsing with it; catching up the words and echoing them over and over, singing like chimes in my head. For a moment, only a brief moment that slipped by so swiftly that it meant nothing at all, desire laid warm, tremulous fingers along my throat. But it was only a moment and then the whole night melted away around me. Everything was so calmly and painfully clear. I could remember my mother standing in her bedroom looking at my clothes in neat piles, ready to be packed for school, and saying in her soft, confident mother-voice, "We'll have no last-minute worries at all, Angie," and again I realized how much she meant it.

And then Jack was standing beside me with his arms tight around me, pleading, "Don't, Angie. Oh, honey, don't do that now. I only asked you because . . . oh, Angie!"

And I was crying with my face tight against his

shoulder, standing in the tall weeds that were cool and damp against my bare legs.

Back in the firelight the others had already gathered up their things and were ready to leave. Swede kicked at the heap of glowing embers till they were scattered in the grass in a shower of sparks like fireflies; and when Jack leaned over to gather up his car robe Swede patted him on the shoulder saying quietly, "That's okay, fellow."

The cars were still parked at the roadside and we put the picnic basket in the back seat again and Fitz got in first so Margie could sit on his knee and Swede and Dollie got in next. Jack opened the door for me and I stepped in carefully, trying not to look at him. He swung round to his own side of the car and slammed his door shut. My breath was still short in my throat and my hands were trembling, so I had to fold them together to keep them still.

Jack waited a moment before starting the motor. Just sitting beside him made my heart pound again. He took a cigarette from his pocket and bent over to light it, striking a match. I noticed his hands were trembling. He held the match with both hands to steady it. In the small glow of light his face was very young and very sad and I saw that his lips were still stained purple from the wild grapes.

And the next morning the swallows were there. I came downstairs early with my eyes small and tired and my heart aching with a weariness that went through me right down to my hands, leaving them limp and heavy on my wrists. I wondered what Jack was thinking then. His thoughts must have dragged as slowly and listlessly as mine with the same painful dullness. The whole night through, lying in bed, memories had corkscrewed through my mind till my head throbbed with thinking and now, in the morning light, everything was still as drab and dismally hopeless as I had dreamed.

The kitchen was filled with the usual fresh smell of morning coffee and my mother was sitting by the window, looking over the garden. "It's the first day of real fall we've had," she said. "We could almost stand a bit of fire." I poured a cup of coffee for myself, hoping the warmth of it would really get inside of me. It was such a dull morning that the grayness of it spread over my thoughts like mold. For the first time I could see brown sticks bare in the hedges and there were a few stiff-petaled zinnias, dull, heavy red, standing alone in the corner of the flower bed, the leaves curling. I tried not to look at the swallows but they were there.

Year after year and every year, we had watched the first flowers drop their petals, the squash turn orange between the corn rows, and leaves thin in the trees, but no one would admit the summer was over until one morning we would wake and the swallows would be there. It never failed. The swallows would come, lining the telephone wires, and from that day on it was fall. The wind would have frost on its breath and the grape leaves would curl and fall from the vines and the dew would be white patches frosted on the grass in early morning. Soon, lonely killdeers would be winging across the sky, their wistful cries hanging in the cool, misty air.

And that morning, sitting by the kitchen window with my cup of coffee, I saw the telephone wires across the foot of the garden dotted with swallows, perched on the black lines like long-tailed notes — a bar of music, stark and sad against the gray fall sky.

It seemed so incredible I couldn't keep the surprise of it out of my voice, "How could it happen, Mom?" I asked. "How could it *end* over night?"

She looked at me oddly and said, "It's always been like that, Angie. You just haven't been old enough to notice before."

We spent a long time over our breakfast, talking about school, planning; just loitering because there were only two days left and we wouldn't have breakfast together again for a long time.

And then suddenly my mother brightened. "Run up and wake that lazy little sister of yours while I straighten the kitchen. She and I have to go downtown this morning. I keep forgetting that you aren't the only one who is going to school. Kitty needs new shoes!"

I was just waving good-bye to them from the front window when the phone rang. I let it ring twice and then again before I answered it, because I knew it was Jack and it takes a moment or two to get your thoughts in order and to make sure your voice is calm. His voice on the other end of the wire sounded as tired as I felt, as if he had just got out of bed and wished he hadn't risen at all.

"Hi there, Angie," he said glumly. "Just called up to see how things were going with you this morning."

"Fine, Jack. How about you?"

"Pretty good, I guess. But we're packing some stuff — that's why I called you. I'm home here with my mother wrapping gunny sacks around some of the upstairs furniture and tying it with rope to ship down to Oklahoma. She wants to get as much of it out of the way as she can."

"Lot of work?" I asked lamely. There was a scratching on his end of the line as if he were scribbling with a pencil on a piece of paper — an aimless, annoying sound and I could tell he was thinking of something else as he talked.

"It's not so much work but I don't think I'll be able to get over to see you today."

"Why not, Jack?"

" 'Cause my mother wants me round to help her. She's got her hair tied up in a dust cap and is really going at it. I can tell by the way she's working herself that she wouldn't like it if I took time off. . . ."

"Does she know I'm going away the day after tomorrow, Jack?"

"Yeah, I told her about it, Angie. And she said to say good-bye to you for her — even if she has never met you."

The conversation was empty, meaningless — there are times when two people can't really talk together without seeing each other. I could just imagine Jack at the other end of the wire, tapping his pencil on the table, his eyes thoughtful, not wanting to hang up and still not knowing what to say next. "I'd better get back to my packing too," I suggested. "There are still little things that have to be sorted out. I want to bring so much but it won't all fit in the bags."

"Okay, Angie," he answered. "But I'll see you tonight, won't I? I may even get a chance to drop round this afternoon but I really don't think so. But we'll have a good time tonight. We'll make it fun, Angie." His voice was warm and almost happy again and after he had hung up I sat holding the phone, as if by doing so I could still hold onto the sound. In two days, I thought, I won't be able to hear his voice anymore.

Margaret didn't come home for supper that night so my mother and Kitty and I were alone. The

273

gray sky of the day was melted into the darkness of a night sky and outside there was a wind that rustled in the bushes.

"I heard downtown that they expect to have a frost tonight," my mother told me. "It's unusual to have it come so early but they say this is going to be a very cold winter for us. The man in the shoe-store said that already there have been hunters out after the ducks over the lake."

Kitty was quiet and contented after the day of shopping and she was eating placidly, her eyes already soft with sleep. "This year when it snows I'm going to make Daddy help me with a snow hill in the garden for my sled," she remarked, half to herself. "We'll build it with boards and put snow over it."

My drawers had all been emptied and my trunks packed and now we were all just marking off minutes till it was time to go down to the train. Now that the day was almost here there was nothing left to say; almost nothing left to think. But we sat and sat at our supper until it was dark outside and the tea kettle had steamed the windows opaque and inside the house seemed very warm and bright. Outside, the wind blew high in the trees, swaying just topmost branches and sending a few leaves floating down to the gutter.

"Not even two days left," kept running through my mind, keeping pace with the other more commonplace thoughts, trying to crowd them out. I was still sitting comfortably in my own kitchen and already my throat ached with lonesomeness and there was a queer, soundless crying inside of me. My mother was just finishing her supper tea and her face was very calm and happy, with her hair brushed up high, just showing white at the temples.

I felt there was something that I wanted very much to say; some little words that would come out warm and shaky because they had been shut up inside of me for so long. But they must have been shut up inside too long, for when I tried then to say that I was sorry that summer was over and that I was going away; when I tried to say that I would miss them — no words came out at all!

And then for the last time Jack came. He came in the front door rubbing his hands together and his cheeks were red with cold. "Did you ever see such a change in the weather, Mrs. Morrow? This is regular football weather." He clapped his hands together and his voice was loud, having come in out of the wind. He had his basketball sweater on, buttoned up tightly, and everything about him had a crisp, fresh-air look.

My mother laughed, just looking at him. You couldn't help laughing at someone so brown-skinned and healthy who brought fresh air in with him when he came. He seemed taller to me that night.

"You wouldn't believe that just this time last week Kitty was running around in playsuits. We'll probably have weeks of Indian summer yet but it feels like real fall tonight," she said. "I was telling Angie that I heard downtown that we may have a touch of frost."

"I heard that too," Jack told her. "My dad told me he heard a warning on the radio to farmers and there was a notice in the weather report in the paper tonight. From the feel of that wind there could be!" and he laid the palms of his hands against his tingling cheeks.

"You're red, Jack!" Kitty laughed up at him and he pulled one of her braids.

"You're a little red yourself," he said.

My mother was worrying away under her breath. "I certainly do hate to have them go to waste when I could can them just as easily as not. A good frost will spoil them for sure."

"You're worrying about the tomatoes, aren't you, Mom?" I asked. Having to gather in the tomatoes before a frost was a yearly occurrence with us. It was all part of having winter come. We were never prepared for that first frost, for we could never quite believe that summer was really over.

"Let Jack and me take them in — will you, Jack?" It will take only about an hour. . . ." I knew he would do anything I asked that night.

"Really, Angie," my mother protested, "if Jack has something else he'd rather do we can just let them go. . . ."

"No, let's get them picked," he said quickly. "I like to do things like that. There's something about tonight that makes you feel good to be outside even if . . . well, even if it's the end of summer."

Kitty brought my old sweater from an upstairs closet and I carried up three clean bushel baskets from the basement. "Just pick the riper ones and don't bother with those that are too small," my mother said as we went out the back door.

The garden lay very square in the moonlight edged with sharp sticks of hedge. I took one basket and Jack the other two, one in each hand — that would be enough for the scattered few tomatoes that were left. Most of the green leaves were dead and the knobby vines were already wet with night dew. We worked side by side, not talking at first, feeling about in the half-darkness for the tomatoes, and soon our hands were wet to the wrists and the rough wool of my sweater chafed. Even my fingers

felt stiff. But somehow it was so natural to be working beside Jack that I didn't want to stop, even for
a moment.

Little patches of spider web shone white and
filmy in the moonlight, stretched from one sprawl-
ing vine to another. Once our hands touched
among the cold leaves and my breath came short
for a moment. Jack looked at me and laughed.
"Funny girl, Angie," he whispered. The tomatoes
were cold to touch and the ripe, red ones looked
black in the darkness and their skins were smooth
and moist. There were green ones with tough stems
that broke with a snap and sometimes a whole vine
would pull out of the earth, trailing from my hands
and sending a shower of cold drops onto the hard
ground. Our ankles were wet with dew but my
cheeks were tingling warm and Jack was humming
a happy, jerky tune under his breath as he moved
among the plants. Small, hard, green tomatoes with
dried blossoms still stuck to them fell on the mud
with soft little thuds. We didn't speak at all but just
tossed the tomatoes into the baskets, our arms moving in an unconscious rhythm, stopping now and
then to blow on our fingers and to wipe the dew off
our hands.

I could feel it getting colder by minutes and the
wind blew harder till the dew on the bare vines and
little clods of earth began to turn white. There were
storm circles round the moon and whisps of dark
cloud brushed across it. Jack picked an over-ripe
tomato and its tight skin burst between his fingers.
He threw it over his shoulder into the darkness and
a moment later it fell softly somewhere in the
hedge. Above us the wind was wailing quietly and
high up in the night the moon was racing with a
cloud. The bare vines stretched like sinews in the

pale light and Jack struck a match to see if we had missed any tomatoes, but the wind snuffed it out. He laughed to himself.

One by one we carried the full, heavy baskets into the garage, the cold wire handles cutting into our hands. The soft blackness of the garage seemed very still after the sharp chill gusts outside — as if the wind were holding its breath. We sat them side by side on the cement floor and when the third basket was in place we covered the tomatoes carefully with newspapers to keep out the cold. Jack found some funnies in a corner and, striking a match, he began to read a sheet of Dick Tracy funnies, yellowed at the edges. The match sputtered and went out. In the darkness we tucked the newspapers in tightly and shoved the baskets into one corner.

"Jack," I said, "I won't be able to see you tomorrow night at all. That last night will be sort of family night. . . ."

"That's all right, Angie. I sort of figured that. I guess tonight's the last then." I nodded my head but somehow I didn't feel sad anymore.

Outside the wind was nosing around the garage windows and slipping in under the door. Jack kissed me and his hands were cold on my cheeks. This is how it should be, I thought. This is Jack. This is how it should be and his lips were warm on mine; soft and warm, and his cheek was cool and firm. It was only moments. A whole summer summed up in a few moments and then we went into the house by the back door.

My mother had made hot cocoa and set two cups on the corner of the kitchen table. Our hands were muddy and we washed them together under the cold water of the kitchen sink. "Angie," my mother laughed, "you should see yourself — you even have mud on your cheeks!" Jack was very busy with the soap and water but his own cheeks were flushed.

We drank the cocoa steaming hot, talking and laughing at each other while our faces still tingled from the wind. Jack's hand looked very brown against the white of the kitchen table. My mother sat with us, sewing buttons on a school dress of Kitty's, and he said to her suddenly, "Mrs. Morrow, would you mind awfully if Angie and I walked out to the lake for a little while?"

"At this time of night, Jack? It's after nine o'clock now." Her tone was disapproving. "I hardly thing it would be wise."

"I know it's late," he added hastily, "But I just happened to think that if the frost comes there might be water in the boat and if it froze in there it wouldn't be good!" Then as if to add strength to his statement he said, "In fact, I know there's water in it."

My mother bent over to snap off a white thread with her teeth and for a moment I thought she was smiling. "All right," she said quietly, "but don't be long. Angie, pull that old sweater of mine that's hanging by the back door on over your own. I'd hate to have you going to school with a cold."

I looked at Jack and he looked quickly at me and then I took the cocoa cups to rinse them at the sink while Jack got the old sweater for me. "We really won't be long, Mom," I told her.

He opened the back door for me and I noticed that in the little hollows where the garage eaves trough dripped the water was covered with a thin scum of ice. The storm circles were dark around the moon and the garden lay very square in the cold light. Our breath rose in vague, misty clouds above our heads.

"Come on," he said happily. "Let's run part of the way, Angie. I'm so glad you could go."

We turned off our street and as we hit the park road the wind swept in from the lake, clean and cold, and breathing the fresh air made my mind feel sharp and clear. I was laughing as we ran. This is how it should be, I thought. The wind sent tears to my eyes and brushed clean through my hair.

The sailboat was rocking against the pier, its mast sticking up like a slim finger, and the white sail was rolled up tightly like a canvas cocoon. Jack pulled in the rope and brought the boat close up to the dock, stepping in. The water was like ink. "Angie," he called against the wind, "will you see if you can find a can lying around so I can bail this water out? There's about three inches in here."

Along the pier I searched and among the rocks that lined the road, kicking among the stones. Waves from the lake itself were crashing madly over the breakwater at the mouth of the harbor, loud as the wind, and the air was damp. Suddenly I ran across an old coffee can, wedged between two stones, half full of old rain water, and I pulled it out.

"Here, Jack, will this do?" I held it up and then realized he couldn't see it in the darkness.

"Toss it over, will you?" he called and I went to the edge of the pier and pitched the can toward the boat. Jack reached out to catch it but missed and it clattered splashily onto the floor.

"This is just swell," he said, bending the can between the palms of his hands so it would scoop up the water better. I sat on a rock and hunched up my knees to protect myself from the wind while I watched him. He stood with feet apart on the crossbars of the boat and ladled the water out over the side. The sound of the can made a rhythmic scoop-scoop that was pleasant and friendly among the wild lake noises.

"Warm enough, honey?" Jack called.

"This is wonderful," I called back. And it was. Just being there with him in the night and the freshness of the wind was enough. The boat rocked as Jack moved back and forth, setting the mast waving gently. It was a little boat and bobbed with every movement, and the water slapped loudly against its sides, sending spray spitting high. It splashed wet against my legs and the wind was cold, playing with my hair and tunneling up my skirts.

A car went past on the road, the headlights nosing aside the darkness. "Almost through!" Jack shouted and I waved back. He bent again to scoop up the water, pouring it over the side of the boat into the darker water around him.

My hands were cold so I slid them up my sleeves and waited. My thoughts went back over the summer and suddenly it seemed inevitable that we should be here at the lake, Jack and I, where we had started. It was like a song that began and ended with the same refrain. Behind it all was the quiet music of the lake. That first night when the water had been calm and the small, bright reflections of the stars had almost tinkled on the ripples; and the afternoons when the lake was wash-water blue in the sunlight; and now tonight, it was dark and bottomless, crashing against the breakwater and rocking restlessly in the harbor. I felt an almost motherly affection for the little sailboat that had spent the summer tethered to this same dock on its short rope, patient as the waves that licked against its sides. The darkness of the sky, the sound of the water — all of it blended into memories of the summer as vivid as the present. But this night wind was chill and sharp with frost.

Just then Jack called, "Pull up that rope, will you, Angie? I'm finished here." I took the rope in both hands and drew the sailboat tight to the pier and he jumped onto the dock beside me.

"There," he said. "Let her freeze." He squeezed my arm. "I think I'll leave this can right here in case someone else wants to bail out." He let it clatter to the rocks. On the end of the breakwater the tall white lighthouse was turning its beacon, slashing through the darkness with long, sharp-edged blades of light, cutting over the tops of the waves. The night was so void of human sounds that the wind was suddenly a roar in my ears. Jack was standing very close to me.

And then I made my mind say it to myself, pinning down the squirm of thoughts till they admitted precisely and finally, "This is the last night." And it was just as it should be. It was right that Jack should have on his basketball sweater and that his lips should be warm and moist and his cold hand rough against my cheek. Over and over again, mixed with wind and the night darkness and the damp, fishy smell of the lake, it was as it should be. This must last for a long time, I thought. I must remember and remember. Every moment of it. This is forever.

Jack's voice was low and husky and his hand was shaking a little. "Angie," he whispered, "I know that you don't want your family to know but I want you to have this. You know why . . . I want you to have it," and he slipped off his class ring and laid it in the palm of my hand.

I held it a moment and it was still warm from

the warmth of his finger, and his hand closed over mine so tightly that my own fingers hurt. And then all so suddenly it was time to go home. For the last time, it was time to go home.

And we walked side by side with the wind behind us and a gray cloud over the moon. And the puddles in the road were skimmed white with the first frost of fall. I was somehow afraid to put it on and I had no pocket in my sweater. There was nowhere to put it. So I walked all the way home with the class ring clutched in my hand.

The next day meant nothing for I didn't see Jack at all. And the next evening I spent with my family sitting in our living room, talking quietly but not thinking about anything. And then, so quickly, it was morning and we were up in the early gray-pinkness of it getting ready to drive to the station. Kitty had begged to be allowed to go down to the train with us but she was sleeping so peacefully, her braids outspread on the pillow, that my mother whispered, "Don't wake her, Angie. We'll be there and back before she knows we've even gone."

In the kitchen we had coffee together and the sunlight had just begun to color the sky. "It's going to be a beautiful day," my father said thoughtfully. "It seems a shame to get you up so early, Angeline, but this train will get you to Chicago before noon and that's what Lorraine wanted. It's good to travel in the clean of the morning anyway."

That station yard was achingly empty with vacant baggage wagons pulled to one side and a solitary taxi cab waiting, with its motor still running. There was an early morning lonesomeness about everything and none of us said much. I kept watching for Jack for I knew he would come. He hadn't said so, but I knew he would.

He drove up in the black bakery truck and I knew from the sound of the car door as it slammed that it was he. "Just thought I'd like to say good-bye," he told my mother and father, and they smiled. Looking at him then I thought of dozens and dozens of things I had meant to say to him and hadn't remembered until now. Little words were eager on my lips but my mother and father stood close beside us, looking down the shining curve of track, waiting for the train to break through the gray mist of morning. Someday I will tell him, I promised myself. After everything else is over.

The sound of the train came riding toward us and its great wheels churned into the station, hissing out steam, and the conductor stepped off onto the platform, waving a lantern, blacked out now in the light of the morning.

"I guess this is for you, Angie," my father said and he kissed me.

"You take care of yourself, dear," my mother whispered, softly. "You will write and let us know everything, won't you?" and she kissed my hair.

Jack stood, silent. " 'Bye, Jack," I said to him.

"Good-bye, Angie. Be good," he answered and for only a moment his hand was on mine.

"Lorraine will meet you at the station in Chicago," my mother called after me. "She promised she would be there on time, so, Angie dear, you won't have to worry about anything at all."

No, I thought, I won't have to worry about anything, and I looked back out of the train window to wave to them and saw Jack in the half-light of morning, standing with his hands jammed in his pockets and his basketball sweater knotted loosely around his neck. I won't have to worry about anything at all.

Quiet, sleeping houses and gray clapboard taverns slid by the window, lined along the track. I could feel the chug-chug of the train beneath me as the wheels turned. The drab edges of the town straggled past, shabby, sad-eyed houses and sagging sheds, trailing bits of worn rail fence around them. Fond du Lac gathered her shoddy outskirts in about her. Bushes in the fields were russet-leaved, catching the glow of the first light of morning and the treetops rocked with the waking birds. And slowly, slowly out of the grayness, morning was coming.

And I saw it all glide past me, lopped off by fenceposts, and I felt myself ache inside with a quiet sadness. And now I knew suddenly that it could come and could come forever, slipping by in the breath of a moment, and yet never again would there ever be anything quite as wonderful as that seventeenth summer!